Ukraine, War, Love
A Donetsk Diary

Ukrainian Research Institute
Harvard University

Harvard Library of Ukrainian Literature 7

Cambridge, Massachusetts

OLENA STIAZHKINA

UKRAINE, WAR, LOVE

A DONETSK DIARY

Translated with an afterword by
Anne O. Fisher

50 years ■ 1973–2023

Distributed by Harvard University Press
for the Ukrainian Research Institute
Harvard University

The Harvard Ukrainian Research Institute (HURI) was established in 1973 as an integral part of Harvard University. It supports research associates and visiting scholars who are engaged in projects concerned with all aspects of Ukrainian studies. The Institute also works in close cooperation with the Committee on Ukrainian Studies, which supervises and coordinates the teaching of Ukrainian history, language, and literature at Harvard University.

ISBN 9780674291690 (hardcover), 9780674291706 (paperback), 9780674291713 (epub), 9780674291768 (PDF)

Library of Congress Control Number: 2023942699
LC record available at https://lccn.loc.gov/2023942699

Timeline of events was prepared by Anne O. Fisher, expanded by Oleh Kotsyuba, and adapted from the timeline prepared for the following publication: Stanislav Aseyev, *In Isolation: Dispatches from Occupied Donbas* (Cambridge, Mass.: Harvard Ukrainian Research Institute, 2022).

Cover image by Mykola Tys / SOPA Images / Sipa via AP Images, reproduced by permission

Olena Stiazhkina's photo on the back cover by Inna Annitova / krymr.org (RFE/RL), reproduced by courtesy of RFE/RL

Cover design by Lesyk Panasiuk

Book design by Andrii Kravchuk

Publication of this book has been made possible by the Ukrainian Research Institute Fund and the generous support of publications in Ukrainian studies at Harvard University by the following benefactors or funds endowed in their name:

Ostap and Ursula Balaban
Jaroslaw and Olha Duzey
Vladimir Jurkowsky
Myroslav and Irene Koltunik
Damian Korduba Family
Peter and Emily Kulyk
Irena Lubchak
Dr. Evhen Omelsky
Eugene and Nila Steckiw
Dr. Omeljan and Iryna Wolynec
Wasyl and Natalia Yerega

Translation of this book was made possible by a generous donation from Yuri Omelchenko of the Coordinating Committee to Aid Ukraine, and Michelle Hu.

You can support our work of publishing academic books and translations of Ukrainian literature and documents by making a tax-deductible donation in any amount, or by including HURI in your estate planning.

To find out more, please visit
https://huri.harvard.edu/give.

CONTENTS

Editorial Note · XII

Foreword · XIII

Ukraine, War, Love: A Donetsk Diary
I don't call you anything · **1**
Zinaida Gippius once said (MARCH 2, DONETSK) · **2**
The Overcoat (MARCH 2, LUHANSK) · **5**
Can you fall in love at a precisely determined time? · **6**
Dima and I are starting a newspaper · **8**
The Former President (MARCH 3, ROSTOV) · **9**
The Beginning of the "Foreign Spring" (MARCH 3) · **10**
The Demonstration at the Church (MARCH 4) · **14**
The First Assault (MARCH 5) · **16**
Today, a "presumed" bomb was found (MARCH 6) · **18**
The Gun (MARCH 7) · **19**
It's March 8 · **20**
The Most Fashionable Word · **22**
The Yid Banderite · **23**
From Letters Not to You
    After the pro-Ukraine Demonstration (MARCH 13) · **25**
The Ides of March · **25**
Quirks · **29**
The uprising was running on an abbreviated
  schedule (MARCH 22, DONETSK) · **30**
From Letters Not to You
    It's bad here (APRIL 7) · **30**
The Assault—The Donetsk People's Asylum—I'm Writing
  for the Paper (APRIL 6–13) · **32**
Words and Meanings (APRIL 12, SLOVYANSK) · **36**

From Letters Not to You

    My friend works for a newspaper here (APRIL 13) · **40**

    Two of our soldiers were taken hostage

      at the border (APRIL 15) · **40**

    Dear Maksim, I have a request for you (APRIL 17) · **41**

    Wait—if you don't mind (APRIL 17) · **41**

Passion Week: Easter Sunday · **42**

Us and Them · **43**

Passionate People · **49**

"Hi. We're fascists and Banderites now" (APRIL 21, MOSCOW) · **51**

I speak about a love that doesn't insist on

   its own way (APRIL 22, MOSCOW) · **53**

We're not leaving (APRIL 23, DONETSK) · **54**

The Eastern Front (MAY 10, MARIUPOL) · **58**

How to Hold a Referendum: A Methodological Handbook

   for New Invaders (MAY 11) · **62**

In the Shade (MAY 15, KOSTYANTYNIVKA) · **66**

The News · **68**

How I'm feeling out here? (MAY 17, KYIV) · **71**

There's a popular topic in the capital (MAY 17, KYIV) · **71**

The *Ukraine: Thinking Together* Conference (MAY 18, KYIV) · **73**

Muratov (MAY 18, DNIPROPETROVSK) · **77**

Thinking Together? (MAY 18, KYIV) · **81**

The Hospital (MAY 19, SLOVYANSK) · **83**

Did you know that, for hunter-gatherer tribes,

   there's no such thing as bad gods? · **87**

Is it possible to accept someone else's god as your own? · **88**

Not _____ Enough · **89**

The Coffin on Little Wheels (MAY 21, MARIUPOL) · **91**

You don't have to be poor · **93**

You can also consider the issue from

   the point of view of love · **95**

Dima and I are meeting the governor (MAY 24, DONETSK) · **97**

There was no presidential election (MAY 25,

   DONETSK, SLOVYANSK, HORLIVKA) · **98**

From Letters Not to You
 The anti-terrorist operation, ATO for short (MAY 27) · **99**
 Our laughter's dark (MAY 28) · **100**
The Tattoo Artist (MAY 29, DONETSK) · **101**
From Letters Not to You
 Headlines. Just Look at These Headlines... (MAY 29) · **106**
Casablanca (MAY 30, DONETSK) · **106**
Victors have to be fools · **112**
Difficult Faces (JUNE 1, DONETSK) · **113**
Rumors (JUNE 1, DONETSK) · **117**
The Photographer (JUNE 7, DONETSK) · **122**
Falling in Love with a Wizard (JUNE 12, DONETSK) · **124**
Announcing the Armed Rebellion
 (JUNE 20, DONETSK–HORLIVKA) · **130**
Like a Woman (JUNE 25, DONETSK) · **133**
The Sign (JUNE 26-27, DONETSK) · **135**
Venya, Katya, and Marina
 (JUNE 28, DONETSK AND MARˋÏNKA) · **142**
Remember, you were telling me about
 your Grandpa Pavel? · **146**
And now the orcs have banned fireworks · **148**
Yet Another Cease-Fire · **148**
Update · **151**
The Police Are with the People (JULY 1, DONETSK) · **152**
New billboards appeared that morning in Donetsk · **158**
Also that morning · **158**
When the minister of internal affairs is an active
 Facebook user · **158**
Olya's mother-in-law used to tell this story · **159**
I have to be happy (JULY 5, DONETSK) · **163**
The question "How was your day today?" is now
 considered indecent (JULY 7, DONETSK) · **164**
Hell in Ukrainian is *peklo* (JULY 11, DONETSK) · **165**
Do you know what burnout is? (JULY 15, DONETSK) · **167**
To Be a Man (JULY 17) · **168**
The airplane (JULY 17) · **173**

In all likelihood, they were alive (JULY 18, DONETSK) · **173**
The "peaceful protesters" are glad · **173**
...and another thing about languages (JULY 18, DONETSK) · **174**
The provocative Russian poet Orlusha writes
(JULY 19, DONETSK) · **175**
Assholes · **177**
The Rat King (JULY 22, DONETSK) · **180**
Astro (JULY 25, HORLIVKA) · **183**
A Civil "Conflict" (JULY 26, DONETSK) · **186**
This war will definitely be conceptualized · **189**
Who's the boss of Donetsk? · **190**
The Game (JULY 28, SLOVYANSK) · **193**
The Checkpoint (JULY 29, LUHANSK) · **196**
Today, they shelled my block, where I live
(JULY 29, DONETSK) · **198**
I catch myself thinking that I'm still treating
her like a child · **199**
Severe hangover syndrome used to help
with everything · **199**
The citizen of the Russian Federation (JULY 30, DONETSK) · **200**
There's nothing they won't do (JULY 31, DONETSK) · **202**
Elche. Tarragona. Barcelona. Figueres · **203**
Girkin has forbidden cursing · **210**
Lyusya and Grandpa have been in Berdyansk for over
two weeks now (AUGUST 3, BERDYANSK) · **210**
We're talking (AUGUST 3, A KITCHEN IN DONETSK) · **213**
It feels like they've already stolen everything
(AUGUST 3, DONETSK) · **215**
Granny Shura's ninety-five years old
(AUGUST 4, DONETSK) · **215**
Yesterday, the Ukrainian Security Service
(AUGUST 4, MARIUPOL, KYIV, DONETSK) · **217**
Good News · **220**
They're Not Refugees (AUGUST 5, THE SKY, KYIV) · **220**

The citizen of the RF, also known as the prime minister
   of the Duh-P-R, comrade Borodai (AUGUST 7) · 223
A mortar has a three-mile kill zone (AUGUST 7, DONETSK) · 224
The Anti-Aircraft Gun (AUGUST 8, DONETSK) · 225
Classified Ad · 230
"Shakhtar," he says (AUGUST 9, LVIV, DONETSK) · 231
I don't like carnations (AUGUST 9, DONETSK) · 232
The terrorists hit a penal colony with a shell
   (AUGUST 10, DONETSK) · 233
Women are giving birth in basements · 233
Not Enough (AUGUST 11) · 233
So Happy (AUGUST 11, DONETSK) · 237
We call explosions "booms" · 238
Antratsyt (AUGUST 11, ANTRATSYT) · 239
Let's call that story from Antratsyt fake · 239
War isn't how it's described in books · 240
"Hey, you heard that over in Crimea, on the Kerch bridge,
   there are thirty-five hundred cars stuck in a traffic jam?"
   (AUGUST 15) · 241
I don't know what things will be like ten minutes
   from now · 241
The "DPR" has instituted corporal punishment
   (AUGUST 17) · 243
The terrorists shelled a refugee convoy
   (AUGUST 17, LUHANSK) · 243
Steinmeier, the German minister of foreign affairs
   (AUGUST 18, BERLIN) · 244
And you know something? (AUGUST 18) · 244
My dad says that you're old · 244
All war diaries are histories of suffering · 247

Afterword · 253
Anne O. Fisher

Notes · 259

EDITORIAL NOTE

In this book, a modified Library of Congress system is used to transliterate Ukrainian, Russian, and other East-European personal names and toponyms. This system omits diacritics, ligatures, apostrophes, and the soft sign ("ь"), and transliterates the iotated vowels of the Ukrainian version of the Cyrillic alphabet "ю," "я," and "є" as "yu," "ya," and "ye" respectively (rather than "iu," "ia," and "ie"), while Ukrainian "ï" is retained. Exceptions from this system only occur when the diacritics or the apostrophe are meaningful in distinguishing the personal or place name (such as Mar'ïnka, rather than Marinka). Furthermore, well-known personal names such as Yanukovych appear in spellings widely adopted in English-language texts.

For Ukrainian Orthodox holidays, the Church used the Julian calendar in 2014, which lags thirteen days behind the Gregorian calendar adopted in the Western Christian calendar.

In the table of contents, a hybrid system is used: titles are used for entries that have their separate titles (with date where available); a combination of the first line, date, and location (city or town only) are used where an entry has no separate title; the first line is used where no other information is available (date or place).

The timeline of events, interspersed as newspaper clippings among the diary entries, was prepared by Anne O. Fisher, later expanded by Oleh Kotsyuba, and edited by Michelle Viise.

FOREWORD

I can't come up with a first line. I know it has to be vivid; sad, funny, smart—yes, but definitely vivid. A line with a guarantee: keep going, it won't be boring.

But no. As of February 24, it's like all my words, phrases, and sentences are stuck between my teeth. Sometimes they fall out, like baby teeth. But the tooth fairy's not coming to collect these. My sentences are short now, economical. They're more like telegrams. There's absolutely no air between words. There's nothing to breathe. Ever since February 24, 2022, there's been nothing to breathe for any of us.

Later we will give this war a name. Our day of victory will be this war's end. But this war's beginning was in March 2014.

My name is Olena Stiazhkina. I was born and raised in Donetsk. I have a daughter and a son. Their significant age difference has allowed both of them to feel like the family's only child. When the Russians entered Donetsk, my daughter organized pro-Ukraine demonstrations, while my son was tearful (because it was scary to hear bombs exploding next to our building) and ashamed (because he thought that at nine years of age a man shouldn't cry).

In March 2014, Russians came into Donetsk and Luhansk—or rather they drove in from Russian oblasts just across the border—dressed up as "protesters." In April, the Russians were no longer cautious or circumspect; they came in as armed special forces. In August, before the battle of Ilovaisk, Russians came in openly, as regular soldiers.

The catastrophe of occupation unfolded gradually, hour by hour, day by day. That's probably why, at first, we couldn't believe it; then we couldn't stop it. For the entire world, this part of the Russians' war against Ukraine was invisible, hidden behind the smoke screen of a crudely cobbled-together "suffering people of Donbas."

We too were invisible: all of us who woke up one fine morning as Ukrainians.

We—I—have reasons for self-reproach. Being unaware doesn't mean you don't care; it means you've been stupid. In our case, fatally so. Before 2014, my answer to the question "Who am I and what do I do" wasn't overly clear: a historian, a writer, a mother, a university faculty member, a grateful reader of good books, a friend, a wife, a daughter. I ranked all these things in different order depending on the circumstances. The hierarchy didn't matter.

These days I still switch around the order of my self-definitions, except for the one that's permanently in first place now: I'm a Ukrainian. And that matters because it determines everything else.

The diary I started writing in March of 2014 seemed at first to be a way of "not forgetting." It seemed that all that stuff couldn't be happening. The "local" (bused-in) protesters who went off to "seize" the Oblast State Administration building but walked right past it because they didn't recognize it... The "people's governor," Pavel Gubarev, who used to work as Grandfather Frost at children's parties... The flag of "New Russia," opportunistically stolen from the Confederate side of the American Civil War... All this was so absurd, artificial, and clichéd that, at first, it wasn't even scary.

But then "all this" started taking hostages, started raping and killing.

Life left the city gradually, drop by drop. The number of dead, the degree of deadliness, kept increasing: the

Russians brought in tanks, mortars, Peonies, Carnations, and Tulips (the "flowers" here—Pions, Gvozdikas, and Tyulpans—being different models of heavy self-propelled artillery). The living attempted to resist.

At some point, I realized I was writing the history of a slow descent into hell. Resisting what I myself knew, refusing to believe in the finality of the occupation, I tried to laugh. Probably just as a way to stay alive.

And, if I didn't stay alive, this diary had to (or was supposed to) explain something important, something I was trying to explain to myself. What's it like when Russians come to "save Russian speakers," and then kill them? What's it like when Russians come to us with war in the first place? What's it like when that first stage of denial—denial that this is even a war—happens not on a personal but a global level? What's it like not to believe that all this is really happening but still try to live in it?

What is it like when your love for your country makes you free? What is it like when the Ukrainian language becomes the language of safety and life, when it is the only indicator of something living?

* * *

In February 2014, my short stories were short-listed for the Russian Prize, an award given in Moscow for the best texts written in Russian by writers outside Russia.

For me, this is now a source of shame and guilt. Now I think about how the Russian Prize was part of a larger war; this prize, among other things, legitimized the "Russian world" in Ukraine, Belarus, Israel, Germany... everywhere. My award was a weapon turned against my own country. I will always live with this guilt.

The award ceremony was to take place in Moscow on April 22, 2014. By that time, the dressed-up Russians ("protesters") were in Donetsk, and Russian Federation special forces had already taken over smaller towns: Kramatorsk, Slovyansk, Kostyantynivka. We already had the first cases of people being tortured to death, of people being killed on the main square of Donetsk as a way of making an example of them.

Back then, I still thought you should talk to Russians because it wasn't meaningless. My concept of Russian civil society was false from the get-go because I was seeing it through the lens of the revolution on the Maidan, through the lens of the possibility of our being, and of fighting for our right to be.

The text of my acceptance speech is in this diary. Things I'd never say today are in it, too. I had the chance to cross them out, not to publish them, to pretend this never happened.

But it did happen.

Besides the phrase "Vova, stop getting on mama's nerves," which I'm still proud of today, there was also mention of Aleksandr Pushkin and of my next trip to Moscow. I said that it wasn't Putin, but Pushkin, who could save us, and I said I'd like to come again and talk not about war, just about literature.

Both of these theses are repugnant. One of my friends, who lost his mother, his wife, and one of his children, now says very calmly: "I would like to go out and have a look at Moscow. But only once it looks like Mariupol." I almost agree with him, it's just that I'm not willing to actually go there. A few good pictures will be enough for me.

As for Pushkin... No. I don't want him to save me. Not him, and not any other kind of "great Russian culture"—may it rot, seeing how it has created, and continues to create, monsters who rape children and steal washing machines.

By cultivating and nurturing the "little man," Russian culture has blessed multiple generations with the prospect of never getting big, of never being responsible, self-aware grown-ups. The little man Raskolnikov used his own capacity for killing a woman—two women, actually—as the measure of his identity. A little man, the giant mute Gerasim, was a serf who obeyed his owner's order to drown his dog, the only living thing he loved and who loved him. He didn't hide the dog, he didn't take it away to other people, he didn't drown the lady, he didn't drown himself along with the dog. No. He looked in its eyes, its loving and trusting eyes, fastened a stone to its neck, and threw it in the river.

"Great Russian literature" exhorted us to feel sorry for Gerasim. In March 2022, during the chaotic Russian shelling of Irpin, a young woman with multicolored hair led eight disabled dogs out of an animal shelter to a safe place. The picture of her taken by Christopher Occhicone for *The Wall Street Journal* has become not just one of the symbols of the war, but a symbol of Ukrainian culture, in which good people defeat loathsome "little men."

* * *

This diary was never published in full; just two short excerpts in 2015 for *Krytyka* and *Eurozine*.

Why not? I have many answers to this question. In the fall of 2014, after my family moved to Kyiv, I tried submitting this text for publication. One publisher responded that it wasn't finished. The other publisher didn't respond at all.

I didn't show it to any more publishers, but I did show it to my friends. Especially at times when I had neither the words nor the strength to describe, over and over again, everything that had happened. In time, it grew painful for me to keep messing around with this diary. It felt as though I was forcing a wound on those near (and far) and dear to me, a wound that kept bleeding but that nobody could do anything about... so they turned away. And later, the diary, the entire text of it, prompted nothing in me but pain. I hadn't read or looked through the diary since 2015. It just sat there quietly in its folder on my desk. Whenever my gaze happened to land on it, I quickly closed my eyes. I also turned away from it. From myself, too, probably. At that time, thanks to Russia's carefully conceived and well-organized propaganda, people from Donetsk and Luhansk seemed, to all Ukraine and all the world, to be "separatists." It took long years and hard work to change that paradigm and begin to see occupied Ukrainians, Ukrainians deprived of their voice and subjectivity, in the people who were still there.

Argumentation worked better than emotion. College classes were more important than personal experience.

But a completely different tragedy was now unfolding in the occupied territory. My friend, who had stayed behind in Donetsk to take care of her and her neighbors' elderly relatives who couldn't walk, once commented that Tadeusz Borowski would've been able to write about the city better than anybody else. Our "Here in Our Donetsk" still hadn't devolved into Borowski's "Here in Our Auschwitz." Or rather: it had, but not everywhere. Because the Isolation prison, which its prisoner Stanislav Aseyev has written about, was (and still is) an actual concentration camp. It remains unseen through clean Western-style windows up to this very day. And now, in 2022, new camps have been added to it: filtration camps, where kidnappers send Ukrainians to be shot because they are Ukrainian and because they want to live in their own country.

In comparison to the suffering of those living on Ukrainian lands that have been occupied since 2014, the texts in my diary seemed to me to be frivolous, impermissibly funny. There was a lot of love in them, and a lot of hope. But, by 2022, the occupation had lasted for eight years (and continues to this day). Light-hearted hope is not the best medicine for the dispossessed. But there was a lot of just that—light-heartedness—in my diary.

Many occupied people had, and still have, a great love for Ukraine. They, not I, are the ones who could become that love. My friend says, "I'm here because somebody has to welcome our army with flowers."

* * *

Why now? Because...

Because... the pain we are experiencing now has stopped being invisible. Nobody is turning away from our wounds, our deaths. And we ourselves aren't yielding.

Because... the purely theoretical question that arose in March of 2014, about whether a Russian soldier could shoot me, now has a thousand real-life answers. And it's not just about shooting. A Russian soldier is capable of anything: theft, rape, torture, lies, robbery, dismemberment, beating, bombing. And of doing all this not just to me. The Russian soldier has come to Ukraine to show the entire world, the world he scornfully describes as "civilized," what the price of civilization really is. If Ukraine does not prevail, the "Russian world" will kill and rape adults and children far beyond the borders of Ukraine. But Ukraine—we, all Ukrainians—we will prevail.

Because... I'm keeping a diary again. In Kyiv. And in Ukrainian. Maybe that one publisher was right: the story needs to be finished. But the only thing that can finish it is victory for Ukraine. That last sentence looks a little flat and formalistic. Like a telegram. But one that's even shorter, like this: "Ukraine is victorious." That's what I would like to send, if only it were possible, not only to our present, but also to our past.

May 13, 2022
Kyiv

BEFORE THE WAR...

After long negotiation with the European Union on an EU-Ukraine Association Agreement, Ukrainian president Viktor Yanukovych is scheduled to sign it on November 29, 2013. But a secret meeting with Vladimir Putin takes place on November 9, 2013, after which Yanukovych about-faces to pursue agreements with Russia instead of with the EU. On November 21, 2013, mass protests erupt in Kyiv and throughout Ukraine, initiating what comes to be known as the Euromaidan Revolution, or the Revolution of Dignity, lasting until Yanukovych leaves office in February 2014.

FEBRUARY 18–20, 2014

Escalating violence between protesters and state forces peaks with the shooting and killing of several dozen protesters.

FEBRUARY 21, 2014

President Yanukovych meets with opposition leaders to come to an agreement and stop the violence. Within hours of the meeting, Yanukovych secretly flees Kyiv.

FEBRUARY 22, 2014

With Yanukovych's actual whereabouts unknown, a pre-recorded interview, in which he refuses to step down from office, is broadcast at around 4 pm. An hour later, Ukraine's parliament—the Verkhovna Rada—votes to remove Yanukovych as president, effective immediately, and to hold a presidential election on May 25. Oleksandr Turchynov is elected speaker of the parliament.

FEBRUARY 23, 2014

Defender of the Fatherland Day: from Soviet times, an official Russian holiday, but only quasi-official in Ukraine; later in 2014, this holiday will be replaced by an official Defender of Ukraine Day celebrated on October 14. Oleksandr Turchynov is appointed by the parliament the acting president of Ukraine. A pro-Russian demonstration takes place in the city of Sevastopol in Crimea where the formation of "self-defense units" is announced.

FEBRUARY 26, 2014

Units of Russian military secret service (the GRU) arrive in Crimea from Toliatti. In Yalta, trucks with conscripted personnel of the Russian Black Sea fleet arrive. In Simferopol, the capital of Crimea, two large demonstrations take place: a pro-Ukrainian one demanding the preservation of Ukraine's unity, and a pro-Russian one calling for the peninsula's annexation by Russia.

FEBRUARY 27, 2014

In the night, "little green men"—later identified as members of various Russian special forces, wearing unmarked green uniforms—take over the parliament of Crimea. A large-scale takeover of government buildings, Ukrainian military bases, and key infrastructure begins in Crimea.

EARLY MARCH 2014

Separatists occupy government administration buildings in Donetsk, Luhansk, and Kharkiv. A well-coordinated campaign of attacks on governmental buildings begins in Dnipropetrovsk (now Dnipro), Zaporizhzhia, Melitopol, Mykolaïv, Kherson, Odesa, and Mariupol. Former Euromaidan protesters form the first volunteer battalions for the defense of Ukraine. Partial mobilization of the population for the Armed Forces of Ukraine begins.

I don't call you anything. I don't know how to address you. And, at first, I didn't even think I was writing this to you. *For* you.

No, I am not looking for understanding. I am making an accusation. Although I probably have no right to.

Do you think you and I know each other well? A hundred mindful days together... Is that enough for you to come to know me, and for me—you?

You don't read my books. Sometimes you say this snidely, other times wearily.

Sometimes you see a diagnosis in them, other times a monstrous complexity that fills you with grief and longing.

I promise, this time it'll all be simple. The way it is only in war.

What do I want?

For you to understand? No. I'm convinced that's impossible. Right now, that's impossible for you. And you don't have twenty more good years for "maybe someday" anymore. My friends and acquaintances don't even have tomorrow. You will not be able to understand this.

Do I want you to be ashamed? Probably. Do I want you to be hurt? Yes.

Well, here's your diagnosis: everything's just the way you wanted it. Sadism at its finest.

But I promise to be gentle. And my accusations will be touching. And—yes—simple.

I will address you here the way I've always addressed you. Without using your name. "Hey, come here," "Oh, look at that," "You know what?"

You are my limit, the most I can manage. You're probably the only, or the last, person I can and should explain anything to.

On the other hand, if you have to explain it, don't...

My first diary entry begins with that quote. A text about love. Which you don't understand.

Sometimes when I look at you, when I listen to you, I think you don't know the first thing about love. But sometimes I think I'm wrong.

* * *

SUNDAY
MARCH 2, 2014
D O N E T S K

Zinaida Gippius once said, "If you have to explain it, don't." But that rule applies to love. To those who know how to love.

You probably have to explain it to the ones who want to hate...

I'm Russian. After January 16, I saw myself as an extremist.[1] After February 20, I saw myself, very clearly, as a Banderite.[2] And for a long time, way back since Tuzla Island in 2003, I've seen myself as a Ukrainian.[3]

I don't know what made the sinking of Atlantis-the-USSR into the sea be followed by this ever-growing sensation, one that was slightly painful, and distressing, yet also sweet: "there once was a faraway land," but it turned out to be my own Motherland.

Ukraine is my motherland. Russian is my mother tongue. So, fine, it's Pushkin who saves me. And it's Pushkin, too, who frees me from sadness and worry.

Pushkin, not Putin.

I'm a Russian Ukrainian, an extremist, a Banderite, and a nationalist.

And my own interest—no longer theoretical—centers on the feeling a Russian soldier will have as he shoots me.

Will it be a feeling of duty fulfilled? Of deep satisfaction? Of sadness that I betrayed Russia the Great? Will he cry as he fires?

Forgive me, Russia, and on this Forgiveness Sunday, I will forgive you.[4] Forgive me for writing books in Russian, for giving talks and even loving in Russian.

Forgive me for continuing to dream, think, and worry in Russian. But your soldier will come and "free" me from distress.

It's difficult, most likely, to kill people who speak the same language as you.

Right now, there's a unique opportunity to try it in person.

Forgive me, Russia, but there will be no Banderites coming. They didn't come for revenge after the war, either. They died over there, in western Ukraine, for their land, for their language, for their right to be free. And almost all of them did die. Some from bullets, others from age. There are no Banderites anymore.

So, you'll have to kill us. Not just the Russian Ukrainians, but also the ones who're chanting "Russia"—"*Rah-see-ah, Rah-see-ah*"—today. Sure, bullets are bimbos while bayonets are heroes... But that army shovel, now, she's a lady with a real head on her shoulders. You get her in a good fighter's hands, he can do some damage...

Do you have a good fighter's hands? Will you do some damage with your army shovel when you come for us? Will you compel us to brotherhood? (Just a quick note here to compel me to sisterhood.) You will make an Ossetia out of us.[5] And wow, yay, the Republic of Nauru will recognize us! For food we'll have our kitchen gardens and for reading it'll be just like in Arkady Averchenko: we'll have words where the letters are made of gallows in different positions... Paradise.

I'm friends with all kinds of people, you know. Everything from total thugs to total academics; from geniuses to office sharks; from neighborhood weirdos to bougie ladies-who-lunch. Ethnically speaking, it's a mixed bag, too. Sometimes my friends don't even know which of their bloodlines to single out as the main one.

You won't believe this, but the thugs of Donetsk are willing to join partisan units to fight for Ukraine.

And the bourgeoisie, whose last day still hasn't come (sorry, Mayakovsky), are getting ready to stock up on guns. Stolen ones, by the way. Stolen from Russians.

It makes me sad that many of the people I care about slapped on a sailor's cap (figuratively speaking), drank their ration of 200 grams of vodka (literally), and are roaming the streets shouting "Our proud Varangian won't yield to the foe"—lines from the old wartime song.

That's correct, if you remember. The warship *Varangian* does not yield. It is deliberately scuttled.

Forgive me, Russia, but I don't understand why you want to sink your own Varangians in the steppes of Ukraine, taking my and your countrymen down with you.

It's hard for me to make you understand this, but Donetsk is my city. Ukraine is my country. And if you're going to kill me for that, well—who'll speak Russian with you then?

Forgive me, Russia. And I'll forgive you on this Sunday. Because I know the Russian people aren't those rubber-stamp puppets from the Russian Federation Council. They're people, who you don't see, the exact same way you don't see Ukraine.

Not seeing Ukraine is a disease. Ask Viktor Yanukovych what that disease does to you.

And here's another thing: I went to a protest today to demonstrate for my country and against war. It was sparsely attended. In any case, it didn't have quite the level of military and tactical readiness as the one that gussied itself up with your flags, Russia. With flags and, for some reason, with vodka.

Your guys, dressed up to look like sailors, yelled at us: "Get out of our country!" And, of course, *"Rah-see-ah, Rah-see-ah!"* A couple of times they even promised to kill us.

But the Maidan has this one rule: whenever you don't know what to do, whenever you're afraid, whenever you lose heart, you sing the national anthem.

The Ukrainian national anthem is really good for driving out devils.

Give it a go. It's a tried and true method. "Ukraine has not yet perished, nor her glory or freedom..."

* * *

THE OVERCOAT

SUNDAY
MARCH 2, 2014
LUHANSK

My grandpa kept an overcoat that smelled like war. It would be cleaned and, in the summer, it would be hung on the balcony in the sun, and then it would be tenderly packed away in a specially-made garment bag with pockets. The pockets held mothballs. But the overcoat still smelled like war.

We've always lived in close quarters. Still do. But the dinner table was always set with a starched white table-cloth. We called our late supper "dinner." And no elbows on the table, not nobody's, not ever.

Torn away from their motherland—which, according to various versions, was already dead and gone, had degenerated over the past twenty years, or was rising up again from the hell and ashes—they felt like orphans. The city Grandpa had come back to after the war had barely changed at all. But there had been a border separating them for over twenty years from that motherland that had collapsed, then returned.

The overcoat smelled like war. The youngest of them, the one who was almost forty, took it out of the wardrobe and removed it from its garment bag. He put it on and went outside.

He walked the streets of his city, returning to his Motherland. He was shouting a name happily. Others were also shouting it: "Putin! Putin!" Like-minded gents. But their smiles were missing. So were their teeth. Their eyes were glazed with fury. They were broken men. He knew these were the people. Enraged and desperate. Unemployed, destroyed by drink, willing to do anything: both to wage war and to wipe away that damned border.

"Hey, buddy, got a smoke?"

"I don't smoke," he replies sternly.

"You a plant, or what? You're from Kyiv, aren't ya?! Men in winter hats surround him. Someone hits him in the shoulder, then—despicable—just below the knees. He falls down.

"You gonna fess up, buddy? Or do I need to cut you?"

There's not enough air. He closes his eyes, so he won't see. He wants to tell them "I'm one of you." But for some reason, he can't.

The overcoat smells like war.

* * *

Can you fall in love at a precisely determined time? On Saturday, say, at seven twenty-two p.m. Moscow time?[6]

I used to think that the time of birth written on the oilcloth at the hospital was just some medical formality. But then my friend said it's important for horoscopes. The hour and minute, not just the day and month. This is where the mind-boggling variety comes from. A person's fate depends on the sun's position in or out of perigee and apogee.

To go good and crazy, you have to give birth.

The digits on the oilcloth establish the exact time of love's arrival.

Probably not for everybody. But many people know it, remember it.

You take your offspring into your arms and look into its eyes—and you're a goner. You drown. With no resistance whatsoever you drown, you float away in a happiness that has no borders.

Later on, after all the grown-up considerations about how children mean a lot of work and being tired all the time, about them not growing up to be who you wanted them to be, about you getting no thanks from them, so don't hold your breath, plus while you're fussing with diapers and boo-boos you don't even notice how your life passes you by and old age sets in, but don't expect them to take care of you when you're old, and "how sharper than a serpent's tooth," and if they ever do love someone unconditionally, it'll be their own children, our grandchildren...

Later on, afterwards, almost all the predictions will be fulfilled, but almost none of the hopes. Almost. Later on, nothing'll be as sharp, as clear, as pure, as it was that first time. But there's nothing you can do about that.

"Oxytocin. It's all just hormones," says my male doctor friend. "Everything's different for men."

And it's a good thing everything's different for them. Explains why they all go ga-ga for their Napoleons and Batmans.

Though, to be honest, my own current delusions of grandeur are way worse.

On Saturday, at seven twenty-two p.m., I took Ukraine into my arms. It was a long labor: twenty-three years. The birth was high-risk, might have failed.

I took her into my arms, looked into her eyes, and was lost. My little one, my golden girl, poor little thing, my one and only... My happiness, my foolish happiness. My joy...

The diapers, tiredness, and anger are all behind us now. Sometimes, she behaves badly. But if we give all our shrieking disobedient children up for adoption, then what'd be the point of living?

So, I kiss the top of her head and breathe in her smell. Such love. Sometimes she even lets me sleep a little.

The Motherland is a child. Not a mother.

Something like that, anyway.

* * *

Dima and I are starting a newspaper. We will not register it. But we will pay the printer. The money's coming from a "business" who delivers it himself to our friend in the mayor's office. It's a secret. We still aren't using the word "underground." But we realize that's what it is. That's exactly what it is. And probably what it will remain.

A defeatist thought. But a realistic one.

Clarity is a gift and a curse.

It comes to everyone. But at different times. And not everyone gets it. Not everyone accepts it.

You don't.

Accepting clarity as a gift means accepting pain, too, and freedom, and responsibility for what's happening. This is where the curse part begins. The punishment part. Clarity offers the possibility of seeing. But then you have to acknowledge, and then, probably, fight.

It's easier to close your eyes. Best to cover them with your hands. In hopes that afterwards, once the game of hide-and-seek is over, everything will be back to the way it used to be. And you don't have anything to do with what's going on because you're safe on your "home base."

But you do have something to do with it. Not just you individually; all of you.

We are starting a newspaper and a smart business is giving us the money for it.

It has "The Angry Citizen's Manifesto" in it.

We're all different. Some of us were for the Maidan. That's the minority. Some of us were for the brutal Ukrainian riot police, the Berkut. There's a lot of those. But right now is not the time to figure out who's further left or right. The enemy's at the gate. Or I should say—the brother.

You are at my gate. You're the one shaking your gun in the air and shouting "Crimea's ours" and "Our blood was spilled in Sevastopol."

You're the enemy. Do you understand?

* * *

THE FORMER PRESIDENT

MONDAY

MARCH 3, 2014

ROSTOV

Now there are words in his head he doesn't know the meaning of. This happens to him a lot. Sometimes, it's just getting people's names mixed up, but sometimes it's outright hearing voices... The elders had been warning him he might be overcome by devils. So he built his own personal church, where everything was deferentially gilded, where he didn't let anyone pilfer anything, not even the marble chips or the Canadian cedar.[7]

Who is this? Marduk? Is it him? Yes. It's Marduk. Just and strong, righteous and courageous. He comes to aid those who call on him. He destroys Her. He tears Her to pieces and from Her pieces he creates heaven and earth, and the rivers, and the oceans, in which all is honest, all the way he wills it. He is not afraid. He has absolutely no fear. Because he doesn't believe that Tiamat is his mother. She is chaos, the emanation of the abyss. And she never loved him.

She left him when he was small. She died. And his father also got involved with snakes and turned into a dragon. His father threw him out and forgot him. And nobody ever told him what it's like to be loved.

"Marduk!" he shouts, waking up in Rostov sticky with sweat.

"No—Main Dork," someone corrects him. Not politely, like they used to. They're disdainful, irritated. "You're the Main Dork."

"I'm here," he says, almost weeping. "I'm alive. I'll show you. I'll be back."

But the others are in his head again: the little Ugandan girl, Hiroshima, a half-ruined wattle-and-daub hut, hunger, filth, hands tied behind backs. He gets people's names confused. And people's names confuse him. He wants to shave and put on a clean shirt. But his hands shake, so someone else shaves him, someone he doesn't know. Someone with no face.

* * *

THE BEGINNING
OF THE "FOREIGN SPRING"

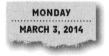

MONDAY
MARCH 3, 2014

Political defeatists were the ones who organized the first You'll Hear Donbas demonstration. To them, the "voice of Donbas" was like a weapon, something they could use to blackmail Kyiv, demanding not just the preservation of businesses and preferential treatment, but, even better, the creation of an autonomous principality, what in the popular parlance is called a *pakhanat*, i.e. a society run by *pakhans* (gangsters). Workers were bused in and had to sign an attendance sheet. That's the way it had always been done. For twenty-three years, government employees had been treated like slaves of the regime. The illegal workers in illegal mines *were* slaves of the regime. Something had gone wrong from the very beginning. From the very first minute...

The defeatists, confident in their omnipotence, could never have imagined that their money-lust and political arrogance were just all part of the script. Someone *else's* script.

The crowd on the square was surly and aggressive. Pavel Gubarev, the self-proclaimed leader of the people, appeared out of nowhere like the fabled imp popping out of the snuffbox, and he and his accomplices pulled all the untouchables and so-called-head-honchos from the stage. Gubarev and his men kicked them, and beat them, and knives were employed, knives that, for now, were only being used to cut through expensive coats...

The crowd turned from surly to scary. Not yet all the way to brute rage, but still thirsting for blood and calling down shame on the ones who had turned people into cattle for years to support "our president's course of stability."

The jollity started flaring hotter. The square "caught fire" from many sides, the crowd roaring and rampaging. It wasn't saying anything that could be clearly understood. It was just reacting aloud, like an old port whore who happens to land a rich john, maybe the last one of her life.

"Yes!" it shouted: to the Russian language, to federalization, to becoming part of Russia, to the referendum, to a separate republic, to a "people's governor," to everything. "Yes! Yes! Do it!"

The crowd moaned. It was all but weeping from the first taste of freedom, from swallowing that first mouthful, after which there's not only no hangover but not even an awareness that there could possibly be a hangover. Heads happily spinning with fervor and with fearlessness. There's a roaring sound. And the less thinking there is, the more roaring, noise, and shouting there can be.

Ask me sternly: "Don't you like people?"

I don't like people. I don't like people who can be turned into a crowd. I understand them, but I don't like them.

From time to time, this fundamentally Russian square would shout "Down with the authorities!" in Ukrainian: "*Vladu—het´!*" These defenders of the purity of the Russian language didn't even notice themselves switching to Ukrainian. It was just switching to a different register for them. Thus, the hated Ukrainian sound of *het´* was heard as frequently as the nice, acceptable Russian sound of *da*.

The excitement was mounting. It was time to storm the Winter Palace, or the Bastille. But neither of them were around. So, everyone decided to storm the oblast state administration building.

There was shouting on the way there, too. "Oh! Oooo-oooo-oooo! Aaaah-aaah-aaah!" They sounded like Comanches all of a sudden. They overturned trash cans and flipped benches. They acted out against any trace of civilization. They tore down Ukrainian flags, the ones they could reach. If they couldn't reach the flags, they ran up to them and jumped at them and shook their fist at them. At the head of the column was the proud leader. The guiding figure. The one known as the "people's governor".

He elbowed his way to the council chamber podium. He said a lot, but slowly and thickly. It was possible to listen to it, but not to actually hear anything. He was rambling, incoherent, meaningless. All his ideas started out decisively, but then ended with (or rather got bogged down in) long pauses, from which the orator, like a donkey loaded down with wineskins, often emerged going in exactly the wrong direction, toward some kind of alternative world perceptible to him alone, a world with grass, water, and young jennies.

You could have excused it as inexperience or excitement. Or as the cup. The overflowing cup of the people's rage. But it wasn't. It was an imitation. It was a rather lackluster imitation of the inarticulate mob's manner of speaking.

Or maybe the "people's governor" was just a drug addict.

The next day, when the city and oblast councils all came down with bad cases of resolutionitis and started moving to have a referendum, join Russia, and entertain other forms of "independence," one of my colleagues publicly called the local authorities "jackals" for not resisting.

A classmate of mine who was with the Ukrainian Security Service called me that night. "Yura's wrong," he said.

"Is he?" I replied. "But still, we couldn't call on people to come out and resist. People would have... there's a lot of us..."

"Unarmed. A lot of us that are unarmed. But they are armed. Just guns, for now."

"How many?"

"Up to two thousand in the oblast. There were three or four hundred on the square. Plus knives. But that's not really the issue."

"What about the police?"

"They've been bought off. For a long time now. As if you didn't know."

"What about your guys there?"

"Mine too. Almost all of them."

"So, what's it going to be?"

"War. We were attacked, Lena. We were attacked, but so far nobody wants to either see or admit it."

* * *

THE DEMONSTRATION AT THE CHURCH

TUESDAY
MARCH 4, 2014
Mom and Dad are funny. They always were. On the one hand, they allowed her to do anything she wanted, but, on the other hand, they questioned her sternly about everything. Masha only remembers one time when her mom said no. This was the tongue scandal. Masha was in Hungary and wanted to get her tongue pierced as a souvenir of her trip. She called her mom. Her mom said, "If you get a hole in your tongue, don't come back." Dad had advice instead of vetoes. "If you're going to kiss a boy, make sure and ask what his name is. And his last name. And who his parents are."

"Don't go today. The city's full of orcs today. You hear me? They're armed. They're not local. They're tourists. They'll kill you and walk away. And nothing will happen to them! I forbid you!" her dad shouts.

"How do you know they're not local?" wonders Masha. But if somebody doesn't want to hear, they won't hear. So, she's redirecting the flow of conversation toward something she needs. Masha isn't just good at this. She's the best.

"Because I pay attention. I pay attention! Their time is two hours off ours. Get it? It's two o'clock here, but where they're from, it's four o'clock. On their watches, on their phones. I see them all over town. In stores. In buses. They don't change their watches. They're on tour!"

Dad nervously lights a cigarette. He doesn't speak. Mom tags in.

"I'm going to be honest with you. We're the ones who made a shitshow of this country. So we're the ones who have to answer for it. This is grown-up stuff. We're the guilty ones. Not you. This is our demonstration. This is our war. Do you get it now? Do you get it now, why you can't go?"

"I get it," replies Masha, in her best A+ student voice. "We have to sit back and wait while they kill you! Right? And then we go out and build a new life? Is that right, Mommy? You'll leave us our country in your will?"

Masha smirks and shakes her head. She sighs. They're so funny.

How can she explain to them that it's nothing they can't fix, and that they didn't make a shitshow of the country, and that she is the country. Because the country isn't the state, it's the people. And everything's going to be okay. And that she and her friends sewed a ten-foot flag, but it's very light and you can sail it high like a kite.

"Come on, Dad," Masha cajoles. "I know her first name, and her last name, and who her parents are. So, please, can I go?"

"But who exactly are her parents?" says Mom, frowning.

"Kyi, Shchek, and Khoryv, and their sister Lybid."[8]

"Nice. But that's not parents. That's some kind of promiscuous polyandry," notes Dad. "And you still can't go to the demonstration. We'll go ourselves, but tomorrow. *Tomorrow.* You may not go today."

Masha acquiesces. She's obedient. Why argue?

So, that evening, Mom and Dad see Masha at the demonstration, on the local streamer's livestream. She's singing Ukraine's beloved song "Chervona ruta" and laughing. She says into the mic, "Everything's going to be okay. You'll see. Everything's going to be okay. Glory to Ukraine."

*　*　*

THE FIRST ASSAULT

On Sunday, an ultimatum was issued: either federalization, Russia, and independence, or an assault.

These demands were so fundamentally contradictory that the terrified authorities were in no condition to enact them.

But the protesters were.

They collected at the building's main gate. They shouted.

The head policeman of Donetsk oblast, General Romanov, opened the back gate for them. Gubarev shook comrade Romanov's hand, saying that he was now and would always be with the people, and that this was a prerequisite for success. Regardless of the complete absence of resistance from the police, these "peaceful protesters" broke in rather than just coming in. Turns out that walking in a slow, respectable manner, while at the same time maintaining your dignity, posture, and smile, requires a lot of skill. Not everyone is fated to master it...

There were journalists and deputies in the building. The deputies left through a service door. But not all of them. There were some who said, "You can carry my dead body out of here, but I'm not leaving."

A whole two deputies said this. Two.

The journalists couldn't get out. Below, at the bottom of the stairs, the "peaceful protesters" shouted at them: we'll break you on the swastika, we'll shoot you dead, we'll cut you some new holes and send you naked to Africa.

Knives. Handguns. Smoke bombs (not stun grenades, but they did make a nice loud bang).

There was no escape for the journalists. But right then nobody was thinking about them. The people needed the servant of the people. But he's so precious he's only saving himself. The police? Well, they're "with the people," although their minds are on their Russian salaries and pensions. What do they care about an assault, or journalists, when there are more important things to sort out? They are diligently converting hryvnias to rubles in their heads. They spend it then and there. And they'll get some nice new stars on their epaulettes. And a pay raise... These are busy people. They're dreaming.

The journalists had Gubarev's cell phone number. Tanya called him and put the conversation on speaker. She said, "If you rotten scum, you sons of bitches, you fetid assholes don't let us out this fucking minute I will strangle you with my own hands, you piece of shit..." Many more words followed. Tanya had been a philology student and her advisor had written a monograph on obscene prison vocabulary, with an accompanying dictionary... You get the picture...

"Of course, Tanya. We'll do it right now," babbled the cowardly "people's governor" ingratiatingly.

The journalists were let out.

The real governor, the one appointed back in the day by Yanukovych, ran away.[9] He wasn't wearing a dress, thank goodness. Video of him running away was uploaded to the internet afterwards. His natural athletic ability and runner's build—and a bodyguard who got knifed in the leg—allowed the "eye of the Sovereign" to scram without health repercussions.

Once he was safe and sound, the governor submitted his retirement papers.

Kyiv appointed a new governor.

I catch myself thinking that the video of the escape is embarrassing because it's so intimate. The fear, the long legs leaping over the curb. It's like he's naked. He's not a man, not even a human being. It's how animals run. The mechanics of his movements are superb. Pure instinct.

No moral duty or human dignity here. It's how roe deer and flushed boars run. Or rabbits. Though rabbits might not be quite as amazing. The governor didn't flatten his ears while running.

What would I have done in that situation? Would I have run, too? No. I'd have frozen in fear. And from fear I'd have started shouting terrible words from our professor's dictionary. Or maybe just: "Aaaaaaaaahh!"

You can't run. You can't. If you run, that's it: you're a defeatist. And the mob will always howl and nip at your heels.

But, on the other hand, you're alive. And being alive means having a chance to correct your mistake.

Those long legs, the leaping, the apprehensive turn of the head: is anybody coming after me...

I'm glad I'll never have to be governor.

* * *

THURSDAY
MARCH 6, 2014
DONETSK

Today, a "presumed" bomb was found in the oblast state administration building. The "peaceful protesters" had to leave the building. Because what if something happened to them?

But it wasn't the bomb they were afraid of. It was the broom. A sweeping new broom that could prove mean in its manner, temperament, or fists (all the usual components of power).

The police were performing admirably. Because they were also scared. Their Russian pensions would come along who knew when, but this new guy is here now. He could fire them, even. Put them in jail. And that's just for starters.

Here, in these parts, we fear authority. But when the authority has a flat-out mean temperament, we worship it. Write books about it, paint pictures, icons, even. With the authority's ugly mug in the middle. Jesus, if he's required, can be over to the side.

Then Gubarev was arrested.

The "peaceful protesters" had their first coherent idea: "Free Luis Corvalán!" Free Gubarev, that is. Nobody in the USSR of the mid-70s knew who Luis Corvalán was, and none of these "peaceful protesters" knew who Gubarev was, either. But, for some reason, they still wanted to free him.

* * *

THE GUN

FRIDAY
MARCH 7, 2014
C R I M E A

A knock at the window.

"*Who's there?*"[10]

"The Crimean Self-Defense Force."

"*We're sleeping. Keep on going.*"

"Give us your cow. Then we'll go."

"*Suit yourself. Petro, shoot them.*"

"What the hell! *What the fuck!*"

"*Petro, I'm telling you, shoot at the self-defenders until they get out. Aim for the legs!*"

"*For fuck's sake.* Where's your revolutionary spirit. *Well, good night then.*"

"Same to you."

But there's actually no Petro. There are the sisters, Granny Manya and Granny Dusya, along with the widowed and divorced Lyuska, plus Yeseniya, the abandoned orphan, named after the film where everything turns out good and right. Granny Manya can't sleep. She's the one on watch.

There is no Petro. But there is a gun. Left over from Lyuska's bandit, back in the nineties. He was a mean, shiftless guy. They cursed his name for all they were worth both while he was alive and after he died.

"We'll get through this okay," they decide together. "We'll have a farewell service for him. We'll see him off with our prayers."

* * *

It's March 8. You call to wish me a happy Women's Day.[11] You call me because I'm a woman and wishing me a happy Women's Day is the polite thing your calendar tells you to do. It sets the right tone. Maybe you're being tactful. You don't call often. You don't want to intrude.

But I can't talk to you. There's a lump in my throat. I see the Russian forces taking Crimea. And Donbas, too.

I see it. We all see it. It's just that the suffering of Crimea is obvious. It's a malignant swelling. But our suffering is overshadowed. So people don't believe it's real. The same way people don't believe a disease is real—they don't accept the fatal diagnosis. As if the disease won't exist if you just hide the doctor's report in a desk drawer.

But there it is, right there, walking the streets of my city. It's a terrible, killing disease. A fatal Russian disease.

I can't talk to you.

"The main thing is love, health, and family." Your voice, just like you yourself, is completely vertical. You believe in yourself one hundred percent, at all times, in all things.

Your words are correct.

But I don't believe them. I yell.

For many years your triad was mine, too. Ours.

But not the word "motherland." That word was worn down to the nub by the late Soviet era, droned and displayed too often in party congresses, speeches, and slogans. Until it was empty.

So it's hard for me to say that word.

But I shout it into the phone. Strange as this is, you're the first person I say it to. I say it out loud: "My motherland... this is my motherland. This is my country. What are you doing to us?"

"*Our* motherland's the USSR," you say, cool and triumphant. What, you think you caught me in some kind of trap?

No. It's just that it's hard for me to talk about this. It's hard for me to keep from sneering with pretend pathos, but also hard for me not to suddenly burst into real tears. Because I can't get hysterical, right? Because that would be embarrassing?

You take my silence for agreement and add: "You people are poor, who needs you?"

How can you refrain from arrogance? How can you withstand the temptation to humiliate us, to flick us on the nose and then snicker and walk on by?

I calm down because I have a response.

"*We* need us. It's our country. And we will fight for it."

"Against whom? Who's attacking you?"

You. You are my enemy. I have to hang up. But I keep holding the phone up to my ear. I still want to say... But you sigh and, as usual, change the subject. Is this your tact, again? You being a grown-up? Is this your love?

"Why are you talking to me like this? Come on, why? I just wanted to wish you a happy Women's Day." Pain in your voice. I hear it. And that's probably why I can't hold back anymore.

"Picture this," I say. "It's the first winter of the Leningrad blockade. Can you picture it? The city, the people, the deafening silence? It's New Year's, but there's no celebration, no presents, no food. The phone rings. It's from Berlin. A cheery voice on the other end of the line tells you 'The main thing is love, health, and family.' How do you respond to that, my little prisoner of the blockade?"

"I'm not little," you say.

And that's it.

* * *

THE MOST FASHIONABLE WORD

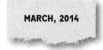

MARCH, 2014

The most fashionable word of March is "junta." Women of ill repute say it suggestively. Respectable women say it scornfully. It's more interesting when the respectable women say it. Pronouncing this word "junta"—*khunta*, so irresistibly reminiscent of *khui*, "dick"—is the only sexual perversion these women have allowed themselves in their crystal-clean, missionary-only sex life. They're embarrassed to have to say it, but you gotta do what you gotta do.

Men like talking about the "khunta," too. A *khu*...—ahem—a junta is something small. Something so small it can't compete with what they've got. They scoff: "Pff. A junta... that's not a junta. I'll show you a *kh*..." You can imagine the rest.

There is no answer to this question: "What makes it a junta?"

At the end of the semester, my students are taking an exam on our current unit in "The History of the USSR." They'll explain the factual background, the chronology of events, and the semantics of Soviet jokes. Here's one of them: "It's Khrushchev's Thaw. A Yugoslavian delegation arrives in Moscow. It's met by thousands of people holding signs saying, 'Long Live Tito's Faction!'"

Somehow, I just know that if the *pakhanat* has its way, then in a week there'll be a "welcoming group" of state employees in the Donetsk airport holding signs saying, "Long Live the Kyiv Junta!"

By the way: my students don't recognize the historical meaning of the word "faction" in relation to Tito, which may (or may not) be why they don't think this joke is funny.

* * *

THE YID BANDERITE

MARCH 2014
....
E A S T E R N
U K R A I N E

We did learn to wear suits. We studied languages, just a little bit at first, but then it became mandatory. Philanthropy? Yes! Now, we didn't begrudge charities our money. We practiced our handshakes: dry palms, a hard, challenging grip, but don't break people's fingers. And sitting: sit up straight, and keep a straight face, too, since it might end up on the cover of a magazine. We quit smoking. We went on diets. We smiled and talked more. The words "yard" and "Forbes" had gotten old, but we hadn't come up with our own yet. We were now global citizens. Palaces, islands, clubs. Among our honored guests were former presidents and current kings. Nice people.

But this guy had always been a black sheep. Bits of fried egg in his beard. Cigarettes in every pocket. Demanded discounts at every restaurant. In shops, he'd sometimes just not pay at all. A filthy pirate. He stole deals, factories, and women right out from under your nose. He was a loud laugher, and spit would fly from his mouth. He'd sit for hours talking about his hangovers or the last chump he'd suckered. There was too much of him. We said it in English: *too much*. But he also had too much money. The French deputy said he was an *enfant terrible*. He agreed and asked to borrow a pen. He didn't give it back.

When the war happened, everyone started weighing risks. But this guy plunks himself right down on Dnipro as the governor. The East and the South are covered in separatists and the Russian tricolor every weekend. But this guy's keeping things quiet. Spring plowing, farm work.

Everyone was calculating risks and benefits. Lustration, escalation, aggression, emigration, sanctions: the only options were bad and worse. And there wasn't enough evil. Not enough evil in this guy who'd planted seedlings, mandated city clean-up days, and paid for tanks and APCs. On TV he said "I'm a Yid Banderite, my good fellow citizens. I was shocked myself when I found out."[12]

There was something in it for the guy. Had to be. He saw something, he saw some angle that others didn't see. It was obvious he was going to make a lot of money. He was in it to make bank. And just thinking of him drove out anything respectable and holy. Made you bite back a curse. It was so tempting to call him and see. But being the one who calls first ... that's lame...

He called. "Look: you're all putzes. Or sons of bitches. You tired of dicking around yet? This is the third week those little shits have been taking the flag off your house and putting up their own. Turn on your freaking brains. Put our flag up. It's the pretty one with the nice blue and yellow, just in case you forgot. Get it up! I'm asking nicely, because you know me and what I can do... And you tie it tight and then cut the extra bit at the end right the fuck off... and yes, I'm still talking about putting up your flag here... And we'll repair the building later. I'll send you climbers to go up there and fix it. For free."

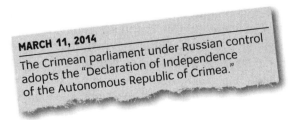

MARCH 11, 2014
The Crimean parliament under Russian control adopts the "Declaration of Independence of the Autonomous Republic of Crimea."

* * *

FROM LETTERS NOT TO YOU

AFTER THE PRO-UKRAINE DEMONSTRATION

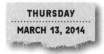

THURSDAY
MARCH 13, 2014

...twenty-two years old. Died in the ambulance from a knife wound. We don't know his name yet. Pro-Russian protesters killed him. Ten more people are having brain surgery. They made children get on their knees; they tore down Ukrainian flags; they beat people with rebar they got out of some big car while the police were right there, watching.

I don't have the foggiest idea how we're going to keep going. We had a really nice city, a sleepy southern city, hasn't been bad since the nineties, and even in the nineties the gangsters didn't touch women and children, they only killed each other. But these guys are killing everyone...

* * *

THE IDES OF MARCH

They clearly needed a Caesar. But only for one thing: to kill him. The faces on those "peaceful protesters"... Faces like that are ready and willing to kill.

Maybe it was some kind of disease. A disease that progressed according to the calendar: symptoms got worse on weekends. And another thing: on days when "Russian fever" was spiking in Donetsk, Luhansk had a quiet day. And vice versa.

On Saturdays, people gathered on the square and shouted. They really did, they shouted. As loud as they could. But every week they shouted something different. On March 15, they dredged up Yanukovych all of a sudden. They called him back home with a nice little sign in English: *Viktor! Go home*. Why was the sign in English? Why was there such a glaring mistake in the English, which should've logically been *come home*, not *go home*? And why'd they even bring him up at all?

Although it's better to ask: why'd they then forget him? By the end of March, there were no more Yanukovyches on any more protest signs. Maybe people just got tired of it.

From the very first day, the agitated crowd on the square felt the need to take something by storm, to occupy something and entrench themselves there. This little game was called "What about the Maidan? Why's it okay for them but not for us?"

"But you're against Kyiv, right?" we asked the ones who were willing to talk.

"Yes! The government there's illegal! It was a coup!"

"So maybe you should go to Kyiv, then? Why are you seizing buildings here if your beef is with Kyiv?"

"But what about the Maidan? How come *they* can do it, but *we* can't?"

"You can. But see, people were upset at Yanukovych, so they went to Kyiv and chased him out. You're upset at Turchynov. So maybe you should go to Kyiv, then, huh?"

"So *they* can do that on the Maidan, but *we* can't do that here?"

What we failed to realize at first was that this "*they* can but *we* can't" wasn't a logical argument, it was a mantra ensuring the preservation of their universe. Made no difference that in their new/old understanding of the world the earth had become flat again. And sat on top of whales that, in turn, sat on top of a big turtle. And that turtle sat on top of a snake eating its own tail. A snake that is a closed circuit: "*they* can, but *we* can't; if *they* can, so can *we*."

This snake's job is just to keep that circuit closed, keep eating its own tail. Otherwise, the turtle will stumble, the whales will tilt forward, and the earth will go sliding off into the starry sky.

Monday through Friday, there were absolutely none of these "uprisings." But on Saturdays, "if *they* can, so can *we*" announced that Lenin Square was Russia and set out to expand the Russian sphere.

Once, on the ninth of March, they marched out of the square to take the oblast state administration building by storm. But they missed. They were off by a whole block. So they marched ceremoniously back. Their return to the square was bewildered and sad.

Could you imagine people marching out to take the Bastille but ending up on the Place de la Concorde instead?

They weren't locals.

The overwhelming majority of the people who wiped Donetsk off the face of the earth weren't locals.

One time when the column of people was stretched out along the city's main road—and yes, in our city it's named for the main Ukrainian Bolshevik, Artyom— the people at the end of the column started shouting up to the people over on the right side: "Hey, guys! Where are you going? What are we storming?" The ones who were ahead of them shouted back, "It's already four. We're going to the train station. Time to catch the commuter train, head home."

On March 15, they didn't want to have to get off the couch and uprise twice, so they went ahead and decided to take the train station by storm. The train from Lviv was about to arrive. The Right Sector was supposed to be coming in on it. All two of them. Four, tops.

It was a very warm, sunny day. They passed out icons to the grandmas and riot batons to the "peaceful protesters." Everyone was invited to lie down on the railroad tracks. Only a few men agreed. The grandmas refused point-blank, saying they'd stand on the platform and drive the demons out from up there.

Anyway, they lay down or stood up, respectively, and got ready. And that's how their images were preserved for posterity. Afterward, a Moscow journalist complained, "I sent the photos to my editors, but they told me the only way to get people that ugly was photoshop, because real people don't look like that. They got mad at me, too, and said I'd done it to get them in trouble."

But there are people that ugly. There are. I can show you that photo.

And the train? The train was fine. Nothing wrong with the train. It stopped a little ways away, before it got to the people lying on the tracks. The passengers got off. Families with children. People on business trips. Same old, same old.

So they all went to the Makiivsky station to wait for the Right Sector. But it didn't show up there, either.

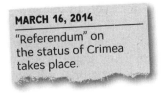

MARCH 16, 2014

"Referendum" on the status of Crimea takes place.

MARCH 18, 2014

"Treaty on Accession of the Republic of Crimea to Russia" is signed in Moscow at the Kremlin.

* * *

QUIRKS

MARCH 2014

STAROMYKHAILIVKA

During Great Lent, people go to confession more often. This year spring has come early, there's a lot of sun. But the churchgoers have sinned. They ask to be absolved before dying. They're afraid to kill, but not to die. Mariya, a housekeeper, has tormented us all and is tormented herself. She says, "I've lived a good life, I'm grateful for everything. But now it's come down to war. Tanks at the border. Will they come? I can't shoot at them, Father. I can't shoot and kill other people and go on living myself. Because they're our people, kind of. Russians. But we can't give them our land, either. But now if I blow myself up, see, with a grenade thingy on my belt, so that both me and the tank... And then I won't have to see anything afterward... Is that a sin?"

Father Pyotr sighs and crosses himself and Mariya. He says, "God will take care of us. He will look after us. Our hope is in Him."

MARCH 21, 2014

Ukrainian prime minister Arsenii Yatsenyuk and EU leaders sign the political provisions of the EU-Ukraine Association Agreement, with the economic and trade sections to be signed after the presidential election on May 25.

MARCH 21, 2014

Pro-Russia rally in Donetsk demanding a referendum

* * *

The uprising was running on an abbreviated schedule. They went to seize the police station and free Gubarev, the "people's governor." He'd done time once in Kyiv, a long time ago, so he was being detained in the Voroshylov district station. The protesters saw this as unjust and incorrect. They shouted "Junta! Junta!" a few times. But the "junta" didn't respond to them either. To ease their suffering, the protesters tossed two smoke bombs and listened to a patriotic WWII song three times in a row: "Arise, my country, homeland vast, arise and join the battle, against the dark fascistic power, against the cursed horde." As a taste of what was to come, they broke two windows. They stood around arguing a little more. Then they looked at their watches and freaked out: "The soccer's on. We're late, guys!"

They quit freeing Gubarev and went their separate ways, some heading home by commuter train, others rushing to the stadium.

Shakhtar, the Donetsk team, beat Dnipro two to zero.

* * *

FROM LETTERS NOT TO YOU

It's bad here. "Tourists" again. And our own idiots too. Now with grenade launchers and automatic rifles. There's shooting in the streets. Turns out it's very hard not to get dragged into civil "conflicts." Our guys are trying as hard as they can to hold back. All our people who are willing to defend the motherland have guns by now. The only thing holding us back: some of the idiots out there are ours, so we've got to find a way to live with them.

APRIL 6, 2014

Beginning of the separatist insurgency, with armed separatist groups forcing their way into government buildings in Luhansk and Donetsk oblasts. In Donetsk, separatists force their way into both the Donetsk city council building and the building of the Donetsk Oblast State Administration and Donetsk Oblast Council. The separatists occupying the Donetsk oblast state administration building demand a referendum. Pro-Russian separatists attack a flashmob singing the Ukrainian national anthem.

APRIL 7, 2014

Donetsk residents issue an open letter calling on the Ukrainian government to protect them from the separatists. Separatists force entry into the building of the Ukrainian Security Service in Donetsk, but are removed some twenty hours later. Ukrainian forces repel an attempt by separatists to seize the Donetsk oblast state-run TV and radio company. Separatists occupying the Donetsk oblast council announce the formation of the "Independent Donetsk Republic."

APRIL 8, 2014

Separatists cancel the formation of the "Donetsk Republic" after garnering weak support from Donetsk residents. A pro-«Donetsk People's Republic»(«DPR») rally is held in front of the Donetsk oblast state administration building.

APRIL 11, 2014

Ukrainian prime minister Arsenii Yatsenyuk visits Donetsk, attempting to defuse the situation; he promises to have a new constitution that will ensure more local governance by the May 25 presidential elections.

* * *

THE ASSAULT

THE DONETSK PEOPLE'S ASYLUM

I'M WRITING FOR THE PAPER

SUNDAY, APRIL 6 –
SUNDAY, APRIL 13,
2014

"The Donetsk People's Asylum News"

There's oodles of work to do in our repeatedly proclaimed, and just as repeatedly repealed, "Donetsk People's Republic."

Despite the fact that the new government entity exists only in the Russian media and the minds of its creators, you have to acknowledge how unique this global "superpower" is. Its power structure is literally vertical: every floor of the building (country) functions independently of the rest.

Recently the sixth floor got into a fight with the eleventh. They haven't gotten to the point of establishing new borders and dividing up the remaining desks yet. But give it time...

Ever since the orderlies from the GRU abandoned the Donetsk People's Asylum, its patients' illnesses have progressed unchecked. Some patients aren't taking their pills. And the provocateurs aren't sleeping on the job, either—they keep bringing in vodka and more vodka.

As a result, the "ministers" and "commanders in chief" are locking themselves in their offices, failing to respond when addressed, barricading themselves in with bits of old tires, and "writing laws."

The Russian language, along with the federalization of Ukraine, those go without saying. They also want to get rid of vaccinations and biometric passports. Next up is a ban on washing your hands before meals, a treaty with flies (vectors of infection), and a debt restructuring initiative for office number 707. There's also the struggle to counter the subliminal "twenty-fifth frame effect," which has clearly been stunningly efficient at turning regular Ukrainians into Banderites.

Our DonODA—Donetsk Oblast State Administration—aka our "Don't-ask Dumbass Administration"—has problems, too: they haven't been recognized in Geneva (hurtful), while one of the competition's "allied enterprises" by the name of Oplot (that is, Bulwark) took over the Donetsk city council building (despicable). And they still haven't passed the resolution stating who they're declaring war on, Geneva or the "allied enterprise." But mobilization has been announced.

Although there's this nasty little trick that goes with that, too, apparently. Seems the governor's gun amnesty program—a bounty, in other words—is a powerful thing. Because yesterday a gun was just a gun. But today it's a very real thousand bucks in your pocket, which is easier to understand and more useful than federalization and decentralization.

So, the people of the Donetsk People's Asylum are starting to cast appraising glances at their armed brethren, while a few of the more enterprising are trying to lure in some "little green men," even just a couple of them. Because twenty thousand greenbacks for two captured "little green men" is some real good money.

Apparently, there are even wholesalers who've popped up to take advantage of this: they round up seven to ten guys, enough to make a brigade, train them to talk about the curb using the word *porebrik* instead of the usual *bordyur*, print up a Russian passport on a color printer, and pack them off to Dnipro. Not to fight, of course. The chumps go straight to Kolomoyskyi and the wholesalers pocket the bounty.

But there are serious people in the building, too, of course. They're the ones raising the issue of money and Jews. The economic policy of these chronically ill patients could be summarized as "money don't smell." Thus, our Donetsk People's Asylum demands not only that all entrepreneurs register, with some even having to buy excise stamps; they also insist on hard American currency. Seventy US dollars for registration, two for each excise stamp. The people of the "Donetsk Republic" disdain Russian rubles, for some reason. Putin's gnashing his teeth, but his "green" orderlies have been out in Slovyansk all week. There's nobody here to bring the "republicans" back in line.

And these "republicans," they're struggling, poor guys. They're struggling with their own poverty and with that ubiquitous fascism of theirs. They struggle the only way they know how. Or, rather, the way Hitler did. Because another one of their orders was a requirement for Jews: pay fifty bucks and submit a list of family members and property. Those who don't will have their property confiscated, get removed from their homes, and be left to the mercy of the nationalists, a group not known for ethnic tolerance. True, the "republicans" haven't made it to executions or gas chambers yet. But—again—give it time...

Malicious gossip claims that many people's "spring fever" has broken and dwindled to nothing. There are fewer and fewer "republicans" on the square and in the oblast state administration building. On weekdays, there are only five or ten grandmas cheering at the barricade made of old tires. The "corridors of power" are also fairly deserted, in addition to being trashed. Some offices are closed for good, since the only thing they contain is filth. There's nowhere else for it to go. It just might be that "General Filth" and "Field Marshal Stench" will defeat the "republic" faster than the antiterrorist operation.

The "ministers" and "commanding officers" organize campaigns every so often, purely for fun. Sometimes they go to the airport where money and space aliens await (space aliens being the only ones, we joked, who were going to actually land there). Other times they go to military bases to steal a few weapons, then turn around and sell them to—well, everybody knows who's buying. But our "military campaigns" are nothing compared to the ones in Kharkiv, where "the people" gather at the psychiatric hospital for thirteen hours every day. Apparently, their leader is being held there...

We're not Kharkiv. Our hospitals have less capacity. And so, there are talks, in which the "republicans" eagerly participate. Especially when the talks are with each other. But they'll meet with government representatives, too. They can't promise anything yet. They deny any involvement in terrorism or separatism. And they're super-upset at the "federasts." To strengthen their position, they've surrounded themselves with posters showing the horrors of the Kyiv government. It's difficult for them to read so many letters. Still, it works just like Viagra: exaggerated and of limited duration.

Every day is full of fear. They share their fears via radio: first they're scared Putin's abandoned them, then they worry there won't be any more money from Russia and they'll have to go underground. They're expecting a big assault. But they're a bit listless in their expectation. What they're not expecting is Yanukovych. They completely forgot about the old man. So it goes with worldly fame. Just last week they were chanting, "Come back, elected leader!" but today they're over it and have set up their own presidents, prime ministers, and parliamentary speakers. To be honest, though, Yanukovych would fit right in here in our "Don't-ask Dumbass Administration." A bird of a feather.

But who needs Yanukovych when spring is so fresh and love is so strong; when for days on end the radio messages pour out of our Donetsk People's Asylum: "Maksim the Mexican is requesting Pasha the Russian to return..."

Hurry up and return already, Pasha. We might not care, but at least Maksim the Mexican will be glad.

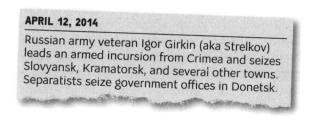

APRIL 12, 2014

Russian army veteran Igor Girkin (aka Strelkov) leads an armed incursion from Crimea and seizes Slovyansk, Kramatorsk, and several other towns. Separatists seize government offices in Donetsk.

* * *

WORDS AND MEANINGS

SATURDAY

APRIL 12, 2014

S L O V Y A N S K

Orderlies from the GRU. The GRU being the GRU of the Russian Federation. The G stands for "we're Giving the orders now." The April assault in Donetsk is a completely different animal from the one back in March. This April one's mean-spirited and cynical. Well-armed and well thought out. And the local alcoholics have no role in this one, not even a supporting role. No sir...

Afterwards, they went into the building. They all took their places. They spread filth and got into fights. But at least they were funny again. They posted a sign: "Bringing Hard Alcohol into the Oblast State Administration Building will be Considered a Provocation." Sure. Right. "Bees Against Honey."

We thought their "curators" had abandoned them.

But we weren't that lucky.

The "curators" had gone out to "do" the oblast. They were organized, disciplined, and focused. Slovyansk, Kramatorsk, Horlivka.

They brought us a word.

And that word was *porebrik*.

In our parts, where Ukrainian is spoken using Russian words, where being educated isn't something people respect, where for a long time the marker of quality for books and newspapers was whether their paper was soft and non-staining, where glasses and "fancy" hats— shaped hats with brims—are going to get you punched right in the nose, so it's better to walk around blind and in a cap... In our parts, where the black faces of our miners inspire great pride but somehow no desire to build high-quality banyas...

In our parts, we don't know the word *porebrik*. So, when the guy in camo says "Hey, you. I'm talking to you. Get back behind the *porebrik*," this causes bewilderment. Puts us in a stupor, even...

"What? Behind the what?"

The guy gesticulates, showing where to go.

And this video winds up on the Internet.

Porebrik means curb. The part of the road that sticks up and divides the pedestrian sidewalk from the vehicular roadway. In our parts we call that the *bordyur*.

Petersburgers think the *bordyur* is one of those architectural excesses on walls, while the thing on the street is a *porebrik*.

What are you doing here, Petersburger? Or whatever you call yourselves out there: Saint Petersburgers? Leningraders? Citizens of Russia? Russians?

Hm. But you're not Russian. The way you're behaving, you're not Russian. *We're* Russian. So, what does that make *you*...?

In any case, these watershed words were identified immediately. The newspapers were the first to use them. Then they got picked up as a verbal signal. It was hard to get used to. It required a difficult pause, filled with intense pain and confusion: how can you be a fascist if you're Russian?

"We're the Russians, *russkiye*," Dima explained. "We're Russian, while they're citizens of Russia, *rossiya-ne*. But there are also Russians among them. Let's think that. And let's write that. Otherwise, we'll go nuts."

I watch that clip of the *porebrik* scene over and over. "What are you doing here, *rossiyane?*" I ask.

And he, or rather they—the men in camouflage—answer me almost immediately.

The first thing they built in Slovyansk was a prison.

A prison.

Michel Foucault would just cry.

Surveillance and punishment. Power over the body. Death in the name of the people. Government in the name of death. Public disciplinary procedures. Who is in their new prison? TV and movie directors, journalists, regular townspeople, activists...

...and *patriots*.

That word is hard to pronounce at first. It's wrapped in a packaging of false pathos, of Soviet teachings on the proper education of the young. The packaging features frenzied caricatures of spasmodic, rambunctious Ukrainian pseudonationalists, the kind who grabbed seats in Parliament so they could get rich and live it up.

It isn't a clean word, this word "patriot." It's a little bit foreign to us. It's been deliberately forgotten, shoved into the storage cupboard with the old stuff and skis. It's a word that doesn't come easily. It's a word that's mad at us because we took it the wrong way, we rejected it, we betrayed it. We left it to die. But without it we couldn't have drawn this line between "one of us" and "not one of us."

Anyway, you'd have laughed at this, and you can laugh now, but the first thing I ask about a person, whether I know them or not, is: "Is he a patriot?"

I know this makes me sound like an idiotic pre-school teacher. Who cares.

Because, after *porebrik*, I have no skin anymore. Their prison is my punishment. My skin has been peeled off, crudely, as a lesson to everybody. I hurt everywhere. Turns out I even had skin on my eyes. But now that skin's gone too. My eyes are wounds. They ache and bleed when I see the flag with the crucified chicken. Or the other one, the one without the chicken but with the three stripes. White, blue, and red. Aquafresh. My friends betrayed that toothpaste in an ecstasy of disgust for those colors. That poor toothpaste never hurt anybody.

"They're hysterical," you'll say. That's okay. But I'm not going to waste any more energy on pointless conversations with people who betrayed the country.

This isn't a civil war. It's a fatherland war. "We were attacked, Lena."

I hear that voice in my own head. And there's not a single minute now when it doesn't hurt.

APRIL 13, 2014

Palm Sunday in the Ukrainian Orthodox liturgical calendar. The National Security Council of Ukraine, without declaring martial law and with the involvement of the Armed Forces of Ukraine, announces the beginning of the Anti-Terrorist Operation (ATO). The first battle takes place near Slovyansk. In Mariupol, the building of the city council is taken over by separatist forces.

* * *

FROM LETTERS NOT TO YOU

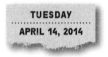 **SUNDAY**
APRIL 13, 2014

My friend works for a newspaper here. He's editor of the regional edition of *The Moscow Komsomolets*. He got a secret letter sent only to editors of all the regional editions of the paper requesting "all regional departments to reserve the headline story due to the changing situation and the probable deployment of troops to Ukraine tonight."

That's it, huh?

TUESDAY
APRIL 14, 2014

Two of our soldiers were taken hostage at the border. I don't know how. The other side's demanding that we open the border, or they'll kill them. The information's being distributed everywhere, in all news channels. To give our guys a chance to at least get out there and maybe get them back, trade something for them. It's in Amvrosiivka, a fair distance from Slovyansk. On the border with Rostov oblast.

They set up a no man's land without invading. They're still talking about a civil war, for now. They're reinforcing the Kramatorsk aerodrome with extra people, to "protect" it from the Americans and the Right Sector. At first, there were around 150 people there. But then some provocateurs started passing around vodka. You get the picture: some of the "protectors" have surrendered, in a pretty bad state.

The "men in camo" are moving from Slovyansk to Donetsk. They're in civilian clothes. We're having a pro-Ukraine demonstration on April 17. We all know what the dangers are, but our demonstration will be peaceful, quiet. It's Holy Week, Maundy Thursday. It'll all be okay, God willing.

APRIL 16, 2014

The Donetsk oblast state administration building is occupied by insurgents.

APRIL 17, 2014

Geneva discussion takes place between Ukraine, the USA, the European Union, and Russia. A large anti-separatist rally in Donetsk is underway.

THURSDAY
APRIL 17, 2014

Dear Maksim, I have a request for you. Today, we're demonstrating for peace and for Ukraine. They're saying they're going to shoot to kill. We're still going. I have a bullet-proof vest. If something happens, could you give my little speech for me at the award ceremony?

And if the really bad something happens, then please end the little speech with the phrase "Glory to Ukraine." But, if everything turns out okay, I'll come and say it myself.

THURSDAY
APRIL 17, 2014

Wait—if you don't mind, please end it with *Putin—khuilo*, "Putin's a dickhead."

APRIL 20, 2014

In the Ukrainian Orthodox liturgical calendar for 2014, Passion Week is celebrated from Palm Sunday on April 13 to Easter Sunday on April 20.

* * *

PASSION WEEK: EASTER SUNDAY

DONETSK—
MOSCOW—
DONETSK

I can't talk to you. So, I text: "Christ is risen!" You will write: "He is risen indeed."

We are polite people.

Other "polite people"—with strong accents from the Caucasus—killed three men. First, they tortured them. Then they opened their bellies. The victims were still alive... And they were still alive when they were thrown into the river... That's Slovyansk. That's the "Russian world."

Now churches are not just places to bow to icons, they're places to store weapons. There's a priest from Slovyansk in the front lines. People say he actually does some shooting. When he's not drinking.

I don't judge.

I won a literary prize. It's in Moscow. It's called the Russian Prize. I don't know whether to go accept it.

A year ago, I'd have wept with joy and dreamed narcissistically about my first big prize. But now it doesn't matter.

Do I go or not?

The "peaceful protesters" are taking over the airport. They're not killing anybody, they're just raising that rag of theirs with the crucified chicken. It doesn't really fit Easter, though. The eggs are missing.

Do I go to a city where they're serving up war as appetizer, main course, and dessert? Where they eat and drink war? Get drunk on it? Do I go to Nazi freaking Berlin? Even if it does have antifascists in it?

"It's not a state prize," says my friend Maksim Osipov. "You can take it."

I'm writing for him, not you. It's his pain I'm making worse, not yours. His conscience and shame allow me to discharge my own hate.

And I send him the text of a speech that has to be given.

* * *

US AND THEM

APRIL 2014
DONETSK

"You want the Banderites to come and burn us alive? Have you read our paper? Come on, what are you thinking?!"

There's a time and a place. A time and a place.

Her name is Larisa. I buy books from her. In our city—which turned into the center of Europe this year and very resentfully shared the fame with its suburbs, also competing for the honor—in our city, there were no bookstores. Just a market. Rows of stalls, hastily thrown together, cold in winter, stifling in summer, they all needed work (but renovation or demolition?)—they stood as a monument to the dying reader, whose fate they shared. The layout: square numbered stalls with a nest of books in the middle. One sixty-three carried children's books at wholesale. Two seventeen was textbooks, answer keys, and visual aids. One ten called itself "Paragraph" and posted a slogan: "Buy something just for fun." Regulars deemed this stall tawdry. The market had its own oligarchs and its own poor. There was a Quonset hut where the retailers used to be crammed in, but the oligarchs kicked them out and took over. They privatized it and announced it was a book supermarket. They handed out shopping baskets at the entrance. The poor were left out in the open. Summer or winter, they worked at their stalls. They sold enchanted stones, old books covered in oilcloth, CDs, and even videotapes.

Larisa was a representative of the literary middle class. Last year, she had dealt with the door to her little kiosk. This year, she was planning on upgrading the fan with an air conditioner. She and her husband liked "the classics" and crime novels. They had Balzac, Faulkner, Steinbeck, and Tolstoy, both collected works and individual volumes in nice, embossed covers. Their shop was known as the smartest. But they made their living not from smarts but from bad habits, mine along with everybody else's. The series Medicine for Boredom, started way back when by the late Ilya Kormiltsev, turned detective stories into an almost elevated genre. This reconciled Larisa with reality. And with me, since I would on no account agree to "get a new Balzac." "After all, Balzac is not a car," I said, trying to convince Larisa. "Pages that have been read by someone have meaning, right? What do I need an updated model for? Even in a nice buckram binding?"

"But when yours crumbles into dust and is completely useless, you'll get your new one from me, right?"

I promised I would. In the meantime, I bought crime novels. Back then, I still believed that it was fundamentally impossible for Balzac to crumble into dust.

"I mean it! Tell me! Don't you keep quiet! I never expected this kind of thing from you! Look around! The junta's taken over in Kyiv! They'll come out here and kill us all! I'll never forgive them for this! And I'll only vote for Communists because they tell the whole truth. They're not afraid of anything. But you—you're an idiot, or else you're a fascist yourself."

She and I are sitting on the floor. Back-to-back. On the fifth story of the oblast state administration building, the building that declared itself a "republic." Our hands are tied behind our backs. Our feet are almost free, if you don't count the chain that's attached to the wall at one end and to our ankles (my left, Larisa's right) at the other, with this special clasp that looks like a bracelet.

They "got" us for disseminating fascist literature. Or, rather, they got Larisa, and I went as a witness since I talked a lot. Larisa was done in by her passion for the classics. She thought Taras Shevchenko was eternal. But he turned out to be a Banderite, too. And let's not forget Lesia Ukraïnka. Sure, she was in Russian translation, but—the name alone!

Three armed "peaceful protesters" demanded that we surrender "all the agitational propaganda." Larisa, insulted, said that this was books. She even tried to defend them, shielding them with her body, comically throwing out her arms and even trying to lie down on top of them.

"I won't give them up!" she shouted. I was shouting, too. Not for the police. Because the police couldn't help us. Ever since March, when the police had sold all its weapons for a song to the "peaceful protesters," and then April, when it sold all its body armor (but to patriots), the police hadn't been able to do squat. I shouted something ridiculous: "Get your hands off her! Shame on you! Shame on you!" My "shame on you's" made me sound like the washstand from Korney Chukovsky's poem about the dirty little boy who wouldn't wash. I should've added the line about dirty chimneysweeps too. But I missed my chance.

"Tie her up. That one, too," ordered the "peaceful activist," his voice breaking. "We'll see. We'll get it out of them. Then we'll shoot them if anything's wrong with them."

"Where do we put them?"

"On the fifth floor. The NKVD."[13]

There really was a little sign on the fifth floor, by the elevator, with the letters "NKVD" on it. The elevator hadn't worked ever since the new government was founded. Things had started going wonky the very first day...

"Wait for the captain," grunted one of them. He was fashionable. His balaclava was green. It looked like it had been knitted by hand. Somebody loved that revolutionary. Maybe it was his grandma. Or maybe it was the handiwork of his girlfriend. It's very romantic to knit a cap with eye, nose, and mouth holes.

We sat and waited. I kept quiet. Larisa didn't know how to keep quiet, nor did she want to. Buying a crime novel from her without hearing who the killer was—yeah, right! Once, a long time ago, back in winter, they had been my joy, part of my own march of liberation with a dollop of secrecy and small victory.

"No! You don't understand! You don't see! Those Banderites of yours have already taken over the dorm of the cultural-educational school. Two thousand people. They'll come by night and kill anybody who looks at them funny! And they'll send us out into the streets to beg! You mark my words!"

"Have your hands gone to sleep?" I asked.

"Don't you start! Don't you be making your comparisons here! Sure, we're sitting here—but we're *alive*. You get the difference?"

Who among us doesn't love being the smartest, the one who wins arguments? I don't. Not anymore.

A person can get used to anything. A month ago, I might have gotten so furious that my commanding voice would've been heard on the Golan Heights, whose position we'd been so strenuously supporting in matters of new status and being a good neighbor. Thirty days is a long time. In that time, I had calmed down, learned to tell whether strangers were "one of us" from their tone. And to remain silent with them in unison. Because there was still hope. It was weak, with a terrible diagnosis: breech presentation, heart defect, respiratory failure... But it was still there.

Larisa wore out after an hour. We spent five minutes in silence. Then the door opened and the "captain" came in. His face wasn't covered up. It was the face of my student Vasnetsov. Third-year student. Second desk from the window. From a mining village. He always looked out the window during my lectures. I know his profile better than my own.

Everything that was outside that window in our big, well-fed city was more important and more interesting for him than anything I could tell him about.

We tried to expel Vasnetsov. Twice. His father came. A former miner. When his mine was closed, he switched to a small, illegal private mine. A *kopanka*. A hole in the ground. You mine by hand with picks, carry it up to the surface by hand in buckets... No machines, no nothing...

"I'll do everything I can to get him out of this hell," his father said. "I've given everything I have for his education. Don't destroy him. You're human beings, too..."

We've seen the kopankas. We understand...

If you look down at the oblast from an airplane, parts of it look like the moon. Like craters on the moon. But there are people inside.

"Whoops," said Vasnetsov, blushing furiously. "There's been a small mistake."

"You're a son of a bitch," I said grimly. "You made no mistake with me. But you did with her. Go on, let her go. And make sure she gets home."

"Of course, absolutely. I'll send a guard with her. The city's full of thugs with assault rifles. They pretend they're part of our movement." He lowered his voice. "They're profiting off of it. They even rob people." Then he said, "Well, anyway, you're free to go!"

"See?" Larisa said. "They figured it out. They saw the situation. They're honest guys. Not like your Banderites."

I saw Vasnetsov's back go tense. He stopped in the doorway and turned around and looked at me with grim sadness. The same way he used to look out the window.

"That's right," I said. "You made no mistake with me. Don't you need political prisoners? To complete the set? I'm ready and willing. But send Larisa home. Hurry up."

"My word is my bond," said Vasnetsov. He unlocked the leg cuffs, first from Larisa's ankle, then from mine. There was something acutely awkward about it. A feminine awkwardness, sure... I can't say the *only* person ever to have knowledge of my legs so up close and personal was my husband. But Vasnetsov's the *last* person I'd ever want to make that acquaintance. (An acquaintance with my legs. Not with my husband.)

"May I escort you?" asked Vasnetsov at the exit from the "republic."

"Won't that look bad for you?"

"I have a plan for you. You know, every state has its dissidents. The stronger the dissidents are, the stronger the state is. And you're a strong lady. Not easily scared. Am I right?"

We were walking through the city. Spring was winding down. It wasn't hot yet. It wasn't cold. It hadn't rained. The apricots weren't blooming. We'd missed the lilacs, too. They were already over there, on the other side. And in this world, the one Vasnetsov and I were walking through, there wasn't anything. We'd let it all slip away.

"We're not like that, you know. We just want to be heard. That's what we want. We want everyone everywhere to hear us."

"I've been ready to hear you since class last winter. You still have an incomplete, Vasnetsov. And I really do want to hear you."

He sighed. We stopped at the crosswalk: he with his AK-100 automatic rifle, I with my bruised wrists. We waited for the green light. It was a very long light for a big traffic junction. There were still cars on the roads, still traffic jams. We darted across on a blinking yellow.

Two cars, three, five... Nice cars. German and Japanese. Expensive and clean. The car washes were still working then. Only the jewelry and fur stores had closed.

Vasnetsov sighed again.

"I'm never going to be a big shot. And nobody in our new republic's presidium will be, either. But after me and the people like me, different people will show up. And they will create a universe. And we'll have our own astronauts, our own Gagarin. And we'll have everything. You see? Everything will be the way it should be, for the people to live, and for the people to be proud. Not like it is now.... Do you believe me?"

I quietly shake my head no.

* * *

PASSIONATE PEOPLE

At the pro-Ukraine demonstration. Who would ever have thought it could be so scary? All day the radio has been broadcasting exhortations from the mayor's office: "Don't go! It's dangerous! No one can guarantee you won't be killed! Don't go..."

This is a civil war, you say?

Then why can't we go to a pro-Ukraine demonstration? Why are the orcs promising to kill us if we do?

If it's a civil war then we should all still be for Ukraine, right?

Some of us for a unitary Ukraine, others for a federal Ukraine—right?

Why is the tricolor okay, but the yellow and blue will get you killed?

Where are we? Where *are* we?

But wait—do you know why the first thing the "peaceful protesters" do is to seize the TV tower?

An object of strategic importance, right. Pravda.vru (i.e., "it's.true.I.lie"), not pravda.ru (i.e., "truth.ru"). Dead-24 (not Live-24). LieNews (not LifeNews). And all the rest of them.

Now those channels are all we have.

Incidentally, I know what they're stuffing your head with. Poor guy... I feel sorry for you...

No, really, I do.

Whereas I, on the other hand, know what it's like to live your last day. It's nothing special, actually. Before the demonstration, I wrote my blood group on a piece of paper, along with the phone number of someone who can identify me.

Children shouldn't take part in something like that. But it'd be even worse for parents to have to do the identifying. I wrote down Zhenka's number.

My last day. It's Maundy Thursday.

I didn't say any goodbyes, I didn't want to scare anyone.

I watered my plants. Wiped off all their leaves.

If it happens, they'll have to wait forty days. My little loves. They'll have to wait until the initial pain passes.

They'll dry out, though...

Enough. No more of that.

A regular day. Just a very scary one.

But you know what? We got through it.

The vulgarity's what I remember most. After the demonstration, a woman my age was walking down the middle of the street, waving a flag on a stick.

The orcs were in a car. They couldn't work their way up to getting out. She was very convincing, this woman. She was tall, and threatening, and cheerful.

The orcs shouted at her: "Suck my dick, you old Banderite!"

She stopped walking. She set the flag down at her feet. She put her hands on her hips. The whole nine yards.

Then, loudly, so the whole boulevard could hear: "Get out of here, you little half-pints! I don't suck wee-wees!"

* * *

MONDAY

APRIL 21, 2014

MOSCOW

"Hi. We're fascists and Banderites now."

"Hi. We're traitors to our country and fifth columnists."

Maksim Osipov. He's a writer and a heart doctor. A cardiologist. We're sitting in a sushi bar. The Zamoskvorechye district. Lemonade, a very tasty ginger lemonade. The ceremony's tomorrow.

I went to Moscow.

Moscow's like Berlin. But like Kyiv, too. I look at the crowds of people in the metro and realize I could start a pro-freedom demonstration right here. I could also sing the Ukrainian national anthem. The metro's a good place to start a revolution.

And the square stones of the road here... they're loose. They waggle back and forth like loose snot. You don't even need a crowbar, just bend over and pick them up. And then along the Kamennyi Bridge to the Kremlin. Nothing to it...

Another thing about being here is that I get enough sleep, which I didn't expect. But when there's no people with assault rifles or shoulder-fired rocket launchers around, you sleep better.

"Why don't you leave Donetsk?" asks Maksim.

"Why don't you leave Russia?" I answer.

We sigh. We grin. What's happening doesn't seem real to us. We're living the good life in our imagined worlds where good defeats evil. Or where good at least exists...

"Well, now we can understand the Jews who didn't run from Hitler until the very end..."

"By the end there wasn't anybody left to run."

That's right: we're not running because our beyond-the-looking-glass is so absurd that it can't be real. The acting is bad, the actors are bad, the screenplay's riddled with plot holes. It's not even a farce. What's the point of running...

Maksim says, "Even so, there's a point past which you can't live."

"And we haven't reached that point yet."

It's not nineteen thirty-seven yet. It's not nineteen thirty-nine yet. And I don't think it's nineteen forty-one yet...[14]

There's still a lot that's comical. Parodic. I talk about that to dispel the fear. For example, the "prime minister" of the "Donetsk People's Republic," Denis Pushilin, is a member of a Ukrainian political party sponsored by the Russian Ponzi scheme MMM. Or there's the chairman of the Central Election Commission ("Oh, they have one?")... This chairman is famous for legally changing his name ten years ago, so he'd have the exact same name as the incumbent mayor. He went to vote with his new passport. You could take a picture with him for ten thousand dollars. He'd say, "I just need a million dollars—that's it, nothing else. I don't know how to do anything but take the fall for someone else. Just make me an offer..."

Maksim nods. "Looks like he got his offer."

"Yup. The people's mayor of Slovyansk lives off his sugar mama. That's the sum total of his accomplishments. And comrade Bezler, the one who took Horlivka, wanted nothing more than to be a cemetery manager, but something went wrong..."

"Are there any of them that *don't* have a long and complicated medical history?" laughs my friend Maksim. My husband shakes his head: "No. They're all either chronic cases or having a relapse..."

APRIL 21, 2014

Pro-Russian activists in Odesa proclaim the establishment of the "Odesa People's Republic."

APRIL 22, 2014

In Donetsk, separatists yield the council chamber of the Donetsk oblast state administration building, along with two floors of the building, to state officials. The stalled Anti-Terrorist Operation (ATO) is renewed.

* * *

TUESDAY

APRIL 22, 2014

M O S C O W

I speak about a love that doesn't insist on its own way; that isn't jealous; that derives no joy from untruth, but rather shares in the joy of truth. About a love that never gets tired. About Ukraine.

Instead of "Putin's a dickhead," I pronounce a long statement about how the person who wants war is so strong he's crazy, and in that lunacy he's capable of conquering whatever he feels the need to conquer. Conquering Ukraine is something he can probably do. But he can't kill Ukraine. To kill Ukraine he has to kill me, *russkaya*, a Russian. And he has to kill other Russians, too.

I read my printed-off speech. I don't look out into the audience. I'm scared. I'm very scared. Even though it doesn't seem to be nineteen thirty-seven yet.

You know what? This may be the first time in my life that I haven't wanted anyone to like me, I haven't tried to lay on the charm. I don't care about what all these people might think about me. These more or less liberal, sympathetic, understanding, even kind people. These *rossiyane*, Russian citizens.

I'm not talking to them. Or to Putin. In this speech, I'm talking to myself.

"Don't be afraid in love. Don't be afraid. Don't be afraid to love... Ukraine is such a great joy..."

The cultural attaché from the Embassy of Kazakhstan pulls me aside and says, "Hold on. Hold on out there. We're neutral, of course. But we are aware that we're next. Those people will come to 'protect' our Russian-speakers if you give up. So don't give up! Hold on..."

* * *

SATURDAY
APRIL 23, 2014
D O N E T S K

We're not leaving. Because this is our country and our city. The orcs are building checkpoints and, on weekends, they usually storm something useless. Just another prosecutor's office, courtroom, or police station. Nobody bothers filing criminal charges against them.

One of my graduate students is defending her dissertation: "The Image of the Enemy in Soviet Print News Media of Ukraine from 1928 to 1939."

That's not the past anymore. That's our present. The "Donetsk People's Republic" shut down the newspapers, even the most loyal ones, "for publishing faked photographs." The orcs don't like their own faces. We understand this feeling and share it: we don't like their faces, either. But now they have their own "correct newspapers," the ones that toe the party line.

The image of the enemy is simple and clear: fascists, the junta, Eurogays, pindoses, the American military machine.

Now here's an interesting moment. Just in case you didn't know, *pindos*—singular—is the ethnic slur for American.[15] Any American, of any color. But what you see all over the pro-Russian new-old newspapers is pictures of "American Negroes." Not just any old pindoses. Specifically "Negroes." Because how can you tell if some random dead white guy is American or not? But a dead Black guy—the pro-Russian press calls them "Negroes"—those have to be American. Get it? There's the proof it's Americans. So. Back to the pictures. "Negroes" with no legs lying in the hospitals of "Russian Slovyansk." "Negroes" jumping out of helicopters next to the TV towers of Kostyantynivka and Mariupol. Never mind that there never were any TV towers there. There still aren't. But there are "American Negroes"! And there are also "Negroes" in the photographs of corpses that the "valiant defenders" toss out when they land.

The "Negroes," once again, are Americans. And wow—they're everywhere.

Lev Trotsky wrote somewhere that, if you believed the Soviet newspapers, then his people, Trotskyists, occupied all the key posts in the government. And if that was the case, then it made no sense why Stalin was still sitting there in the Kremlin, and not him, with his "army of Trotskyists."

The opponent, the external challenger, on my graduate student's committee is from Kyiv. We make him sick. He hates us. It's our fault. We're not Ukrainian enough. He says he'll teach us to love our motherland, he'll show us how it's done.

I know he's hurting. And I also know that, for years to come, we, the inhabitants of this cursed region, will bear the responsibility for everything. Collectively, as is the custom.

APRIL 27, 2014

Regional broadcasting centers are captured by separatists, who replace local programming with Russian television channels.

APRIL 28, 2014

A pro-Ukrainian demonstration in Donetsk is attacked by masked men armed with baseball bats, resulting in heavy injuries and the disappearance of some of the participants in the demonstration. The Donetsk police do not interfere as pro-Ukrainian protesters are being attacked.

MAY 1, 2014

Labor Day. Separatists seize the prosecutor's office in Donetsk. Acting President Turchynov decrees the reinstatement of military conscription.

MAY 4, 2014

The flag of the "Donetsk People's Republic" ("DPR") is raised over Donetsk police headquarters.

MAY 3, 2014

Ukrainian armed forces establish control over Mount Karachun near Slovyansk. Separatist attacks continue, resulting in the collapse of the tower of the Kramatorsk radio and TV transmitter station, located on Mount Karachun.

MAY 6, 2014

Pro-Russian separatists install checkpoints controlling all traffic on the main streets of Mariupol, while briefly vacating and then retaking the building of the city council.

MAY 9, 2014

The Soviet-era "Victory Day" (in Ukraine, starting in 2015, replaced by the Day of Victory over Nazism in World War II). In Mariupol, around sixty armed fighters attempt to take over the local branch of the Ministry of Internal Affairs. Fourteen tanks of the Ukrainian Armed Forces enter the city, and fire breaks out in the building of the city council and the local prosecutor general's office.

MAY 10, 2014

The Ukrainian government decides to withdraw National Guard troops from Mariupol in order to avoid further bloodshed and loss of life. The local police also leave the city. Looting of local shops is reported.

* * *

THE EASTERN FRONT

SATURDAY

MAY 10, 2014

MARIUPOL

Kolyan and Grishka liberated an IFV from the Ukrainian army. It was a total accident, but still, Kolyan was driven by ideology: he didn't like Banderites. Although, as he himself admitted, he didn't know what a Banderite was. Grishka was not driven by ideology. Grishka liked his vodka. But here's the deal: it's buddies hangin' in the city, right, plus you can make a few kopecks, so why not do a little fighting? Grishka wouldn't mind ending up among the fallen, actually. He's got no place to live, no money—so, screw it. And besides, ever since he was a kid, he'd known that bullets are bimbos while bayonets are heroes. So, anyway, they liberated an IFV. It was their striped military undershirts that did it—scared the bejeebus out of the little soldier boys.

Kolyan tore at his "Abibas" shirt, screaming as loud as he could, "Shoot me right in my communist chest! Shoot, you scum!" The boys were young, inexperienced; they got flustered. But not Kolyan. Bang! He popped one off. He and Grisha'd gotten the pistol the day before from some cops. It had come in handy.

At this point, Grisha wanted to say the Lord's Prayer, but the only part he remembered was "Let death, once come, be quick; let wounds, once got, be small." He screwed his eyes shut and roared this as loud as he could. When he opened his eyes again, the little soldier boys were gone. Pissed themselves at the thought of shooting a good working man.

Grisha knew how to drive. A tractor, not an IFV, but what's the difference? He and Kolyan got in, called over some more guys and took off. Nice. Went by some shops, went past Kolyan's house, so the homeboys could see, and then went up and down the main drag, Lenin Street. Up and down, up and down.

They sputtered to a stop right in front of the city council building.

"That's the fucking army for you," said Kolyan. "They fob off all the broken-down old junk on everybody else and build themselves dachas. Fat-faced generals. Here, lemme take a look. I'm dynamite with engines."

Grisha was not dynamite with engines. He moved over. Kolyan poked around for a while and clicked his tongue pensively. Their comrades also eyeballed the equipment. They tore off a panel. There were more wires behind it.

"Americans must've made this. Doesn't look Russian, somehow."

"No way, man, they did this on purpose to mess us up. Just lemme catch those pindos sons-of-bitches, I'll kill 'em," said Kolyan angrily. "What the crap we supposed to do with it now?"

"How 'bout a campfire?" suggested Grisha. "We'll go out and bake us some potatoes and have a drink, huh?"

In warm weather, Grisha lived in a little wooded area outside the city. He'd recently stolen one of those little pop-up promotional tents with promises of imminent stability and prosperity plastered on its waterproof walls. It was a good tent: big and kept the rain out.

"A campfire!" agreed Kolyan, excited. "We'll burn this Banderite machinery to the freaking ground. Boys! Got any Molotov cocktails?"

They did. But in plastic bottles. Kolyan and Grisha each threw one. Nothing happened. Insulting.

Some nice folks, their people, started telling them they needed to use glass. The cool thing about glass, you see, is that it breaks. So, when it hits you get that combustion, that larger area of things catching fire. Fire burns everything the gasoline lands on.

They got their cocktails together. Easy enough: they snagged a plastic bottle from a passer-by. Why not? Now they all had a Molotov cocktail, a knife, and a mask each—some in briefcases, others in backpacks. The masks were cut out of women's black winter tights. And they scored more than one glass bottle, and more than one full one, in a shop. For free. To support the revolutionary uprising of the people. But the hardware store had an insulting sign on it: "All inventory stolen. Kindly leave us alone." But that's no big deal. Just one more reason for us to separate ourselves from them by means of war and to insist on our rights.

Anyway, they laid into the IFV. It burst into flames. They lit it up from both sides, just to be sure and also because it looked better.

Guys started coming over to admire it. They took pictures, to show off to their girlfriends.

They also took pictures of Grisha. He looked good throwing stuff. He'd gotten an A in gym. Old-school Soviet style.

Once he ran out of Molotov cocktails—he only had a couple—he threw rocks. He also threw sidewalk paving stones the lollygaggers gave him. Some dug the good ol' pavers out with fancy manicured nails, others with fancy hunting knives. Terrific.

Except that suddenly that Banderite bastard let out a huge bang. And then another one. And another one, and another...

"Hey, who's in there?" yelped Kolyan. "Who's in there?"

"Freaking Americunts," people said, scared. "There's Americunts in there. And NATO!"

"Shit, it's an assault," someone behind Grisha shouted. "Assault!!!" echoed down the street.

Kolyan and Grisha thought for a second and ran for the city council building. Yesterday, it had been the revolutionary headquarters, but last night half of it had burned down. The mob did it, thinking they were flushing out the Right Sector. But the only victims of the fire were the desks and chairs nobody'd managed to cart off home yet.

"Everybody into the building!" shouted Kolyan. "We'll take cover there. Take no prisoners. We'll defend ourselves down to our last bullet! Follow me!"

Two other folks joined in. Guys they didn't know. Three people total, if you counted people they did know: Mar'Pal'na, the coat-check lady. She wailed, "My dears, please, in the name of Christ the Lord, I beg you, don't break anything here... There's nothing else to break, but still—it's government property... In the name of Christ the Lord, huh?"

From inside the building, Kolyan aimed the pistol he got yesterday from the cops at the IFV. "Ready! Aim! Fire!" he commanded.

"Fire!" shouted Grisha.

They fired and shouted.

Then they fired some more.

And, all of a sudden, the IFV went quiet.

So, they won. Kolyan and Grisha. Well, and those other two guys.

But then Grisha got sad. He felt really bad for Mar'Pal'na, the coat check lady. Not because he was drunk, but for real. He'd already guessed what was up with her, because it was all plain to see: she lived in the city council building. Maybe her kids had kicked her out, maybe it was something else. And so, she'd quietly found a warm, dry spot for herself, either by cunning or by the watchman's kindness. But what now? Everything had burned up here, everything, both her little alcove and her paltry possessions. And she was no longer of an age for year-round begging. Spring and summer, sure, no big deal, but winter? It brought tears to his eyes. It occurred to him that he could take Mar'Pal'na back home with him. There were some nice potatoes there, and nature... And the tent, of course... As long as it hadn't been stolen by thieves covetous of the declaration that stability and prosperity were just a day away...

MAY 11, 2014

The "independence referendum" takes place in Donetsk.

* * *

HOW TO HOLD A REFERENDUM: A METHODOLOGICAL HANDBOOK FOR NEW INVADERS

SUNDAY

MAY 11, 2014

D O N B A S

Get some *vata*—some nice, fluffy cotton wool.

Also get a lot of Kalashnikovs and Rahshah-TV journalists.

The vata is very important. Vata is a new concept that should enter the international lexicon along with "sputnik" and "glasnost."

Vata is the brain structure of one-seventh of the earth's land mass and the fringe elements that go along with it.[16]

There is no blood in the vata brain. No blood vessels. No wrinkles, hemispheres, or grey matter. None of any of that.

There's just vata—nice, fluffy cotton. It is very absorbent. It is excellent at being tamped down. You can make it into cotton balls, or cotton swabs, or cotton wadding...

The Russian Federation manufactures vata at a massive scale. Schools, higher education, and television are all part of the production process.

Although television alone would be enough.

Vata's other advantages? It scares easily. It's not inclined to see cause-and-effect connections. But it's very proud of itself.

Oh, and vata is definitely not a fascist. Quite the opposite. When it's twisted into cotton wadding and dressed in camouflage, it pretends it's fighting fascism by drawing swastikas and other "Sieg Heil"-type stuff on its arms.

Vata is irreplaceable for referendums. It's the whole foundation. It posts fliers and conscientiously takes payment for participating in protests. And for a token pittance from Yanukovych the fugitive, vata is happy to throw itself at tanks and sit on vote-counting committees to tot up any number of votes.

People with automatic rifles are another important component of referendums. You have to have a lot of them. Don't be shy about the automatic rifles you bought at the grocery store: distribute them to the aborigines. But you must make sure to put your own specially-trained man, an officer, in charge of the locals. Otherwise the locals will steal something, and then drink it, and you'll find them later lying in the bushes, useless. But if you set one of your own over every five or ten locals, it works pretty well.

Locals are really excellent when it comes to bashing down the doors of schools where they never did manage to get diplomas. Don't even think about opening all the polling stations. Otherwise, there won't be lines and you won't get that accurate picture of an entire people expressing its will. Better to do less but better, as the great

Lenin used to say. Stop at ten in the big million-population cities, four in cities of a hundred thousand, and just one in all the other cities. For the aborigines, that's plenty.

You can print out ballots on any printer. No need to be delicate here.

You can have a lot of ballots. Or not. The quantity's not important. Later you'll count them as instructed anyway. If you need more, add some. If you've got too many, toss some.

Nobody's asking you to *keep* the ballots.

After the referendum's over, the best thing is actually to burn them.

And, last but not least: journalists.

They should only be at the polling stations in the morning. Pay special attention to the Western ones. Ply them with drink, flatter them, seduce them, offer them your own car, your companionship, your cameraman, but stay with them all day. Don't let Europeans make it all the way to evening sober. Never let them stop by the polling stations as they're closing "just in case"!

In the morning! Only in the morning!

Keep in mind that your crowd is, one, grandmas dreaming of sausage for two twenty a kilo, and two, ideologically-driven losers whose lives were better the day before yesterday than today.[17] The latter group is often heavy drinkers. They have headaches starting first thing in the morning and they're highly active then. Take advantage of that.

From eight to ten get video of lines, grandmas, and members of vote-counting committees. Whatever you do, don't get any footage of automatic rifles. Send them around the corner. They can't be in the shot. It has to look to viewers as though the people's expression of will is free, transparent, and of sound mind.

Announce 80% turnout, even if you only see one person at the polling station.

Remember that at twelve the coach turns into a pumpkin: the polling station will be empty and unattractive, which won't be helpful for our common cause.

Never, ever film at night. You might get beat up!

Count the votes the very same day. Don't delay the announcement of the results, even if this means you announce them in the middle of the night.

Don't use numbers over one hundred. Be aware that certain people don't believe that something can win a hundred and fifteen percent of votes. Well, right now they don't. But we'll fix that.

When announcing the results, don't forget what the vote was for. That doesn't look good.

Finally, we need the picture and sound to coincide by at least ten percent or so. The vata will fill in the rest on its own.

Now go for it, dear builders of the "Russian world"! Let our truth be your guide!

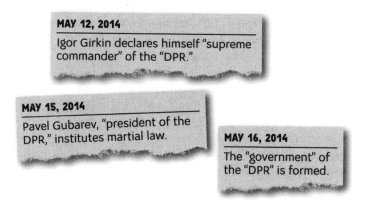

MAY 12, 2014

Igor Girkin declares himself "supreme commander" of the "DPR."

MAY 15, 2014

Pavel Gubarev, "president of the DPR," institutes martial law.

MAY 16, 2014

The "government" of the "DPR" is formed.

* * *

IN THE SHADE

THURSDAY
MAY 15, 2014
KOSTYANTYNIVKA

So how do you like "big politics,"
Slovyansk?

There are different ways for
towns to make a name for themselves. Usually it takes a war. That's
what makes a town turn from a dot on a map into a sign,
a watchword, a name that makes a foreign or very distant
imagination call up a picture and see it. Actually, see streets
that were still normal yesterday, streets like thousands of
other streets in provincial towns, see them as heroic, tragic, bloody, barricaded, mournful, empty, terrifying...

The first towns get the glory. Or the bloodiest ones.
Then the others follow. But the world doesn't have
enough interest—either elevated human interest or vul-
gar frenetic spectating—for all of them.

The towns that come in second remain dots on a
map. Even if everything's the same, or almost the same,
as in the first cities. Nobody asks them "So, how do you
like big politics, Kostyantynivka?"

Nevertheless, there are also barricades in Kostyantynivka. And burning tires. And the trash isn't picked up.
And the "peaceful protesters" have a lot of Kalashnikovs,
and the tank that was taken down from its pedestal actually started! So now it and a milk truck are both parked
blocking the road to keep out Banderites and space aliens.

My great-grandpa lived in Kostyantynivka. The entire family was evacuated during the war. In the spring of
forty-one, my great-grandpa planted an apple tree. A rare
variety, nobody from my family remembers what kind
anymore. But rare, unusual. Frivolous. My great-grandpa
didn't evacuate, he stayed behind for that tree and for

two feather beds, his daughter's dowry. These were very valuable. He sewed sacks for the feather beds and buried them in the ground. At a distance from the apple tree.

Now there's a satellite of Donetsk university in Kostyantynivka. Higher education moved closer to students' registered place of residence. It was cheaper to send instructors out two times a year for exams than to pay for a dormitory. There might have been some other benefit as well. But that's not the point. Twice a year isn't very often. And it was also obvious that it was unnecessary and served no purpose. My great-grandpa would've said, "You can lead a horse to water but you can't make him drink." But they hardly even bothered to walk up to the trough, these horses. Much less drink. They weren't too keen on reading or writing. Although the Internet access and the digitized books we uploaded for them by the megabyte should have given them a little inspiration. But alas, that was not the case.

Anyway, it was time for final exams and we had to go out there. News media agencies were giving the standard terse updates on the latest round of buildings that had been seized and hostages that had been taken, including identifying information for the hostages' cars and wallets. Kostyantynivka was included in the list of cities, but after the "including." It wasn't in the middle of big politics; it was next to it, on the way to it.

"You have sessions on Monday the nineteenth. Are you coming?" The satellite's director of academics was calling. She was the satellite dean's favorite daughter-in-law. The not-favorite daughter-in-law lived way up north with her fifth husband. All the children from all the marriages were here in Kostyantynivka with their grandma, who was very practical, and a saint of a woman, if you think about it.

"How can I run exam sessions? You're nothing but checkpoints and barricades out there..."

"Pff," scoffed the phone. "What are you talking about? There are only two barricades. And three checkpoints.

They're clean. We wash them every day. They're all our people..."

"The people with Kalashnikovs?"

"Well, yeah. They handed them out. Our Kolya took one, too. He takes turns on guard duty. That's what I'm telling you, it's all our people. It's not dangerous. We get bread and drinking water delivered. And there's electricity almost everywhere."

"Mm-hmm... but your mayor's had two cars stolen, right? What's up with that? Is that not dangerous?"

"There you go, 'stolen'! People just went joyriding!" I can tell she's starting to get offended. She's probably pursing her lips.

"But what does the mayor think of that?"

"The mayor doesn't even know!!" Hurt feelings forgotten, her voice now resounds with broad, sincere joy. "He's in France! On vacation. Oh—but it's a secret that he's in France. We're telling everyone that even though the mayor's office isn't in its regular location because it's gone underground, it's still working just fine... Oh, how do you say that... It's still operating as usual. So are you coming? Or are you still afraid?"

* * *

THE NEWS

 **MAY 2014**
DONETSK

What we say about ourselves is "Yes, we're hysterical." But some, the especially smart ones, the ones who used to study medicine, disagree: "This isn't hysteria, it's psychosis. You need to know the difference..."

We don't quibble about the little things. We're learning to love our condition. Being on a seesaw is good, actually. It's inherently optimistic, as long as you look around when you're at the lowest point.

A comrade writes... Well, comrade, I guess, but what other option is there? We've still got some issues with the lexicon... A few rough patches... Let's stick with comrade, even if this one is acting like a gossipy grandma.

He sends me a text: "There's been nothing but culture all morning. All channels, all social media: just culture and the weather. This lull isn't a good sign."

I am positive he's looking in the wrong places. And I am correct. I text him a reply: "A mining equipment factory was taken. A pump station was blown up. A glass bottle warehouse was shelled. The finance minister got into a fistfight with the minister of internal affairs. It took the entire fifth floor to separate them. Two cars were stolen from a parking lot. Don't worry. Everything's fine."

News is like gossip. Rumors send an electrical charge through the informational field. Everyone's a passive witness and everyone's an active participant. There are no middlemen. We all hold our vigils, we all weep in utter solitude.

If somebody stole something, it's good news.

If somebody calls in the military, though, it depends what floor they're calling from. If the call's from the seventh floor, it's no big deal. The local radicals are on seven. They call in the military five times a day. The neighborhood weirdos are on eight. Even their own death is afraid to enter their room without a psychiatrist present. If they call in the military, it's actually funny.

But when floor five calls in the military, it's scary. Five's the professionals. They're in it for the money and do what they're told. If they're the ones making the call, it's because they were told to. Scary.

It's scary when they take hostages but don't demand a ransom.

It's scary when they burn apartments because of flags.

It's scary when we find bodies with the stomachs sliced open.

There is a lot of news like this. Too much. Two, three, four stories an hour.

They're like shells that keep hitting closer and closer: your neighborhood, then your street, and then your building. They've been personal for a long time now, all these news stories.

There's a lump stuck in my throat. Just sitting there, like a highway patrolman who's found a lucrative spot. But I don't have anything to buy him off with anymore. I haven't had tears for a long time. Vodka has no effect. The doses of antidepressants keep getting higher, pretending they're just innocent little vitamin C. There's a strong urge to go out there where the shooting is, so it'll all just end instantaneously.

In those moments—always—and I've underlined "always" a hundred times, it's too bad you can't see it, in those moments I always get a text:

"Summer's still on! Tam-Tam Group boutiques invite you to come in and see their new collection of swimsuits and light summer jackets from the world's wildest, most in-demand designers!"

A list of designers is usually attached.

I know these boutiques. But I don't know why they are texting me, of all people. A bra strap from one of these boutiques costs as much as my monthly paycheck. Okay, maybe half a paycheck.

"Summer's still on!" Those boutiques and I are all in the same city. They see all the same news I do.

I swear to you, my dear Tam-Tam Group: after all this is over, the first thing I'll do is visit you. It'll be hard but I'll do it. Because now we all know that money's just paper. I'll come and buy everything you call light summer jackets.

* * *

SATURDAY
....
MAY 17, 2014
....
K Y I V

How I'm feeling out here? Like Professor Pleischner in Bern. Remember, from the Stierlitz stories? The spy who gets out of occupied territory for the first time? Breathing the air of freedom. Giddy from the air of freedom.

Like in *Seventeen Moments of Spring*, I'm carefully examining all the windows for the flowerpot signaling that my handler's been compromised. I'm still trying to talk quietly so I don't get captured... But this dizzying air of freedom... Nope, no way I could be an underground operative...

But out here, nobody's going to capture me.

I stop in the middle of the street, see Ukrainian flags, and start crying.

* * *

SATURDAY
....
MAY 17, 2014
....
K Y I V

There's a popular topic in the capital: give up Donbas. To hell with them, those degenerates. They're beyond saving anyway. They hate us, so why force them? Let them live the way they want.

They'll die off quicker that way. If they don't want to be in the new Ukraine with us, then what do we need them for? Dead weight, suitcases without handles. "Donetsk People's Republic?" "Luhansk People's Republic?" *And Novorossiya—"New Russia"? Really?* Whatever it is they want out there, let them have it. We'll relocate the normal ones and give Putin the fools. What's a million more, a million less. It's hard for a federation to accommodate fools.

That's the condensed version. And yes, it hurts. We might even deserve it.

Although... we conducted a study and we're not really all that foolish, to be honest.

A little more than thirty percent—that is, one out of every three people—dreamed of reuniting with the ur-mother. A few of them meant the USSR, others meant the RF (Russian Federation). And there were some who nurtured hopes of Donbas's self-determination.

One out of three seems like a lot.

But Donbas always was a wild nature preserve where the foot of a Ukrainian person would never tread. Or want to. It was a ghetto that intellectuals and businessmen just wrote off. A slave society, a feudal or tribal order... Communists, and the Party of Regions, and nobody else. Nobody would risk it, try to break through to them, go help them.

"Donbas... that's so yuck. How can you live there in that kingdom of brutes?"

"Lena, honey, forget those cretins and move out here with us." At first, "here" means to Kyiv; then, it means to Lviv, Dnipro, or Kharkiv; eventually, it means to anywhere else at all.

"This place is suffocating. How do you even breathe? Nothing you can do with these people, it's hopeless..."

This hurts, but it's my standard, daily pain, so it's not too bad. And I have a standard response: "The more of us there are among them, the fewer of them there are among us."

But here, in Kyiv, I explode. I shift to a shout: "If your teenage kids start using drugs and turn into animals, do you abandon them? If your parents get Alzheimer's and start pooping their pants, do you drive them out into the street? Renounce them? Wash your hands of them and head off into your happy forever after? Who has a severe case of social Darwinism and fascism now? Who has thick fog in their head now? And if it's not fog, if it's your principled position, then to hell with us. Give us away. Regular people went into that killing machine along with their mentally ill friends and family, and you're offering to kindly close the door of our gas chamber and lock it tight behind us... Adolf Aloisovich is weeping tears of joy because his struggle lives on..."

* * *

THE *UKRAINE: THINKING TOGETHER* CONFERENCE

THURSDAY, MAY 15–MONDAY, MAY 19, 2014

KYIV-MOHYLA ACADEMY

**SUNDAY
MAY 18, 2014
KYIV**

The play *Titus Andronicus* is considered the worst thing Shakespeare ever wrote. It's so bad there's doubt as to whether *they* even wrote it.

There's too much meaningless evil in the play, and almost no logic. Titus takes revenge on Tamora, Queen of the Goths. The Queen of the Goths takes revenge on him.

One Soviet Russian Shakespeare scholar, Aleksandr Anikst, counted it up: "fourteen murders, thirty-four bodies, three severed hands, one severed tongue..." He forgot the rapes and the slaughter of children, even of babies.

And it seems like there's no reason for any of it. It's a series of pointless endeavors. Every subsequent step only multiplies the bloodshed. At some point, the blood, drunk on itself, takes charge of the whole process. Blood and death for the sake of blood and death. And for the sake of the next interstitial victor's laughter. For the sake of this maniacal laughter...

Even for the seventeenth century, this whole bacchanalia of horror came off as a little overdone.

But no...

It's not overdone at all. The play *Titus Andronicus* is being performed on the stages of Slovyansk, Kramatorsk, Donetsk, Horlivka, Luhansk...

Hieronymus Bosch is doing the stage scenery. A ship of fools sailing into hell. Instead of a mast, it has a live tree with a fat goose tied to it, and it has a broken branch for a rudder. Going nowhere, for no reason. And the church. Yes. The church. Playing the lute. In hell. Sailing into hell and drawing others into hell with it.

And the faces... Faces that don't exist, that can't exist. The febrile imagination of an artist. Grotesque, you say?

He just drew what he saw. Faces you can't believe exist. Civilization hides them, and hides from them. It hides from these identical faces, smudged, as though half-erased by the same dirty eraser, blue-grey as ash, with saddle noses, with empty expressionless eyes, with mouths that are not for speaking, only for screaming. These faces will need centuries of faith to find empathy and compassion, to attain reason...

Everything is now Shakespeare here. And everything is Bosch.

Being, just living your everyday life, is hard for people. In choosing it, you have to be willing to suffer. "To be or not to be" is the question of every day, every moment. Freedom is an unbearable burden, in which an infinite "you" carries responsibility for an infinite world. The weight of all that is probably why we talk and write so much. A cosmic roll call: "We're here. We're here. We're here..."

Seems that not-being, not living that everyday life, is easier.

Maybe...

...Except that's death. Death is the one shouting, "Donbas needs to be heard!" It's not the people who are shouting it. Because those people *are not*. They, themselves, as people, *don't exist*. And they have not existed, for all these years.

Yanukovych truly is their president. Through him, they multiplied their emptiness. He was the measure, the scale of their own individual non-being in the world. We are like him. He is like us. He is one of us. He is us.

But not "he is me."

There is no "me" here. The "me," the "I" wasn't taught, it wasn't nurtured, it wasn't acknowledged as a possibility. An agglomeration at the edge of the abyss. One more step and no more you. Whether you're conscious of your "you" or not. Every living thing knows of its own death, somewhere, in its final or first cell. And death chortles, and sobs, and shrieks, "Hear me! I'm here!"

The space Yanukovych left behind was filled by Russia and Putin. Not by people's selves.

Being is a burden. Not being is hell.

People set out on the path to an imaginary, non-existent Russia. These people were given guns. They liked that. And with these guns, by means of these guns, they entered into reality.

The perennial nobody, the perennial zero grabbed a Kalashnikov and became a somebody, a ten. A boss. A commander. Screaming death made manifest. Ready for service...

Nobody is attacking them. But they sleep with their automatic rifles. Because a Kalashnikov has a voice. It has an intonation. It even has meaning. But they only have their screaming, which holds the pain of their poverty, their bad schools, the impossibility of living like so-and-so's son.

They aren't sons. They aren't brothers. They haven't got patrons. But there weren't any other social elevators in Donbas, and there still aren't.

They've been robbed and discarded. Forgotten in towns where you can make any war movie or disaster film you want... Forgotten in buildings where half the windows are boarded up... Forgotten in beds that no longer remember sheets or pillowcases. They're twenty years old, forty, sixty. They are men and they are women.

Somewhere inside, this thick clot of "we" sounds a song of mourning for justice, for imperfection, for the inability to live this way. The mourning is for ignorance, too: what is this "living"? What is this "being"? What is this "personal agency"?

They need a boss. An alpha, a leader. Whatever. They're wandering cold in the darkness, trying blindly to find someone who seems near and dear.

The USSR is the country they consider their "golden age."

The West hasn't known this kind of keen desire to "go back." The last portrait of "going back" was painted by Hesiod, and with time it came to be regarded as a fairy tale.

But fairy tales are cruel. They're protective amulets for heads that are breaking their skinny necks trying to look back at the past. Tom Thumb abandoned in the forest because his parents can't feed another child. Little Red Riding Hood eaten by the wolf—and if it hadn't been for the woodcutters... The stepmother's evil mirror. Kai turned into ice at the Snow Queen's whim.

The past is dangerous, my dear children. It was worse in the past than it is now. Even if you have a tinderbox like the soldier in Andersen's tale, there's no guarantee you'll win.

The USSR is an eternal fairy tale. A lure. A trap.

An invented country sings its siren's song, enticing us to come back and fall asleep. And die.

Russia does not exist. Russia was tempted back into the past, where it dissolved; our own weak selves are being tempted, too.

It's impossible to hear death. But you can listen to it. The screaming of people being killed; sprays of automatic gunfire; cannon booms. Victorious laughter. Cameras clicking as men take pictures of other men's deaths as souvenirs.

But to be clear: it's their own deaths, too.

Titus Andronicus on board the *Ship of Fools*.

* * *

MURATOV

SUNDAY

MAY 18, 2014

DNIPROPETROVSK

For Aleksey Muratov, cell phones were complicated technology. Okay, so he knew how to do a few things—he wasn't a blockhead, after all. Like setting an alarm. Text messages. Reminders, too. No worse than the average guy, but worse than his own kids. He also knew how to use Facebook. But it, too, was like a foreign language, one he could read and write with a dictionary. He couldn't do the fancy stuff like pictures, or Photoshop, or changing your profile picture, but to heck with that. He had enough to do without it.

He treated his cell phone like a friend. Lovingly. Everyone else had updated their phones ten times, but Muratov still had the same old thing he'd dropped a hundred times and thrown at the wall twice as much. It was old, but it was alive. Not so much on the outside as on the inside, in the actual phone, which held what Muratov could not throw away.

It was painful, sentimental, and yes, probably womanish. But he couldn't bring himself to delete the messages, dry and curt, like telegrams: "Zaitsev died," "Ivan is gone," "Igor died in a crash."

He had this idea that, as long as he carried them around in his pocket, they existed. Old man Zaitsev, a funny guy, a physics teacher and a great storyteller, who'd seen Lenin in his coffin and been glad Lenin hadn't seen him. And Igor, his childhood best friend, renounced with all the hate a teenager can muster... Forty years of silence, yet Igor had instructed his wife, "If I die, write Muratov. Might as well..."

Ivan also lived in the message saying he'd died. As long as the message existed, Ivan did, too. Or something like that. But Muratov didn't want to dig into it too deeply. The pain was not sharp, but rather constant, breathing in sync with each step.

On the other hand, there were "letters of happiness." "Three of us now!" "It's a boy." "Anna, 3220 grams. That's all for now." "Katya had a boy." "You're a grandpa!" Various children and various parents informed Muratov about these new lives. Whenever there were more kids than deaths in his cell phone, Muratov knew his life was going more or less the way it should.

He didn't write text messages like that himself. He preferred to call or to visit in person. But to each his own.

He used Facebook to read other people's thoughts at a distance. He himself almost never wrote.

Until the war, that is, when he, Muratov, a surveyor and landowner who hadn't done half bad in life, started spending money making sure soldiers didn't go into battle in sunhats and bare feet. So: army boots, bullet-proof vests, helmets. He was afraid to fight himself, but he knew how to keep the equipment coming. Facebook was pretty much his logistics center: what to send, and to whom, and how much. He required reports, photographs, receipts, signatures. He was fully aware that lots of people were just out there making money, but he still went pale whenever he saw that the helmets he'd moved heaven and earth to get were sitting around unused while the bullets fired by "peaceful protesters" were landing in soldiers' unprotected heads.

He did not write his first post himself. He copied something from underneath a photo of some equipment he'd bought. Yes, he was bragging. It was quality stuff, he'd have worn it himself. People were praising Muratov in the comments and calling him a pillar of the nation. But among the praise there was this, which hit him hard: *Stepan Moskalenko, 45, died fighting for Ukraine near Slovyansk.*

Moskalenko worked in his company. He hadn't asked for time off to go to the front. He'd just left. He'd taken vacation days. Their last conversation had been noncommittal, about nothing in particular: "When the cars get back from Obukhiv, unload them but don't let them drive off empty." "What are we moving?" asked Moskalenko, looking over the rims of his thin-framed black glasses. "Let's take a look here..."

They were moving pallets for vodka, as it turned out. Business was booming in this war. All the inspectors were either hiding in their hidey-holes or waiting for someone to come save them. And when inspectors are hiding, expenses go down by twenty percent... Muratov still hadn't had time to calculate his net income...

Stepan Moskalenko, 45, died fighting for Ukraine near Slovyansk.

Muratov posted this as a monument. The first and only one. And no more photographs of supplies he'd bought. Not until victory. The next post—Muratov could see it clearly, down to the last detail—would be this: "Never again. The war is over. We are together. But never again."

People went to Moskalenko's monument on Facebook and laid words under it, like flowers... Like paper flowers, artificial memorial wreaths... The days and nights went by, but someone would always go in and write a stern, simple "Kingdom of Heaven," or "Eternal memory," or "Let the earth be soft as down." Or the one this war had made common: "Heroes don't die."

But one day, instead of words, a photo of a bullet-proof vest appeared in the comments. One of the ones he'd stocked up on at the very beginning, the ones he'd had marked with his own company logo in a fit of empty boasting—explaining, to be sure, that he'd done it as a practical consideration: "That way they're accounted for, people won't walk off with them."

There were dents clearly visible in the bullet-proof vest.

Let there be no holes... No holes... No holes...

This message with the photo could be a good message, or it could be a bad one. The "peaceful protesters" were armed with rifles that could penetrate this vest's armor.

But there were no holes! No holes! Just dents!

Muratov couldn't work. He sat there looking at the bullet-proof vest, whispering an incantation over it, casting a spell on it like an old peasant woman had done for him when he wasn't coming out of a fever, and was sinking deeper and deeper... It had been a long, long time ago, in his now-forgotten childhood... In the village, where there were no medicines, no cars, no roads, no telephones... He remembered going towards that whisper: rhythmic, but irrational, or incoherent... There was nothing magic about it. The peasant woman was just calling on him, telling him to come back, to get well, to live. And Muratov was calling on that bullet-proof vest, asking it to keep the next post from including the words "died near Slovyansk."

And it didn't. But it did include a picture. This photo wasn't as clear as the first one. It had been taken on a phone, in bad light, or maybe even in the dark. A tiny, wrinkled face. And underneath it, no paper flowers, only live words: "My dear friend, thanks to you, my grandson has a father. Eight pounds six ounces, twenty-two inches. We called him Murat. We're Tatars, so the name Aleksey isn't right for us. Don't be offended."

Muratov wasn't offended. He cried. He sat in front of his monitor and cried, loudly. And kept repeating to himself, "Just like on a phone... Would you look at that..."

* * *

THINKING TOGETHER?

SUNDAY
MAY 18, 2014
K Y I V

Franz Boas noted that different chronological orders can exist in one and the same society at one and the same time. To put it more simply: people live in different historical epochs, even though everyone's calendar shows the very same twenty-first century. The fourteenth year of it.

Here, in Donbas, the hunter-gather way of life is perhaps the most widespread. It only *looks* like there isn't anything useful in abandoned mines and broken concrete. But there is. There is, for example, metal. Some of which can be sold as scrap. Manhole covers, the remains of equipment and machinery, weed-choked—but still scrapworthy!—train tracks...

If you can break it off, or saw it out, or pilfer it, or cart it away right in front of your neighbors' eyes, you can bring it to the scrap yard. Get some money for it. Live on that money for a while.

Theft is bad. But it's only theft when you're stealing from your own people. And a manhole cover is just what's naturally there. Nature belongs to everyone. Nature gives to everyone.

The local police officer might not agree with that. But it isn't because he feels bad about government property. It's because he's higher in rank. He's the boss. You have to share with the boss. And then your hunt for manhole covers, or cemetery fences, or train tracks will be successful.

The police officer-boss has connections "up there." Somewhere up above, in the sky, live the gods. The boss has to share with the gods. Their names are Prosecutor, Judge, Mayor. The gods have to be sated and smiling for the hunt to be successful. And they do smile: they beam down from campaign billboards and show up on TV.

Then the people know: the gods are satisfied, the hunt will be successful...

There's not just scrap metal, by the way. There's also the *kopankas*.

A *kopanka* is a private mine. Sometimes they're deep. But they don't have lighting, or insurance, or any kind of machinery. Well, except for the pickaxe. They're dark. They're scary. And they're also natural. Nature gave some people fish and bananas. It gave other people coal. In small pieces. You haul it up from the kopanka, bucket by bucket. And you carry it in a bucket. But you don't carry it home; you can't eat coal. You carry it to a working mine. Because a mine director is also a boss. And you have to share with him. He doesn't pay much. He records your coal as part of his own mine's output.

There is no "tomorrow" for hunters and gatherers. The future isn't clear; it's blurry, dangerous. The future is a threat. And nobody is strong enough to deal with it. In these new, Ukrainian years, every day has been worse than the last.

But we have the "great yesterday" to make up for it. The Golden Age. Today's manhole cover thieves used to be steelworkers or miners. They got a salary. The boss sat in the Kremlin. He was just and stern. Very stern. Back in the great yesterday, when he was boss, nobody would ever have stolen anything.

Life was sated. Predictable. Good.

Paycheck advances and regular salaries. Lunch breaks. Severe reprimands for being late. Recurring absences got you fired, maybe even put in jail. But in jail you get fed. And there's a daily schedule. And education through work. Nobody's afraid of work. Nobody's afraid of jail, either.

Not everybody remembers the "great yesterday" now. A generation has grown up knowing it only from pictures and stories. This generation steals manhole covers out of desperation. It descends into what locals call "the hole" as early as twelve. This generation, along with its fathers and grandfathers, dreams of going back in time.

When you look down from the height of an airplane, the Donbas steppe resembles the surface of the moon. Craters like kopankas. Kopankas like craters. And nothing more.

Adam and Eve. The expulsion from paradise.

Except these people don't know what sin they committed. All they know is that their past was just taken away from them, by some enemy of the human race, some evil and pitiless person.

Not by a local person. By somebody foreign to them.

Grief and longing… such grief and longing…

* * *

THE HOSPITAL

MONDAY

MAY 19, 2014

S L O V Y A N S K

"Last name?"

"Nekrasov!"

"And those two over there are Pushkin and Lermontov?"

"Good thing you're so smart. Go on, fix them up. We'll wait here."

Three guys with automatic rifles. The leader aims his at Klimov lazily. And three "patients," all with gunshot wounds. Klimov knows even without examining them that one is severely injured.

"We need to operate immediately."

"So. You're the doctor. Operate."

The lazy rifle pokes him in the ribs. The non-injured men laugh and talk in their guttural language. They have the profiles of eagles. They speak the language of eagles. Do they have the beards of eagles? Klimov imagines birds with beards. He sees turkeys. He laughs.

"So you *don't* want to live?" the leader asks.

All this already happened, in the nineties. Mafia, guns, shootouts in the operating room. A jeep, the largesse of a thief-in-law who lived.

Back then Klimov had been afraid, but he'd kept his head down and his mouth shut and sewn people up. He'd been glad for the jeep and for everything else besides. He'd overcome poverty.

Now the time had come for his clinic to pay the piper. "Big politics" had arrived in town as Chechens who were killing one kind of Orthodox Christians in the name of other, more orthodox Orthodox Christians. Everyone here had been making this bed for a long, long time. Klimov, too. The bandits he saved had then squeezed the local chumps out of their own businesses, towns, districts...

Everything living was ground into money; the rest, into dust.

It was the Wild Steppe, the vast southern plain that had been inviting colonization, competition, and war since at least the fifteenth century...

The Wild Steppe attracted barbarians. And one of them was dying right in front of Klimov.

"Get everybody out! This is our hospital now!" shouted the leader to the nurses peering into the examination room. "Move!"

He said something else, guttural and quiet, to his comrades. One of them burst out laughing and sprayed the ceiling with bullets.

Klimov pushed the rifle barrel away, looked into the hall, nodded to the nurses, and said calmly, "You have ten minutes to remove the patients. Get to work."

Then he said, "Your Pushkin needs an operation. We can't do that here, we need anesthesia, medical instruments... You want him to die?"

The leader stared coldly at Klimov and said, without any special emotion, "Do it. Or I'll kill you, you son of a bitch."

"Then you assist me," grinned Klimov.

"Brave, aren't you?" said the leader, shoving the muzzle of the rifle back into Klimov's ribs. Then he looked at his rifle, clicked his tongue, and carefully placed the rifle on the floor at his feet. "I'll strangle you with my bare hands if I have to."

Klimov looked at the leader's hands. They were capable hands. Capable of anything.

"These two we bandage," Klimov said, nodding at Nekrasov and Lermontov. "Pushkin gets an IV. Anesthesia. You understand? Move out of the light..."

The leader moved. Klimov could see the hallway where more "guttural" men were kicking his patients out of the rooms and carrying in their own fighters. Wounded and dead.

"What are you doing, you sons of bitches!? What are you doing?!"

Oh, that voice. Klimov would've recognized that one voice out of a thousand. The entire ward's favorite. A chronic case, constant bellyaching and troublemaking, didn't let a day go by without pitching a fit... Porridge cooked with water instead of milk, substandard thermometers, old sheets, nurses smelling of tobacco, and incorrect, catastrophically incorrect treatment that more than once put "me, an invalid with a decade of experience, on the verge of immortal outcome...."

You heard right. Not "a mortal" but "immortal" outcome.

Klimov screwed his eyes shut. Two shots. Silence. No more complaints, now or ever.

"He that dwelleth in the secret place of the most High shall abide under the shadow of the Almighty... I will say of the Lord, He is my refuge and my fortress: my God; in him will I trust..."

"What's that you're whispering, doctor?" The leader poked Klimov hard in the chest. Klimov couldn't keep his balance and fell down, stupidly, his back slamming into the windowsill. He got back up. No big deal.

He got to work. He gave the leader orders: "Hold this here... lift his head... move him over... close this... hand me that... put a tourniquet there..."

He did everything by the book, but he already knew he was no longer a doctor. The Chechen, on the other hand, got so into it that he looked like a real nurse. The two of them worked in concert and in silence. The hallway, however, was noisy. The wounded and dead kept coming. The men spoke with each other in eagle but cursed in Russian. Evidently, there was fighting somewhere in the city.

"And now you'll give him a tetanus shot," said Klimov, digging a package of syringes out of the drawer. Along with the package emerged two grenades.

The two grenades had been given to him by his neighbor, who, as recently as a month ago, burning with the desire to unite with Russia, had manned checkpoints and, in general, thought of himself as a people's militiaman and a savior, delivering his motherland from the brown plague. But last Monday, the man had moved to Kyiv. For business, and for good. To live there permanently. As well as the grenades, and the conversations about those damned Banderites and how you just can't get away from them, the man left Klimov two pistols, a shoebox of cartridges, and a cat by the name of Holmes. Holmes immediately went looking for the ladies. He'd be out all night, come back in the early morning, eat, wash, walk Klimov to work, and then go out again. You can't take spring away from a tomcat. This is the difference between them and humans, as a species...

Klimov had brought the grenades to work, to show off. For the cute nurses, and just... in general. The hunks of metal warmed him, somehow. He knew how to use them; he'd served in the late 80s. Aiming, shooting, throwing: he'd had to do it all.

He pulled out the pins. Carefully, almost tenderly. Like pulling a foreign body out of an open wound. He crouched low and put one grenade on the ground, setting up a "shot on goal" with his right foot through the open door into the hall. The second grenade remained in his hand.

The leader twitched reflexively. But the shot had already gone in. The "ball" flew into the opposing team's goal.

One-and, two-and, three-and, four...

* * *

Did you know that, for hunter-gatherer tribes, there's no such thing as bad gods?

Their gods can be cruel, angry, raging—just not bad.

If a god isn't in a good mood, it's the people's fault. They did something wrong. And that's why their hunts fail, their firstborn are daughters, the rains don't come...

You must propitiate your own god. And listen to him. Figure out his moods, intonations. You must give. Make an offering. Sacrifice something. And wait obediently: will it be accepted? Will he take it? Will he deign to receive?

Your own gods are never bad.

Only other people's gods can be bad.

And other people's gods are always bad. They're the ones who took things away from you, deceived you, mocked and ruined you.

Other people's gods seem stronger than yours; angrier, too, and more despicable, prone to betrayal and swift, brutal punishment.

Your own gods are like children in comparison to them.

And children have to be protected.

People vote for their own gods to save them. They save their own gods. Otherwise, the hunts won't be successful, the railroad tracks won't succumb to your tools, and the coal you brought up from the "hole" will just sit there in its bucket. And you won't have anything to eat.

We know little about contemporary industrial paganism. We're arrogant, for some strange reason, and deny its existence.

But look: if your own god has died, or been killed, or was chased away by other people's gods, then... How are you supposed to go on living?

* * *

Is it possible to accept someone else's god as your own?

If he's as strong, scary, and harsh as a thousand of your own, then yes.

Someone else's god can't be good. People here don't believe in what they've never seen. They've never seen good. They don't recognize it. They won't believe in it.

For someone else's god to win, he has to be threatening, grim, and mean. He's not obligated to be just. Justice, in a god, is a pitiful trait.

Cruelty and murderousness are the usual traits.

The Ukrainian army took one residential area three times. Every time, after the army had set up a checkpoint and left the place in peace and quiet, people would hit it with mortar fire from the courtyards of nearby buildings. Different courtyards every night.

One of the fighters manning the checkpoint was local. He said, "That's it! Time to play hardball."

That night he built—and here you're free to roll your eyes—ten gallows. He followed photos from WWII, easy-peasy.

He built them and set them up in the middle of the village.

The next morning, the locals go up to the checkpoint. They hand out cherries, varenyky, kvas, and fried onions and potatoes.

"That was us... Guys... We apologize on behalf of the whole community!"[18]

"So what the hell'd you put on that late-night dance party for?!" the guys demanded sternly.

"Well, see... We didn't know, right, that you're in charge now... And what are we supposed to do without somebody in charge? Can't have that..."

"All right then... So the gallows can come down now?"

The locals got flustered and whispered to each other, then announced their decision: *"Let them stay a bit. We might let ourselves get out of hand if they're not there..."*

In order for someone else's god to become your own, he has to put up gallows on the main square. And then, next to it, a school.

Strictly in that order.

Because a school is good. It is justice. So, therefore, it's a weakness...

* * *

NOT ____ ENOUGH

Being an impostor, proclaiming yourself to be someone or something, was one of the Middle Ages' main amusements. Our lands have suffered from this whimsical affliction for a long time. For us, the impostor tsar is a familiar phenomenon.

But what about an impostor PhD? What about a self-proclaimed scientist? MD? School director? Journalist?

We have petty impostors all over the place.

In the nineties, you could buy not only a university degree but a high school diploma. A lot of people were trying to change their degrees or careers quick back then. Education and jobs only coincided for the lucky few.

The economic waters were murky. People were hired and fired not for their qualifications but for their abilities. For the ability to stand firm yet be flexible enough to get things done. For the ability to be flexible but keep from getting caught. For the ability to keep from getting caught but also to not turn into a cynical bastard.

It turned out that a lot of the people who'd been forcibly freed from the Soviet cultural yoke were quite talented.

But the "past" twinged and ached like a stiff neck. Made-up college degrees, fake PhD degrees hard-bound in official cloth covers, membership IDs for bogus "Academies" with all of three members... In this strange new world, all these pieces of paper seemed like guarantees that the person holding them was not some random character, but a quite respectable personage. People compensated for any lack of symbolic capital by simply buying it.

But what they bought was old, familiar, Soviet. It was what had been valued and respected in the distant days of yore.

As a result, they suffered from a strong sense of personal self-insufficiency. And the constant threat of being found out. The False Dmitry... Pope Joan... The children of Lieutenant Schmidt... And "Professor" Yanukovych.

The present day seemed to be forged, the kind of space-time gap that is inevitably followed by either purges or the Last Judgment.

A bought degree certificate between real-looking covers is like an indulgence, a pardon. When the

Bolsheviks come back, you'll be able to show yours and get off the hook...

* * *

THE COFFIN ON LITTLE WHEELS

WEDNESDAY
....
MAY 21, 2014
....
M A R I U P O L

In the referendum on a new life, the pensioner Tamara Petrovna voted four times. Twice for herself and her son, then two more times (at a different polling station) for her neighbors who were at the dacha. The new life looked to be similar to the old one, which Tamara Petrovna loved and remembered clearly. The good things she remembered most often were sausage, her youth, and that nobody was rich.

In this current new life, still a little runny around the edges, Tamara Petrovna liked everything: the people's name of the republic;[19] the simplicity with which anyone could walk into any of the republic's offices at any time; the tall, brave men in military uniforms; and the significance of the historic moment.

When Tamara Petrovna's son was picked up on the street for breaking curfew, Tamara Petrovna was not worried. Her little Vitalik was a drinker. And whereas earlier there'd been no way to rein him in, well, now there was. Tamara Petrovna got a phone call asking her to kindly ransom her son; if not, the caller warned, he'd be reeducated finally and irrevocably. Tamara Petrovna liked the reeducation option better.

She had no contact with her son for three days. But the man called her and gave cruel updates: today, they beat her son and sent him to collect corpses; tonight, he'd be sent to stand guard at the checkpoint... "Thank you," said Tamara Petrovna. "Don't mention it," said the caller.

Tamara Petrovna could hear he was angry. His anger was understandable: if anybody knew exactly how hard it was to reeducate her Vitalik, it was Tamara Petrovna. She knew better than anybody...

Vitalik was released on Friday. He came home and told his mother he'd never drink another drop, but he cursed the "republic" and its executioners down to the seventh generation. "You've turned into a fascist?!?" wailed Tamara Petrovna. But she was faking most of it, truth be told, because in her heart of hearts she was relieved. Her thinking was that if it had taken the people's authorities just one week to stop Vitalik's drinking, then they'd be able to build a bright future for the more conscientious members of society even faster.

A week later, on Sunday, they picked Vitalik up again. Notably, he was taken while sober and at the wheel. He'd cobbled something together from pine boards and tied it to the top of his old Niva. It was a coffin. He'd gotten the boards from the garage. Ten-odd years ago he'd planned to use them to build a cupboard at the dacha. He'd never gotten around to making the cupboard, but the coffin he got around to. Vitalik had covered the sides of the coffin in flags of the "people's republic." On the open coffin lid, he put the "republic's" coat of arms and a sign reading "Dead Meat." If only that had been all he'd done, it would've been fine. Nothing factually wrong there. He could've said the coffin was for ceremonial burial processions for peaceful people's militia members returning from the left bank of the Don. But underneath it, Vitalik had written: "May you all drop dead! Man was born free! Get out of the city!"

He had filled the coffin with scrap metal, empty cans, and a Chinese-made remote-control car. The car bellowed some song in a foreign language. Eyewitnesses said, it was ABBA's "Happy New Year."

Vitalik was arrested again. Then—well, maybe they had him drink himself to death, or maybe they executed him. They offered to let Tamara Petrovna ransom the body. Otherwise, they threatened to bury him in a mass grave. But she had no money for a funeral. And Vitalik had always liked being with people. The man who was calling got angry at her again. But Tamara Petrovna wouldn't budge: *you* killed him, *you* bury him.

* * *

You don't have to be poor, or poorly educated, to have absolutely no sense of yourself and no sense of self-worth.

The absence of selfhood is a complicated problem. At some point in childhood it starts with toxic shame and a lack of love. "You're bad. Nobody's worse than you. You don't even exist, you're nothing…"

Yet another variation on the theme of death. Dying, when you're a little kid, is a sharp feeling. You don't forget it. The refrain "There is no me… I'm nothing… I don't even exist…" becomes your call sign for the rest of your life.

Although some people escape. Into a life that's not always healthy, maybe, but it's bearable, even good.

Others don't escape. Their daily dose of dying increases under their parents' stern—or blank—gaze. To keep their hold on life from slipping away, these others search frantically for external attributes: a diploma, success, money, applause, fame.

But if you don't have a self, if you don't exist, then that's all nothing. A great big nothing.

The greater the non-being, the larger the scale of attributes.

Russia is all about large scale.

You can hide your "not _____ enoughs" behind your love of Russia. It'll cover them all up. Russia feels like a mother whose gaze will always be loving. The great return to the womb. It's a visceral, dark, and extremely dependent existence. But the upshot is you're a baby again, you're inside your mommy's belly again. "I'm safe on my home base."

And nobody will bother you. Nobody will ask you: what the hell did you buy your degree for? Why did you steal those medals? What were you thinking, robbing the city coffers?

The warm uterine waters, the gentle permeating noise, the beating of your own heart... In unison with your mother's.

Rivers, vast expanses, snows, victories...

Rock-a-bye-baby...

Sleep. Dreams. Death.

It's strange, dying to save yourself from death. But, on the other hand, it's collective. And it works.

"Mommy will protect me, Mommy will get back at all of you..."

I know people whose success can't be called into question. But they still whine "Mommy!" because they can't do anything themselves.

Or maybe they can, but not very well: their academic articles are plagiarized, not a single kopek of their great wealth was earned, their successful political careers are due to their family connections...

At those moments, when you are being honest with yourself—and this happens even to the most hopeless cases—at those moments, which are difficult for me as well, you admit everything about yourself.

You're good, but not great... In places you're okay, especially when it comes to English... You could be a better mother... And a better daughter, too... And in the book this passage here's just so-so, and that part there's not great, either...

I don't envy people who've taken what's not theirs once it's their turn to face these realizations.

Fear of shame. Fear of being discovered. Fear of the little boy pointing his finger at the naked king. Or of another little boy, the blood-drenched one they see even with their eyes closed...

Fear looks for a safe place to hide.

Russia seems to be just what it's looking for.

Russia seems to *be*.

But it isn't. Russia *is not*.

Like the others, the ones who don't escape, Russia has no self.

Russia has no safe place to hide. So, at those moments, when it's genuinely trying to peer through the murk and be honest with itself, it prefers to do its dying in public, for all the world to see.

Russia's misery loves company.

But, so far, the only ones dying are us...

* * *

You can also consider the issue from the point of view of love. The point of view of basic humanity.

The forgotten children. The forgotten regiment. The forgotten submarine, the Kursk.

The world Donbas entered in the 1990s was all wrong. Unwanted. And unjust. Very unjust.

That world abolished once and for all the bright future the utopians had painted: "from each according to his ability, to each according to his needs."

It turned out that nobody needed capable, smart, or honest people.

It's practically impossible to accept a situation where might makes right and the idiots call the shots. But, if you believe the claim that it's all temporary, it's not for real and not forever, then—why not?

It's just a game. A game that bad parents—usually mothers—have played from time immemorial. They leave their children in the forest, on the side of the road, at the train station, and order them to wait. Just sit and wait.

The days go by, the weeks, the years... And the children wait. They eat something or other, take some handouts, pilfer a few things here and there, and grow up, and then they start really robbing people. But they don't leave that spot. They sit there and they wait.

Mama's definitely coming back. We just have to be patient.

You can describe this in military terms, too. Here's your regiment, and here's your hill. The commander says, "Take it and hold it, defend it down to your last bullet. We'll send backup." He says that and leaves.

And now, again, the days go by, the weeks, the years. The bullets ran out a long time ago. The local women have all had kids. There's nothing to shoot with, except maybe words. But they hold on to that hill and shoot with whatever they've got. They eat the local food, sleep with the native women, but their hearts and minds are fixed on the country that sent them to take that hill. Too bad nobody remembered to tell them the country doesn't exist. And the Kursk—the submarine that was waiting for help, just like them—sank ages ago.

For twenty-three years, a lot of people lived "just pretend" lives. Some of them became "bad" people because the circumstances they were being offered were bad. But it doesn't matter. Because it's "just pretend"...

Don't you remember Pechkin the mailman, from the old cartoon, and why he used to be so mean? It was because he didn't have a bicycle. So he ratted out Uncle Fyodor and got Uncle Fyodor's bike.

Russia is exactly that—a yearning for a bicycle. A yearning for a way to become good, not mean; to become whole and at peace. For a way that's external. A way that's simple, like a gift. And inevitable, like fate.

Russia will come, and everything will change.

Except that "the first person you run into at the train station in Paris will be yourself..."

Our waiting soldiers and waiting children don't know much about Paris.

They think this "bicycle" will magically turn them into good people. It'll finally bring together their internal and external images of themselves.

What we have here isn't a civil war. Not at all. There are people who want to live in Russia. It's the same as it was in the US in the eighteenth century. There were people like that there, too: people sincerely devoted to the English crown...

Civil war is when some people believe the United States of the future won't have slavery, while other people are sure it will.

But, when somebody wants to live in another country, when somebody gets physically sick when they hear the word "Ukraine," when the sight of blue and yellow burns somebody's eyes like acid, then, for goodness' sake, how is that a civil war?

* * *

**SATURDAY
MAY 24, 2014
DONETSK**

Dima and I are meeting the governor. He's good. Smart, cultured. Everyone and their brother has compared him to Woody Allen.

People had high hopes for him back in March. In March, when it was still like the goofy "Russotouristo" guys from Leonid Gaidai's *The Diamond Arm*. Wasn't so bad.

We think it's not too late even now. The first order of business is to down the TV tower. We know how. You can't cut the cable, unfortunately, but there's this thing in there like a light bulb and one shot from a sniper brings the tower out of service. Yes, it's quick enough to repair afterward. But then you can just shoot it again, too.

He's gentle and tired. But we need somebody mean and ready for action.

"You need to be a little harsher. You need to pound your fist on the table. Our people don't respond well to the spoken word. They believe in a firm hand," I say.

"If I was harsher, I would've been dead a long time ago!" explodes the governor.

Well, yes. If the task here is simply to remain alive, then sure—he's earning an A+.

MAY 25, 2025	MAY 26, 2014
A snap presidential election takes place in Ukraine; Petro Poroshenko wins.	The battle for the Donetsk airport begins, with Ukrainian forces taking control of the airport.

* * *

SUNDAY
MAY 25, 2014
DONETSK, SLOVYANSK, HORLIVKA

There was no presidential election. For two weeks straight, the orcs have been kidnapping members of vote-counting committees, smashing voting boxes, and setting fire to polling stations. A few people have been ransomed. Others are still being held hostage.

This morning "they" drove around the empty city with automatic rifles. To scare people.

The polling stations did not open.

On Rahshah-TV, they called this a "boycott."

* * *

FROM LETTERS NOT TO YOU

TUESDAY
MAY 27, 2014

The anti-terrorist operation, ATO for short, began in Donetsk yesterday.

It started when the Vostok Battalion headed out to take the airport.[20] The night before, on the square, Vostok fighters happily announced that now some of Ramzan Kadyrov's men had joined them.[21] People took a minute to think about this. Chechens were clearly not what the people had in mind in terms of their love of the Russian Federation.

Then people got afraid. They started leaving their homes less, driving around less.

Anyway, yesterday Vostok headed out to the airport on two or three KAMAZ trucks. Certain individuals among us think they were lured out there, others say the Russians needed the airport for their planes. No way to know the truth now. In any case, they were destroyed out there. Aviation, then an airborne assault force, then snipers.

The Oplot battalion went out to help Kadyrov's men. Oplot's got a mix of locals, Cossacks, and purported Crimeans. As they headed out, they were so happy, so sure of themselves, that it was just astonishing. They were destroyed, too.

Their Zello radio broadcast said they had 100–150 dead and 300 wounded. The mayor of Donetsk said officially that there were 46 dead and 43 wounded.

The relatives of those killed still haven't come for the bodies. Because, as the dead men's documents show, they come from Grozny and Gudermes. The wounded, too. And there's no way to hide this now. Today, for the first time, the mayor acknowledged the fact that there are foreign fighters among us. But either from age, or from fear, he continued calling them *opolchentsy*, the people's militia.

Today, everyone was expecting things to get intense fast. But there's been nothing so far.

Meanwhile the fighters have recovered from the shock and started grabbing men off the street. They're doing the Abkhazian version, where they shove a weapon in your hand and cart you off somewhere. If you resist, then congratulations, you're our latest hostage. If you're lucky, they'll send you out to be ransomed.

They killed two policemen and shot one woman who tried to defend her husband. They shot her in the face. She's alive, but...

The ATO's afraid to do anything too harsh inside the city, because of peaceful citizens and all that. But as far as I can tell, that's just what the other side's after: they've already taken a school (without the children, at least) and a hospital surgical ward (with the patients, unfortunately).

In a word: Chechnya.

WEDNESDAY
MAY 28, 2014

Our laughter's dark. Harsh.

If you go for a walk in the Donetsk airport, you can assemble yourself a whole Kadyrovite from all the parts lying around there...

Kyiv will definitely hear Donbas—as soon as it finds a Chechen interpreter.

MAY 29, 2014

The Feast of the Ascension in the Ukrainian Orthodox liturgical calendar. The pro-Russian group Vostok seizes the Donetsk oblast state administration building from other pro-Russian groups. Trucks marked "Cargo 200," carrying bodies of 33 Russian citizens killed in the fighting, leave Donetsk for Russia: the first open admission of Russian involvement.

* * *

THE TATTOO ARTIST

For some reason, they decided to take the airport on the last Monday of May. Nobody knew exactly why. It was just that the volunteers arrived—Ossetians, Chechens, Ingush. Hot-blooded guys. War's in their blood. Real war, not like these little playtimes where the entire "republic" is in a single building...

Kalya's crying. She's crying with her arms, her legs, her stomach, mouth, and neck—her whole body.

"Such a good tattoo artist. And just a good man. He was a good man... A good man... A good man..."

It's true. Denis was a good man. He'd studied architecture. He loved Gaudi and Barcelona. He'd never been to Barcelona. He'd never been anywhere abroad. But he believed we could build "abroad" here at home. While he was a student, and then later, while he was looking for a job as an architect, he did painting and tile setting at "properties." The builders got them up quick and did the interior finishing fast, too. But not in a shoddy way—it's just that with ten crews you can get any mansion done on time. Denis never got to know any of the clients, but he did know they had bad taste. These people wanted the Peterhof Palace and Hermitage styles of luxury that had astonished them when they were little: majestic enfilades, golden monograms, velvet, brocade, marble, whimsically-patterned parquetry... The designer, a French woman who forwarded Denis little internet orders and big architectural ideas, used to laugh at his photos of the "properties." "When you have a revolution and the people come to take it all," she wrote, "the owners will be embarrassed." The French woman wrote in English. But she foretold the worst just as good as any of our village grannies.

"He never did a bad job on anything, he worked so hard, he tried as hard as he could to do work people could be proud of..."

Kalya's crying. She hiccups, blows her nose. There's vodka in her. But the vodka isn't the source of her misery now. The source is all around us.

"He was so good... Who told him that was the right way to be? Who told him?"

What is injustice? Denis didn't ask. He gritted his teeth. He scored pictures into skin. He gave master classes. When it was construction season, he worked in construction. He cobbled together his own building crew a couple of years ago. "I'll plane down the rough edges of the broad masses' taste."

The masses' taste didn't budge.

Murals with little angels, ornamental plaster molding, gold-leaf windowsills, suffocating reds, dust-choked browns—the clients were incurable.

His business was squeezed out, too. Men came and told him: "We take half. It's our share." "No shares," replied Denis. "No shares for any of us..."

He closed in on himself. The drawings he made on skin grew sadder. Kalya loved each and every one of them, since they were all unique; Denis never repeated himself. She was his one and only. And every other woman was his one and only, too. They were all unique.

Who told him this was the revolution of the working people? Who told him that the rich were swine, thieves? Not even businessmen, just thugs? Who told him that now justice would reign in all things? Or rather, as soon as we achieve victory, justice will reign, but until then, you force yourself to do what you have to do. And yes, you have to take what doesn't belong to you, but only to serve the needs of the people's revolution. Take it and enter it into a detailed list, so that after we win—once everyone has understood who was right and who was telling the truth—we can maybe even try to give it back... Who told him all this?

Because he was smart. Smart and honest. Kalya remembers how harshly he chewed out one of his dumb buddies. The guy had picked out some overalls, tried them on, and then carefully put his size at the very bottom of the stack, underneath all the other folded-up overalls. He'd even put a yellow sticker on them, so he would be able to find the right ones. "So, I don't make any mistakes when it's time to loot the City Center shopping mall. Because it's going to be looted, right, Denis?"

Denis had just about burst into tears. What a funny guy, a thirty-six-year-old man who almost cried...

Kalya says that at some point he got to where he just couldn't leave. Not because he was being held, or because his family was being threatened. No. He didn't even have a family. Just a grandma, but she'd managed to die a couple of years before.

The reason he couldn't leave was different. It was a stupid reason: because he'd promised not to. And it was a childish reason: because they'd become brothers, and all of them would be facing, as they put it, "a maximum-security fifteener." But even so, it wasn't out of fear. In prison, you're fed, it's warm. It wasn't out of fear. He couldn't leave, because, if he left, then senseless plunder would be all that remained. If he left, he'd be taking an idea away with him—an idea that nobody else believed in anymore, sure. But he believed in it.

"That's the problem right there!" Kalya says, getting worked up. "Do any of you believe in something enough to die for it? Have any of you ever believed in something that strongly in your lives? Even for one minute!?"

Turned out to be a pretty funny question. Right now, we're living in a city where we all might be killed at any moment. For anything. For a pair of earrings, for having a Ukrainian flag at home, for just ending up on the other end of a stray bullet, or a guerrilla fighter's grenade, or an artillery strike by the Ukrainian army... And it's been this way much longer than one minute.

"You know, Kalya, from the looks of it, I'd say, yes, we do believe..."

This city is our home. And these streets are our home. And the cafes that aren't open anymore, and the empty playgrounds, and the trolleybus that doesn't go all the way to Putyliv Bridge because that's where the war starts... That trolleybus is also our home.

"Well, then you should understand Denis..."

"But what did he go to the airport for?"

Kalya's not crying anymore.

Denis and his volunteer comrades didn't manage to take the airport. There wasn't really a fight—just air strikes. And snipers.

The plane fired decoy flares, so the "peaceful pro-testers" couldn't shoot it down with their shoulder-fired anti-aircraft missiles. Every time it appeared, it made a low pass right over the city. The planes were visible from the windows of even the smallest buildings. Sure, it was scary, no two ways about it. It was scary. The time when death by your own hand will be preferable to despicable torture at a stranger's hands hasn't yet arrived. This time will come later. Two weeks from now, the roar of an airplane will bring relief. It will mean that it won't be long until... Regardless of whether we're around to see that "until..."

But on Tuesday morning we were still (or already) joking: "If you go for a walk at the Donetsk airport, you can assemble yourself a whole Kadyrovite from all the parts lying around there..."

Denis was brought to the morgue intact. But he didn't show up there until the third day, Wednesday evening. On Wednesday morning, the "republicans," with childish glee, had looted the one supermarket left on neutral territory that hadn't gotten as much shooting.

Nobody knows how Denis died. Might have been shrapnel, might have been a sniper... But Denis was one of those guys who was made to tame the wild beasts of our nature. He was honest, smart, and strong.

He might've told the looters: "Everyone! What are you doing? We're the people of this country, not a mob! We're the people!"

That's what he used to say to Kalya, too.

The explosions in the airport lasted all night. The wind changed. Sometimes, it felt like they were bombing right next to our building's front entrance. Other times, all we heard was a distant reverberation, like an exhausted bomb's whispering.

Lights flared and faded in the night sky.

Then, late Tuesday night, the booming started up again. Sometimes near, sometimes far. The dark sky lit up in brief flashes. We didn't sleep. We were counting hits.

Wednesday morning, the mayor's office released an announcement: "People," it said. "People! There was a storm from Tuesday evening to Wednesday morning. There was loud thunder. There was thunder in all districts of the city. This is 100% verified information. Don't worry..."

There was thunder the next night, too.

Eventually, we learned to tell it apart all by ourselves...

* * *

FROM LETTERS NOT TO YOU

HEADLINES. JUST LOOK AT THESE HEADLINES...

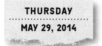

THURSDAY
MAY 29, 2014

"A Day in the Life of the DPR: In One Day, Terrorists in Donetsk Stole Seven Cars, Kidnapped Three People, and Wounded One"

"In Slovyansk, Terrorists Killed Six Berkut Fighters"

"Communication Established in Luhansk with One of the Members of the Kidnapped OSCE Mission"

* * *

CASABLANCA

FRIDAY
MAY 30, 2014
DONETSK

The good-byes picked up as May drew to a close. A lot of people were taking their kids out and leaving themselves. The word "forever" wasn't said, but it was understood: there might not be any coming back, and people might not see each other again.

People didn't call the war "circumstances" anymore. The war was no longer a euphemism. But it still felt completely foreign. The stage of the amusing, chaotic Makhnovshchyna was over. The color scheme was now mostly from the Caucasus—bright and pitiless. You could still pick up the phone and call some minister whose past claim to fame was being the manager of a glass recycling station. But it wasn't him making the decisions anymore. And, sometimes, it took more time to figure out who *was* making those damned decisions than you had life left.

Because you had a closer acquaintance with bullets than with the former "bottle king"...

People weren't obvious about saying goodbye. They were afraid of scaring each other. And themselves. But in the final days of May, when nothing mattered anymore— not money, not age, not skin color, not who you knew—it was understood that the thing you'd regret the most was whatever you left unsaid.

Surikova used to add, "Or whoever you left unhugged."

During the war, words had already lost their meaning, of course. But starkly and keenly, and maybe even before it was too late, we realized what we'd had before the war: Fairy tales read to our children. "Just sit here with me for a little bit," said to our parents. You are beautiful—I became the man I did because of you. It was awful when you left, we shouldn't have split up for good back then. Yes, you're right, there's something about those impressionists (Rammstein, Bosch, Justin Timberlake, paella, Dorblu cheese). But you're also right...

People were departing, leaving, and remaining, all searching not for excuses, but for each other...

Surikova was staying. This was not a final decision. War is a time when even dinner plans turn into a murky, very distant future...

Casablanca.

Nothing but Casablanca everywhere you look.

Every Monday, Serov used to drag Surikova and Kotya to the Newsreel and Second-Run Film Cinema instead of physics class. So there were always four people in the morning showing, counting the projectionist.

Surikova and Kotya were bored. So they kissed. Meanwhile, Serov would sit there being jealous and memorizing scenes. His voice was older than he was. An enchanting voice. He used this voice, as well as quotes from *Casablanca*, to tease and to torment.

As it turns out, he jinxed us.

Serov actually ended up being a "republican." "A separatist," amended Kotya.

Serov, that fifty-year-old idiot, went ("ran!") straight into the government of the self-proclaimed "republic." He was a minister for all of five days. At one of the sessions, he protested the policy of nationalization ("It's looting!"). He was sent to the NKVD on the fifth floor and sentenced to a week of light corrective labor.

The former minister mopped every floor in the eleven-story "republic" without daring to make a peep. After he served his time, he tendered his resignation. They told him, "It costs one ruble to get in, gramps, but two to get out. Grab your briefcase and get to work."

Serov wasn't paid. But he drafted a proposal for reducing the cost of communal services anyway.

He also saved twenty hostages. Whenever new people appeared in the NKVD torture chambers, he'd call his wife and ask her to tell the right people: "Major Strasser has been shot. They've rounded up the usual suspects."

Twenty people. Some were taken for money: hostages brought in a fair portion of the "republic's" income. Others were to exchange for our soldiers, at a good rate of one to one. He got two out himself by saying they were his assistants, people who were absolutely indispensable for some new economic projects. Serov had more bad things than good to say about *Schindler's List*, but even it came in handy. He exchanged his wedding ring for a student, just like in the movie. His wife cried and yelled at him. Surikova did, too. Cried, that is.

"Our brothers from the Caucasus" put a speedy end to Serov's little side business with a shot to the knee. They asked, "What is your nationality?" He answered, "I'm a drunkard." The bullet didn't put an end to things. But Serov was glad he'd been shot. He got an honorable discharge from his position as minister due to his disability.

The three of them, Surikova, Serov, and Kotya, were sitting in a café. The café's name had a pretty pindossy whiff to it: The White House. Little tables on the sidewalk and a boring menu that still had items containing meat and oil. Plus an accordionist.

That accordionist... He sat on a high stool and played... If there had been any chance of resisting the insanity, then that musician could've been the handler for the entire resistance. That, or a nice little neighborhood weirdo. Nice, and fearless. He piled on the Ukrainian songs one after the other: "What a Moonlit Night," then "The Pine Is Burning, All Aglow," next "Two Colors, My Two Colors," and finally, on the bass strings, "The Wide Dnieper Roars and Moans"... But not a single person listening—whether that person had an automatic rifle or not—heard the saboteur in him. All of them, festooned as they were with grenades and Saint George's ribbons, hated Ukraine without even knowing Ukraine.

Although many of them didn't hate Ukraine, actually. They were just working. The war was just a job.

It was evening.

But night was not yet a given.

"We've got to get this cinematic miracle of separatist thought out of here," said Kotya, nodding at Serov. "Before they finish him off..."

"Guys, I wanted to improve things, though. I was being just. I was doing it for the people. Remember the war in Spain?"

"'Guys,'" smirked Kotya. "Surikova, he's insulting you. And I can't tomorrow. I've got stuff to do. But the day after tomorrow I'll take you to Dnipro. Get ready to go."

"She no want," said Serov.

"Still making fun of Chukchi? Or do you mean your Galya doesn't want to leave?" Kotya was now truly angry.

"Don't fight," begged Surikova. "Don't fight..."

"Well, what am I supposed to do!? What are you supposed to do when your old childhood friend turns out to be vata!?"

"You'll answer for those words in court!"

"What court?" Kotya asked wearily. "There's no court in your establishment. Just the NKVD, then jail. You of all people should've noticed, comrade Serov."

"You know why we're doing this?" said Serov, now serious and sad.

"Why?"

"Because Surikova wouldn't marry us. Especially me. As a result, we're incomplete... Unfulfilled... There's a horrible emptiness to my life. Instead of love, I wanted to fill it with justice... For the people..."

"It's a good thing your kids are smart, comrade minister. At least they left, got away from the shame," grumbled Kotya, reddening.

Back in the day, he and Surikova had been all but married. They'd been together for two years. Like needle and thread: where the needle goes, the thread follows. But when the thread (Surikova) wanted to move to Moscow, the needle (Kotya) refused: "You have to choose: me or Moscow..." He said it out of desperation, out of fear, and impatience, and a bunch of other childish nonsense... So the thread didn't leave. But it broke. It fell out of the needle's eye. And never went back. Friendship was all that remained. A good friendship that was so nice and friendly it hurt to look at.

"Thanks, guys," said Serov. "But I've just got a question for you, as patriots: why didn't you come out to resist us? Why didn't you start beating us with your riot batons and shooting us with your fashionable American weapons? Why didn't you give a shit about your Ukraine?"

"We still might, so don't get your panties in a twist," said Kotya.

"Oh, is that so?" smirked Serov.

Yes, it was so. You weren't supposed to talk about it. But for some reason, you wanted to. Like when you were a kid and wanted to go to the middle of downtown and shout, "My dad's is bigger than your dad's! My dad's is bigger than everybody's!" Kotya was a former Berkut fighter who'd been thrice cursed, fired, and forgotten after the Revolution of Dignity. So, he had a sniper rifle. And excellent shooting skills. Every other night he'd go out into the city; train his rifle on one spot; set up his "nest." He attentively tracked the enemy's movements and weaponry. Anyone carrying a shoulder-fired anti-aircraft missile or grenade launcher was fair game.

He went out hunting the day Serov was shot in the knee. As he was leaving, he swore to himself he'd get revenge on every foreigner who brought war into his city. As he got set up on a rooftop, he thought about how that old fool Serov was now going to be on crutches for life. And about how every Colorado-beetle-colored ribbon was now reason enough to kill... He wanted to be unjust. He thirsted not for the rule of law, but for revenge.

Still, Kotya couldn't bring himself to kill someone just for a ribbon. He didn't have enough bad in him. But for aiming a shoulder-fired anti-aircraft missile launcher, though, he could. Easy as ABC. The first enemy died with an expression of absolute astonishment on his face: he'd aimed at an airplane, but landed in the clouds himself...

There was no way he could tell Surikova about it. Nor could he tell that idiot Serov, who'd never shed a drop of someone else's blood.

"As long as we're all here, everything's okay," said Surikova. "And I love you so much, guys... I always have... The only people I love a little bit more than you are my own children. You're in second place."

The accordion player finished a melody that the Russian Kotya had learned to identify just that year. At the

Maidan. "The police are with the people!" voices in the crowd had roared. "Idiots! You idiots! The police have to be with the government!" Kotya had roared back, angrily.

The melody flowed on. And judging by everyone's reactions, only Kotya and the musician himself knew the words of that Banderite fight song: "Ah, belt after belt, give me the cartridges! Ukrainian rebel, don't retreat from the battle!"

Once the music was over, Kotya got up from the table and walked over to the accordionist. Doing his best to replicate the intonation of Blaine/Bogart, the noble ne'er-do-well who Serov had tormented us with back in the good old twentieth century, whose second half had gone by so very slowly, Kotya said, "Play it again, Sam."

* * *

Victors have to be fools. In order for them to celebrate, to breathe easily and freely, to roar with joy without being embarrassed, to embrace passers-by, to cry as they hug the men who came to defend them... Victors have to be fools.

If they aren't, then there can be no celebration. And there can be no complete happiness, either.

We won't be able to celebrate. We'll probably never be able to. Because you feel sorry for the people you defeated. Even if they don't deserve it, even if they would've killed us without a second thought. And even if we leave aside the "would've," because they already have, and did it without any thought at all.

It doesn't matter. You feel sorry for them. And our victory will be muted. Not underground, not secret. No. It'll just be quiet, like love.

* * *

DIFFICULT FACES

SUNDAY
....
JUNE 1, 2014
....
D O N E T S K

Good news, Marco, looks like this:

"Yesterday, in Mariupol, a security guard at the Santa Barbara restaurant knocked a gun out of the hand of a 'raging' terrorist. Then he shot him. The guard shot the terrorist, that is." I'm having a conversation with a friend, who is telling me this story. After a pause, my friend adds: *"And you know what? The guard flew into such a fury that he also took out the buddy of the 'raging bull' he'd just killed. The buddy said he was a sniper and pissed himself from fright. Turned out he wasn't a real sniper at all, but the rifle was real enough."*

I offer my friend some funny news in exchange for his "good news." Well, maybe not funny, exactly... Funny in terms of the situation we're both stuck in: "Yesterday, twenty men with automatic rifles attacked a gay club in Donetsk. All who participated in the conflict survived..."

"Do we really have a gay club here in Donetsk?"

"Nobody knows for sure except the terrorists..."

I tell Marco about that phone conversation. He laughs. Marco's an Italian. He's been with us for two months. I don't have to explain anything to him. He watched as everything went to pot before our very eyes. At the end of March, we talked about the difference. About how, in Italy, there are still Romans and Tuscans, Sicilians and Lombards, up until this very day. About how nothing's permanently glued together in that eternal boot of theirs and their unity is still just a surface appearance, all but illusory. And how it's possible to live with that.

In April, we taught him new words. The first one was "Colorado beetle." "Potato beetle?" laughed Marco. "*Dorifora della patata*?" "Yes, we don't get along with the *dorifora*," we laughed. "Look at the color pattern, Marco... The ribbons they wear have the exact same color pattern. And the people who wear them destroy stuff we could eat..."

"Is it a bad word?" Marco asked.

He didn't need to ask about "Cargo 200." It had taken a long time to get the body of his comrade, a photojournalist from Milan, out of Slovyansk. There had been a homemade "200" decal on the car that brought in the dead.

"Cargo 200 means they're dead, but what if there's some hope?" Marco asked.

"If there's some hope, then it's 300. Cargo 300."

Marco was the first one I told about my pity for them. For the others. And about *She Who Runs on the Waves*. Marco had no idea who this Aleksandr Grin was. I told him Grin had been my great love when I was a teenager. The phrase "sooner or later, the dreams that haven't come true will call to us" hadn't made any sense at all. At fifteen, we're sure that each and every one of our dreams is attainable. But in the embrace of middle age, when "still can" changes to "never did," when "awesome, I still haven't tried that" is replaced by "that's something I'll never do now, too bad," that's when we have to build some kind of a relationship with exactly that, with what we haven't done... Convince it, or convince ourselves, not to sing sad songs... Not to want what we shouldn't want.

"All those people roaring about not being heard— what they're actually saying is that nobody's hearing or seeing their unfulfilled dreams," I said to Marco. "People can't live just on food... Or on condescending handouts... People want to be complete, fulfilled. The things they haven't done sit there and whisper despicably, 'So, what have you even seen? What have you experienced? You're going to die, and your bones will molder, and there won't even be a memory of you left... But you could do something, if you wanted to! You could!..'"

"Oh," smiled Marco. "I understand. I get it. It's Hamlet, right? They're all Hamlets now? Except that they all have very difficult faces..."

I like that. Difficult faces.

It's already June. And I have a "difficult" face myself. I know what it's like. Your face turns difficult after everything human has gradually leached away. I think my face actually got off relatively easy. My face, our faces... We really did hold on for a long time...

There are kids playing on the boulevard, there's the caffe latte Marco likes, there's the black tea with mint that I like...

We talk about Italy again. And about the Ardeatine massacre. I know the story, but it was important for Marco to tell it so I could see, for the nth time, that he understands.

The Nazis entered Rome as enemies in 1944. Italian partisans bombed a Nazi unit. Over thirty people were killed. Within twenty-four hours, the Gestapo had collected victims for revenge, taking them from prison, the Jewish ghetto, or just off the street. The oldest was 74, the youngest 14. Three hundred and forty-four people in all. They were executed to punish the city.

This story is nothing out of the ordinary in these parts. It is out of the ordinary in Italy, though.

"But the Romans—"

"Oh, those Romans," says Marco. "They think the partisans are to blame for the mass execution. They think the Germans are an organized and cultured people, and that the Germans gave the guilty parties the chance to turn themselves in, and that then nobody would've been executed. But that never happened. There were no chances given. The Nazis just shot those people. For revenge. To scare everyone. But the Romans... Those Romans still don't believe this, even now. They think there's no way the Germans could have behaved that way with civilians ... Hitler and Mussolini were like brothers..."

"Those darn Romans," I agree. "I'm afraid they'll never be able to believe that a fraternal people could treat them like that..."

Marco and I exchange a look. I'm grateful for his tact. I want to tell him this, but I can't find the words. All my words are now in another place, one that's full of pain.

A burst of fire from an automatic rifle goes off right next to us, along with shouts and the sound of a car speeding away. We don't hide. We're used to this. But Marco displays a professional interest: "We have to go see what happened..."

What happened?

"*Somebody got popped, that's the lads*"—a line by Burkov (played by Borislav Brondukov) from the film about 1920s gangsters, *The Art of Living in Odesa*.[22]

"*Somebody got popped*" lay face-down on the ground. He was wearing a purple suit. It was hot as hell outside. The flung-open lapel revealed a Zilli label. The name-brand shops had all been looted a month ago. Although the dead man could've bought it, too. Why not?

The police only come once they are sure the situation is no longer dangerous and the shooting is over. Ever since the police stood "with the people," it stopped protecting businesses or risking being shot at, and it only very grudgingly picks up the phone in case of emergencies.

Good people get the dead guy's passport out of his pocket and identify him as the assistant to the chairman of the presidium of the high council of the fifth floor of our Donetsk People's Asylum. The dead man's a Russian citizen.

Now I can explain what a "difficult face" is: it's the face of a person who sees a dead man and thinks, "He got what he deserved, the occupier!" A person who thinks without filtering their thoughts, without feeling horror, without feeling the least bit of shame.

When my professor lectured about the Crusades, she'd repeat this one phrase over and over: "The veneer of Christianity is thin. It sloughs off fast, leaving naked archaism with a light dusting of pagan sacrificial offerings."

A light dusting, indeed...

Father Pavel was killed at a checkpoint for asking Kadyrov's men to leave.

Father Pyotr, on the other hand, would administer last rites for any *opolchenets* who wanted them every time before the assault on whatever it was they wanted to seize that day.

God, we all have "difficult" faces...

And they're all equally difficult now.

* * *

RUMORS

SUNDAY

JUNE 1, 2014

D O N E T S K

Okay, fine. To hell with physics. It's a complex science. Fine! I'll go with it. Straight-C students all round. It's actually better that their Molotov cocktails are in plastic fucking bottles. Better for us. We stay alive longer.

Your English isn't the greatest, eh? "Save Us From Right *Quadrant*"? Come on, you can't figure out how to translate the word *sektor*?! *Sektor*, you benighted gnomes, is "sector." It's "sector" even in Africa. But if you want to be rescued from a Quadrant, then God help you. Don't look at me.

And your rights are also being seriously infringed. Assaulted. Violated, basically. I completely agree with you. But only in your translation. Because for regular people it's "human rights," but for you warriors of the BFD army it came out correctly, in line with your thinking: *"USA Violences Our Hymen Rights."* Hmm. So, the United States is violating your hymen's rights. But this particular membrane is in your head, a giant intact tract of concrete that's even overgrown with moss in places from lack of use. Think of it as birth control that keeps you safe from the pindoses, forever and ever, amen.

My respect to all you teachers of our basic English language. Great job! Your efforts have made our lives much more interesting.

And what have we here? Another gem from our new educational program: "The cut-open bellies of the Volhynian soldiers."[23] Don't even ask what they were smoking. No, ask when. When, exactly, did they use their ABC books for rolling papers? On the first day of school? Or did they manage to hold off until New Year's, so they could smoke away under the holiday decorations? It was their last remaining book...

Who, I ask you, is cutting open the bellies of Volhynian soldiers? Your fucking "peaceful protesters" with combat experience in Chechnya? Ah, what a plot twist. Almost a confession. Congratulations! That'll go over really well at the Hague. Now, I know that in Russian we say "Gaaga" not "Hague." But let's just make sure: I'm talking about the city "Gaaga," not the singer Gaga. Got it, you animals?

Wait—what? I can't hear you! Not "peaceful protesters" but who? Who is doing the cutting?

Americans, you say? Transplant specialists? Fantastic. But why are the Volhynians getting their guts taken out? Why isn't that happening to our guys, our poor guys, as revenge for the—well, what do we call them—"New Russia Russians"? "Russians of New Russia?" Now that'd be something to show your rapacious Russian audience. But what's with this Volhynian thing?

Ahhh, because they're fucking healthier, that's why. Their "uhcology" is better and their organs are cleaner. Yes sirree. And "uhcology" must absolutely be with an "uh," my man. The way you say it. Has to have an "uh."

Let me get this straight: the "Americunts" go out into that oh-so-clean west-Ukrainian "uhcology" and pick out the ones they want, just like you do with livestock. Then they get them to enlist and get them sent out not just anywhere, but right here, to the front, and then, once they're here, they hide in the fields and lie in wait for them, scalpels clenched between their teeth. Then they cut out all their organs and ship them to Pindosia to use for treating the billionaires. Is that right?

I get it. I'm local. For us, sterilizing medical equipment means pissing on our hands and licking off the syringe between uses. Our hospitals are also basic: rats, cracked plaster, wire spring beds, and iodine for whatever ails you. There hasn't been electric light, anesthesia, or surgeons in our operating rooms for ten years now.

You think this is what it's like for Americans, too?

And that's why they yank a guy's liver right out of his belly in the middle of a dirty field, pass it around so everybody can get a good look at it, grab a plastic bag, empty out the pickles, plop it in there, and then trundle it to the train station on a *kravchuchka*, a folding granny cart? And don't forget the ten-spot for the conductor so he hides it from customs!

Sure. Fine. Go ahead and eat that up.

But why the hell are you sending me letters with this fucking "delicate" lead-in about "let *the Westernizers* see it, they're human beings, too..." To hell with them: *I'm* a Westernizer. It's just that, from my window, I see that same old slag heap and that same steel mill as you, but from my mouth, if I'm not being monitored by my audience, comes the most voiced possible fricative "h." An astonishing sound, I'm telling you... It only hardens to a full "g" if I make a colossal effort of will... And for me, a guy who's eighty, that's already a victory, my man.[24]

Right. Back to that letter. A letter that I got by email, which presupposes that the sender has functioning Internet access, for sure, if not that the sender has a functioning brain in their head. And the Internet has the letters of the alphabet in it! And you can also come across encyclopedias on the Internet. Whole libraries even...

But their brains' hymens are as whole and virginal as ever. The letter mentions the "horrer" of biological weapons and the "special reserve chemists" conspiracy theory...

Well—everybody cry along with me now—you deserve your "special reserve chemists" because you're the ones who created the plagues and diseases you'll dump into the water supply and into the water bottles sold at every supermarket, thus causing a biological and humanitarian catastrophe for us all. Western Ukraine and Poland will suffer, too. Along with all of fricking Europe. Because the junta feels no pity for anyone.

And only Russia... Oh, yes, Russia. Only Russia will be saved. Russia will wall itself off with a sanitary corridor made of neon signs reading *Putin—khuilo*, "Putin Is a Dickhead." Not a single bacteria can penetrate signs like that.

Whereas a blind man could see we're the ones who'll be wiped out. And, if someone does manage to survive, then the "junta's" next move will be gas, same as with the Nord-Ost hostages.

I'm not asking anymore what grade they were in when they quit school. Now, I'm asking what century they were in. What the hell *era* are we talking about? Leeches, water from poisoned wells, washing your body weakens your resistance to the Devil's tricks...

Don't forget the rats. They'll see the post marking the border of the Russian Federation, stand up on their hind legs, salute, and then, without even crossing the border, they'll drop dead where they stand. From happiness. Fucking hell.

I wonder, is common sense the only thing they've banned in this "republic," or have they abolished the water cycle, too?

Why? Why must I read this?! Although there's this, too, a patriotic missive, apparently from our side: "Donetsk! Everyone go back home! Don't go anywhere else! There is fighting in the city's Kyiv district! Everyone sit inside at home and don't go fucking around right in front of the window!" But it doesn't make me feel any better. Because I'm old. What else is left for me besides going and fucking around right in front of the window?

If it weren't for the cigars, my man, if it weren't for that marvelous whiskey that was given to me as a test balloon for actual bribes, how could I possibly survive all this?

"The Kentucky Derby is decadent and depraved," my dear. If I'd written my essays on the rhythm and intonations of Russian versification in "gonzo journalism" style right from the get-go, then those people might have been able to comprehend me...

But, as you see, I'm not giving up. I'm still practicing. I'm eighty and I'm beginning everything all over again. And you, don't you think you're too good for it. Study this style. Learn it. It will come in handy, trust me. Because we still have to live with the ones who use it.

* * *

THE PHOTOGRAPHER

There was an announcement posted inside the elevator: "In case of air strikes or artillery fire, you are requested to take shelter in the basement of our building (the drivers' ed office), or in the bomb shelter of the Science and Research Institute of Integrated Automation at 2 Batyshchev Street. Bring your ID, medicine, and a day's supply of water."

The first notes like that from the housing and utility management department appeared two weeks ago, after the fighting at the airport. The notes were hung in the entrances: "This side of the street is dangerous during artillery fire." It's the signs in blockaded Leningrad all over again. I take pictures of them, hoping that I'm working in the genre of the absurd. And that this absurd will end any minute now. And that we'll laugh about it.

But we won't. That's also clear. We are laughing about it now, but—regardless of how this ends—we will never be able to laugh about it afterwards. I don't have anyone I can talk to about this. But I'm trying to get her back.

I'm trying to get my wife back.

I started trying on Monday. I'm not bringing any groceries home. The fridge still has food in it. But what's in there is old. I'm not buying any groceries and I'm not going to buy any. I eat shawarmas. But not hot dogs. I don't like them. They gave me food poisoning during Euro-2012. We were drinking whiskey with some English guys and chasing it with hot dogs. It was raining really hard. And it was windy. Almost a tornado. The match kept getting delayed and we all needed something to calm our nerves. The French were worried the tornado would carry them off into

Kansas. They didn't want to abandon the continent, even for Kansas. The next morning, it became clear that something had definitely been off. And it wasn't the whiskey.

Two years ago, we lived in Europe. And in three days our fridge will be empty. I calculated it. If we don't replenish it, it'll end up empty. Whatever. My wife noticed. She's even asked about it already: "Where are the groceries?"

And I answered, "No money, no groceries."

"So why don't we have any money?"

And you know what? I didn't even explode at her. I kept my cool. "Your new 'republican' friends closed all the newspapers. They kidnapped two editors. And just to make sure, they burned down the typography. I don't have anywhere to publish my photos. There's nobody to commission them. So how could I have any money?"

We're already out of sausage, butter, cheese, and potatoes. There's a little buckwheat kasha left. Two eggs. So it won't take long now... Not long now...

But yesterday she brought home two bottles of Ossetian vodka. I asked her, "How can you do this? What's wrong with you? You made it twenty years as a leading orthopedic surgeon without taking so much as a box of chocolates... What's wrong with you? What are they doing to you?"

She answered, "You don't understand. This is Ossetian vodka. Russian vodka..."

Too bad I quit taking pictures of her a long time ago. Because I could've captured the tear. It was very touching: a vodka bottle in each hand and a tear in each eye.

This is the kind of thing she says now: "I'm with the ones whose 'yes' means 'yes' and whose 'no' means 'no.'"

This is a pronouncement about me, not about the country. About my "shades" and "half-tones." Ukraine's got nothing to do with it. I've always been this way.

She's suspicious of me. No—not that I'm sabotaging the fridge. She thinks I'm connected to the Resistance. She listens to me when I talk on the phone. But she doesn't listen to me at any other time of our shared life together. She's not interested.

But we're even, you see. I also have both a Plan A and a Plan B for her.

In Plan B, I emulate Abraham. We have a son, Kirill. He's only twenty-five. But he's just the right age for defending Mordor. I'll sacrifice him. I'll say, "Here's our dear son. Take him for the *opolchenie*, the people's militia. Let him fight."

And you know the scary part?

I'm almost certain my wife won't be as merciful as God. She won't stay my hand.

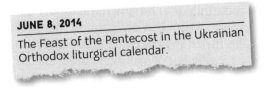

JUNE 8, 2014

The Feast of the Pentecost in the Ukrainian Orthodox liturgical calendar.

* * *

FALLING IN LOVE WITH A WIZARD

THURSDAY
JUNE 12, 2014
D O N E T S K

So, I've finally fallen in love. Two years ago, an astrologer read my cards and told me, "Oh, you will meet a big man really, really soon." I asked, "As in tall? Or as in important?" "No, no... I mean, I see he's an engineer, but he's got a big..." "Weenie?" "Soul! He is a big man *spiritually*!"

But is two years "really, really soon," though? I'd managed to forget by then. This one psychic—you remember him? He opened that sport club in Vetka, in the Kyiv neighborhood of Donetsk, but it failed because that's not his thing? Anyway, that psychic said that sometimes a person's fate, the thing that has been foreordained for them, ends up forgotten. We're moving along, doing our thing, but we end up in a dead end. And we're stuck there. The only thing that changes is the view out the window. Weather, nature, color—everything changes, but the train isn't moving. We're getting older, but our intended time isn't passing. And, if you stay stuck that way your whole life, then, in your next life, you could come back as an elephant or some other lower form of life. I don't have anything against elephants. It's just that they're animal alcoholics. They eat things that have fermented and then the next day they're drunk. For days at a time. They're happy. But us, we're supposed to become gods, create planets, measure out doses of love... We're supposed to become greater beings, not elephants.

And that's when I realized that my train had just been stuck in a dead end for two years. But now I've fallen in love with a wizard. He has the same connection with the cosmos that I do, just stronger. A lot stronger.

He led these funny yoga classes on the boulevard. Everyone could join in. I could, too. He said "Hello" to me. But all the rest of it happened during class sessions. During his yoga classes everyone becomes friends and starts hugging. He hugged other women briefly. But he hugged me once and for all.

It's very difficult to talk about love. Here I am, forty-five years old. I've seen all kinds of things. When I was little, I could kill you with a snowball, I've always been quick. That's probably why it's hard for me to talk about love. He's younger than me. I could tell right away. It took him a little while. But he said that the soul doesn't have an age. As for me—it feels good to me. It feels good.

I'm grateful to *everything*. If it hadn't been for the fighting, he would've left a week earlier. But there was no airport, no airplane, and no Moscow. So he's with me. It's great!

He has these eyes... And his skin's like a baby's. He wakes up in the morning fresh as spring water. Clean.

Me, I'm an old lady in the morning until I put on my make-up. I'm afraid. And I'm not afraid. He says that my love is love for myself. He says it's that I've simply seen myself, finally. And that I'm perfection. And that I can control not only the weather but basically everything that happens. And, therefore, I can't think about the war. It's just not an option for me. I attract it, I bring it on myself. If you think about it, we all do, actually.

I remember not wanting to eat when I was little. My mother would yell at me: "You're not getting up until you eat everything. You'll sleep at this table tonight!" I believed her. She would forget to pick me up from daycare and leave me there all night, and now here she was at home, leaving me at the table all night. She was quite capable of it. And do you know what I thought about? War! I thought about war, about how some children's bellies got distended from starvation during war. I thought about war! So I ate. Against war. My whole childhood. I've asked other people and they did the same thing. We know that to make yourself have an appetite, you have to just start eating; doubly so during war. And you say we didn't bring the war on ourselves? I'm not so sure...

He says this is a lesson. We're all Michelangelo's nudes at the Last Judgment. We didn't think we were naked... These apartments of ours, the money in the bank, all the trinkets, and bling, and nonsense... Although you can pay with it at the checkpoint: a ring will ransom a body, especially a dead body. Even a live person can be ransomed, in theory at least. As for the rest... Well, at least it's crystal-clear now: we don't have anything. Except ourselves. He says that's just it, that is the greatest thing we have.

He calls me "my dearest dear." Not a word about love. That's an important word for him; I still haven't made it to that level yet. But I will. That same astrologist told me that ten years after first meeting him, we'll be married. But, for all the years in between, he'll be distant, a sea-faring wanderer. Fine with me. It's only a tiny bit painful. Really, just a tiny bit.

And take note: this is also a lesson. The hardest one, for me. Because stuff—the stuff isn't that big a deal. You can also learn not to think of everything through war, learn not to think of only the bad. There's this thing you can do—sort of a thought-disarmament technique. I'll tell you about it. But then you get to the hardest thing: there's no past. No future. There's only what there is now.

We don't know whether they're going to mine the city. We don't know what they've already done. We don't know what we'll do when they've done it. But pinot grigio is really a decent little wine. Although I like my wine a little sweeter. And those young ladies at the table over there: just look at that girl's hair. She worked on that hair for probably two hours so she could bring it in here. Hair... Hair's important. Loud music from speakers is shit. I think restaurants are for eating. Not for going deaf. But right now, today, sure. Let it play. The sweet melancholy of Boombox's "Night Watchmen." Let it play. It's not a funeral march—that's a plus.

But something's always happening, you know? There's never a time when something's not happening. And that's why there's no death. Falling, even hitting bottom: those aren't the end yet. Those aren't the end. Yesterday, I went to Obzhora for dinner. They dragged in a guy beaten within an inch of his life and shouted that they'd caught a fascist. They were ecstatic. Kicking him with each step they took. I said, "Lord, I'm being pulled into darkness. Give me a sign. Give me a sign that I can understand with my simple womanish brain." And guess what happened? Just don't laugh. God is like communism: he gives to everyone according to their capabilities. Which is probably why he had me see two rainbows. Two parallel ones, a bright one like usual and a second one that was this wide, sort of washed-out band. I took a picture of it. Here, just a second and I'll show it to you.

The rainbow is protection. It's a sign of unending mercy and love. We are under this protection because we were guiltier than everyone else. Which also means we understood more than everyone else. No coming back as elephants for us...

I think that when he—my guy—looks at the sea, his eyes turn purple. Can you imagine that? I want to go to the seashore with him. He said we can forget about Goa. I never dreamed I'd be the kind of person who could think of forgetting about Goa. I know this is my great good fortune. He said the women there don't wear shorts. But I don't have anything I could wear, anything purposefully long. That reminds me... What was the first thing you bought after they started bombing the airport? Come on, what? For me, it was foundation. I even found some on sale. Everything else you can figure out. You can't buy supplies of everything you'll need for the rest of your life. But at our age it's crucial to have good foundation.

My ex called. My guy heard me being rude to him. And you know what he did? He read me the riot act, like I was a little girl. "You spent twenty years with him. For twenty years you needed something he was giving. Where's your picture of him? Why don't you have one? What's wrong? Are you still mad at him? Are you wasting your time amplifying the bad? But what if it's God dressed up as your ex, testing you? It doesn't matter how he behaves. What matters is how you behave when someone amplifies anger. You are a source of peace. You are joy. Everything is in you. And God weeps when you don't see Him in the face of an untouchable. Put out a picture of him. Make a nice dinner. Treat him. Make peace with him."

I happened to have some mashed potatoes on hand. And two fried meat patties. The pocketbook's a little lean these days. I try to eat less. The meat patties were still there when my guy left. He's meat-free. As you'd expect. Anyway, I went ahead and put a picture of my ex in a frame. He's sober in the picture, and handsome. He's in the army. It was before we got married. I put everything out on a plate. I said, "Eat, please, and don't be mad. I have some squash, too, if you need more... And I can open the tomatoes. My mom pickled them the way you like..." And I even felt sorry for him. To tell the truth: we made up.

The next day, he even called me. He said he was sorry for something or other and wanted to get married again. But what do I need that for? I have love. When my guy's falling asleep, his eyes are still clear and bright. Like the sky. I'll tell you more another time because there's no right word now for what to compare it to.

He said he'd come back with the young corn. He also said that our city is under God's protection. In His mercy and in His debt. My man's indebted to God, too, because his parents are here... You know, my guy can repair any roof under the sun. Our roof isn't the biggest one out there, and neither's the hole in it. For him, repairing that shell hole's easy as pie. I'll get a little more practice and maybe I'll be able to do it myself...

But yesterday, when their tanks entered the city, I thought, "Maybe there's no use in our being so angry. Maybe this is also God, dressed up in the Dickhead's suit, making us see we're not human anymore?" I don't know what all he likes or what kind of food people make for him, but I don't exactly have a wide array of options here anyway. I fried some potatoes, so he'd know I can do something other than mash them. I wanted to get some chicken thighs, but then I remembered they're po-litically tainted—"Bush's chicken legs." Can't offend him. I got a piece of beef, marinated it, fried it up like a steak. Medium-rare. Just a little bloody. I found a photo of the Dickhead on the internet, where he's still young and that

whole country of theirs is ramping up to love him. I printed it, drew a frame around it, and set it there next to my
ex. I served dinner. I apologized for the hate and rage.

That's what I did...

He hasn't called yet.

* * *

ANNOUNCING THE ARMED REBELLION

FRIDAY

JUNE 20, 2014

**D O N E T S K –
H O R L I V K A**

On June 20, the "people's governor" of
the Donetsk region announced: "Tomorrow, the armed rebellion against
the Kyiv junta begins. I won't go into
any more detail; you'll see for
yourselves."

The "people's governor," Pavel (Pasha) Gubarev, is
also my former student. One of the ones whose faces
are hard to remember. It's my fault. I should have understood. Seen. He'd wanted to say something important.

He loved and hated Lenin. I think he approved of
the plan to seize Petrograd. But he thought Zinoviev and
Kamenev's position, their decision to release information
about the planned revolt, was traitorous.

But now he's doing it himself. Writing about a revolt.
Is he Zinoviev, maybe? Or just a spy? An innocent Stierlitz?

"You all in Kyiv are going to have a rebellion tomorrow," I say sadly into the phone. "Gubarev gave an
announcement."

"A rebellion of who? Grandfather Frosts? In June?
What's he been smoking?" growls the person on the
other end of the line, adding, with a sigh, "What an epic
fuckwit."

After graduating from college, the future "governor"
did not find a job teaching history in a school. Instead, he

started an ad agency. He had very few ideas and the same number of clients. But he did have three children. In winter, Pasha worked as a Grandfather Frost. There was good demand for it, and it made good money. Even now you can see happy pictures of his "winter self" on the Internet.

The mayor of Horlivka was taken prisoner a couple of weeks ago. For over two months, he'd tried to "find something in common with the *opolchentsy*, the 'people's militia.'" In addition to keeping up the trash service, repairing the sewers, filling in potholes, and pretending the situation was normal. Which it was, more or less. If you don't count the barricades, hostages, armed robberies, arson... That's even what he said in Kyiv: everything's following the normal civilian routine.

But, at some point, the rebels just had enough of the mayor. And that was that. Men with automatic rifles came and took him down to the basement. He didn't resist. The only resistance a man without a gun can offer is a quick death from a bullet. Which is perhaps not the worst thing. But the mayor of Horlivka wasn't ready for it.

After a few days, the city elders tried to get him back. To ransom him, or just to come to some agreement. A big delegation of them went. Before they left, they said their farewells to their families. But they came back alive. They didn't have the mayor. He's still a prisoner. His captors shot or broke his leg, shaved him bald, and dressed him in camo. They keep him drugged out of his mind and make him sign documents. He no longer owns anything, has no more personal property. And the Russian flags fly high over Horlivka. As per orders by the "head of the city," of course—how else...

The mayor picks up trash in courtyards, cleans toilets, and gets hauled up on the barricades to lift the rebels' fighting spirit. One of the promises they've made is to throw him into the front lines when the direct attack begins. They'll throw him out there wearing camo, so the

Ukrainian army kills him. That'll be a fan-fucking-tastic story for the Russian channels...

In April, after the "peaceful protesters" captured the oblast state administration building in Donetsk, anyone who felt revolutionarily inclined could enter freely. Some people even came from sixty miles away, with their families, to take the tour. Just to go up and down from story to story, to be inside a place that they, simple mortals, would never have been able to enter before that. Not a chance. But a month later the building had been as wrecked and thoroughly looted as though it were the Winter Palace. As though the walls themselves were guilty of everything and now it was time for them to pay.

Ah, the mayor of Horlivka... Handsome, dignified, and most likely rich. At some point, he'd been unattainable, unavailable for a simple handshake. He'd been sacralized, the way we sacralize all power here, whether great or small. And now the townspeople felt sorry for him, of course, but they were also enjoying his situation. A few of them even helped. It was way better to belittle and abuse him than the walls of the oblast state administration building. People said that, when he was high, he was even funnier.

Fun little tales.

A rebellion of Grandfather Frosts. A rebellion of imaginary people. A pseudo-urban legend that only later became a Soviet fairy tale. Mr. Frost had always been mean, actually. But believing in him once a year was easier than believing in God.

Instead of a miracle from Saint Nicholas, instead of sharing the joy of baby Jesus—presents in a red sack. "Hi there, Grampa Frost, beard of cotton wool! Where are our presents, you hunchbacked old fool?"

Note that even as kids, as it turns out, we already knew about the vata.

Not about God, though.

* * *

LIKE A WOMAN

WEDNESDAY
JUNE 25, 2014
DONETSK

The city's like a woman who's been raped. Yesterday, she was carefree and loved. Beautiful, especially in the morning.

And then the thing that happened... happened.

Not one. Many. All with the same faces. All in the same camo. The automatic rifles they jabbed her with were probably different. But she couldn't tell them apart.

Those men raped her cruelly and for a long time. They took turns, one after the other. Afterwards, resting, they spat on her body. They had fun shooting out the streetlights.

They beat her with checkpoints and sandbags. Every day they tore off her dress, which had once been yellow and blue.

They demanded her love while raping her. And they called over friends so they, too, could take her whatever way they wanted. Especially ways they wouldn't or couldn't allow at home in their own country.

They degraded her. They dreamed up new tricks and new bloody poses for the next day, which she now hoped would never come. She hoped everything would be destroyed and left in ruins.

But no.

They laughed, promising she'd die sooner than they'd leave her alone. And they came again, in great crowds. She didn't have the strength to resist. She didn't have a single living part of herself left, either.

Every morning, she, the woman who became my city, got up and washed herself. She scrubbed herself with brushes, doused herself with water through to her very bones, so that at least some part of her somewhere would be clean.

She did her makeup and put on her best clothes; she took out the trash as usual; she did the shopping, stocked the fridge with food, and went to work by trolley-bus or taxi; she went to the post office to send the mail. She even called the plumber or the electrician whenever the previous night's orgy had done more than the usual damage to her home. But she never called the doctor.

Instead of a doctor, she probably bought herself flowers every day. Roses. A whole lot of roses.

And every night everything would repeat all over again.

She didn't even scream anymore. She didn't call for anyone to help her.

Like any other rape victim, she thought she was to blame. She'd given them a reason, brought them into her house, fed them... So, what else did she expect?

She couldn't complain, because everything they did to her was shameful. She had to learn to forget. But they were acquiring a taste for it and didn't let her forget. As they spread-eagled her on the city square or on a stair-well landing, they demanded that she enjoy it.

Everything inside her had burned to ash. But still to come, she knew, was the pointing, accusatory finger: you are ruined, filthy.

Still to come was other people's squeamishness, their desire to keep their distance from her.

A drop of empathy, yes, but only from those who, like herself, had been degraded. The initiates.

There were moments when all she wanted was an airstrike. A powerful, large-scale airstrike that would take out her and all her torturers, just wipe them off the face of the earth, change everything from suffering into desert wasteland.

The days went by. The weeks. And then only this dream was left.

They raped her over and over. She smiled, anticipating the screaming of a thousand jets.

I don't remember whether it was Michael Kimmel who said it... Yes, it was him where I read that what men are most afraid of is being laughed at. For women, it's being raped and killed.

This is true. We are afraid of that. If my Donetsk had been a man, we would've easily made it through any amount of mockery. We'd have had the strength.

But here she is, a woman. And I'm not sure if a century of love will be enough for her to stop remembering, and feeling shame, and trembling at the slightest touch.

* * *

THE SIGN

THURSDAY AND FRIDAY
JUNE 26–27, 2014
DONETSK

The military unit had been under fire for seven hours. With breaks for talks and bringing in more shells. Our general spoke on television, ordering the troops to fight to the death.

Our neighboring country's TV bleated that the Right Sector had taken over the military unit.

It's unlikely that any of those actually participating in the process were watching TV at the time.

This military unit is in a residential area. *My* residential area.

Playgrounds, shops, a gas station. A gym. The treadmills in the gym are by the windows. They're French windows, all the way down to the floor. You can see the slag heap from them, and the road, and the barracks, and cars going by, and, sometimes, just a little, the soldiers. It's a police and security unit. All the contract soldiers are local. Almost all the conscripts are.

Whenever I started feeling like it'd be better to be fat than to fall down like a fool right on that damn treadmill, I'd tell myself: "Look! Those boys over there have it worse... They have strict regulations, tight discipline, and heavy meals. For a whole year. You've only got to last forty-five minutes. Keep going... Keep going... Keep going..."

For seven hours, it thundered and boomed. If you have a good imagination, seven hours is an infinite number of pictures of the Apocalypse. A shell in an apartment building. A shell in the gas station. Fighting on the streets. Mortars moving through a residential neighborhood.

Eventually the unit gave up. All the personnel were taken prisoner.

I learned to tell the nighttime explosions apart.

"Is that an anti-aircraft missile?" I'd ask.

"It's a mortar," my husband would answer. "Don't worry, it's a mortar..."

"What do you mean 'don't worry'! How is a mortar any better than an anti-aircraft missile?"

"The kill zone's smaller."

He'd served in the army.

A mortar. A machine gun. Individual shots. Then a mortar again.

"Where are they getting so many bullets and shells from?"

"Humanitarian aid."

Algeria was also playing the Russian national team that night. Soccer. Russia scored first.

Mortar fire. A goal. Roaring from the stands. Another burst of fire. Then another, and another, and another.

We've got two men in the house. The second is our son.

He thinks he's grown-up. In his opinion, it's bad, embarrassing to cry or be afraid.

"I can't sleep for some reason. Maybe we should turn on the air conditioner?"

It's fifty-three degrees Fahrenheit outside, quite a cold snap for summer. The wind is howling and the rain is thrashing. It's chilly. Really chilly.

"Or maybe you could turn the sound down? Maybe it's just the soccer game that's keeping me from falling asleep?"

My hands felt his tears in the dark. I stroked his hair and said, "Hey, listen, we're not idiots, right? Or we would've left. But we're here. We didn't leave. And our windows face the other direction. And a mortar has a significantly smaller kill zone than an anti-aircraft missile. And they'll eventually run out of shells, and the shells won't make it all the way out here to us. And, if something does happen, all you do is just fall flat on the floor, and then crawl over to the door, nice and easy, and then we go down to the basement."

Embracing him, I wasn't sure we weren't idiots. The presence of a basement (where the driving school used to be) was a pretty thin justification for our nonchalance.

As long as we're here, nothing bad will happen.

As long as we're here, there's a here...

As long as we're here, there's a we...

I wanted to flick my grown-up son's nose with my finger, just lightly, to stir up a fun little fake fight. But he took off his glasses and sighed heavily. It was a sob, to be honest. I touched his face and happened to brush his eye. The corner of his eye sheltered little tears that ran in a tiny stream over his nose and fell neatly on the pillow. My son, my little boy, was lying on his left side. So it was a lot easier for his right eye to cry than for his left.

"Fascism's not going to make it to the quarter-finals. Algeria tied it up. Shhh. Everything's going to be okay," said our husband and father, and then hugged us both close, shielding us with his body. "Everything's going to be okay! You hear me?"

We didn't hear any more shots. They'd run out of shells and bullets. The Grand Ceasefire had been filled out with a teeny-weeny one. A hopeless one.

"Don't get on the Internet! Everything's going to be okay! Algeria tied it up!"

It was the first time my friends had wanted Russia to lose. It was the first time the Russians in Donbas had wanted the Russian national team to lose. This region, a region that had been so carefully turned by its brother into a place of murder and death, was watching the soccer world cup.

My husband was also watching it. But it wasn't the defeat that made him so happy. It was the sign. Or rather, the Sign.

A lot of new suffering came in with the morning news. A lot.

Our Ukrainian checkpoints had been attacked by tanks and Grads—the multiple rocket launchers whose name, aptly, means "hail." Five soldiers dead. One of them, as he lay dying in his comrade's arms, said in Ukrainian, "*Brother, I'm falling down...*" Five deaths in the sixth night of the cease-fire.

The editor of the *Druzhkivsky Worker* was kidnapped. The terrorists decided that fifty thousand was insufficient for our friend, who'd been captured at a checkpoint, and asked for another ten thousand on top of that. Like that line from the movie *Irony of Fate*: "Don't be a skinflint, Nadenka!"

They shot up the Artemivsk–Chasiv Yar *marshrutka*, the jitney minibus. Just shot it up for no reason. The driver was killed on the spot. A female passenger died in the hospital.

But the attack on the military unit turned out to be "by agreement." There were no casualties. Just two dents in the main gate. Some broken windows. They even fed the prisoners breakfast. And a few of them admitted that everyone who'd been part of it just fired into the air.

The only casualty was my son. And the other children who heard and remembered the voice of war.

They decided to extend the cease-fire for three more days. There are still too many of us—the living and unbowed.

By Monday, there will be fewer of us.

The university was open. Its—our—news was merely bad, as opposed to full of utter suffering. What lies ahead is unclear. There might be no incoming first-year class. Enrollment will happen in August, although it'll probably be more like September. But what student's parents will want to hang around waiting for that spectral September? None, probably. The juniors and seniors are running away. We should have taken them hostage, like the med school did, by transferring the summer exam session to the fall. Although what would they have transferred with? No grades, no transfers... It's like in those bad jokes: "Ah, if only we'd been as smart back then as my Sara always is in hindsight..."

The last faculty meeting was the last one of the year. Maybe the last one, period.

I said to myself, "Lord, I want something like what my friend Inna got. So please, give me a sign that everything will be okay. A simple sign, one my terrified woman's brain can understand, one I can't miss. Please, if you can, give me a sign..."

On that note, I headed home to make borscht. I wanted green borscht, with sorrel. I don't like chopping cabbage, but I do like sorrel. It's light, tart, and happy.

There are lines on Fridays in the Rizhky ta nizhky (Horns and Hooves) meat market. People need meat for shashlyk, for weddings... It's good meat, from the countryside. And there are long lines for quality when there's a surfeit of surrogates.

But today, after the bombing, there's nothing, nobody—an empty shop. And Lenochka, the gloomy salesgirl.

"Aw, come on... I wanted ribs, or brisket, for borscht...! Aw, what is this!" I wailed, lowering my eyes, so my tears wouldn't spray everywhere like a clown's, but would instead stream down my cheeks in a cultured fashion. I lowered my eyes and... saw some pork ribs, hiding all curled up in the farthest corner of the shop. They were the only ones left.

"That worked out real nice!" said Lenochka. "We tried to give them away, so they wouldn't go bad and be wasted... But the customer before you didn't want them—his wife told him not to get two... And now here you are, getting them for borscht..."

I walked out of Rizhky i nizhky clutching the package of ribs tight to my chest. Like a bouquet of flowers. My joy made me rude. I got all pushy. Smiling beseechingly at the clouds, I whispered, "So, as long as we're doing the pork ribs, maybe throw in a little sorrel, too, huh?"

Nobody would believe this later. And I myself even went on to think it'd never happened. Afterwards. But in that moment, I know I heard HIM sigh.

And there was sorrel in the fruit and vegetable store. Fresh sorrel. Gorgeous.

Then, once I was home, I saw that one of the very moodiest of my potted plants, one of my most—no, not capricious, just really apprehensive—sad... (This happens to everyone, I know: the little guys eat well, and put out leaves, and the root is healthy, but they don't smile. They miss their homeland, their freedom; maybe they miss their mom or their friends from the greenhouse...)

Anyway, the thing is that this little one put out a flower bud: delicate, long, white, and fragile... The first bud it ever put out in five years of living in my window.

None of my little potted friends give me blooms for no reason. Some of them let me know there'll be children soon. Others, like my orchid, only bloom in a year when I write something worthwhile (and get an award for it). Then there are the "moneybags," whose flowers signal money. And there are also just good friends, who put out buds whenever I start feeling like everything's just going not all that great.

This particular one had kept silent. It had lived until now in total silence.

The flower, white with a little pink, is still waiting for me inside the bud. I don't know what it'll look like. Maybe it won't even be pink, but orange, or yellow, or blue... I don't know yet.

But I'm smiling.

Everything's going to be okay.

Everything's going to *be*...

Someday, when people I don't know, or people far away, ask me how, on one of the very worst days, I knew everything was going to be okay, I'll tell them about this flower. Those who've been there will understand; the clear-eyed realists will think it's nonsense, but elegant, respectable nonsense that's worth indulging. Everyone can agree with a flower as a sign.

But we... But I... Me and my terrified woman's brain...

Little pork ribs. Borscht.

JUNE 27, 2014

Ukrainian president Petro Poroshenko signs the economic provisions of the EU-Ukraine Association Agreement.

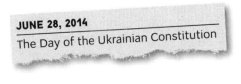

JUNE 28, 2014
The Day of the Ukrainian Constitution

* * *

VENYA, KATYA, AND MARINA

SATURDAY
JUNE 28, 2014
DONETSK AND
MAR'ÏNKA

Veniamin—Venya—always had more women than he had sense. It was because he wasn't raised right. His mom steered him toward a good girl from a Jewish family, while his dad told him that a woman ascends to God through her husband, so don't get Mom all worked up, it's pointless anyway.

His dad's teaching laid the foundation of Venya's great capacity for love. In this foundation, Venya saw himself as a stepstool or folding ladder: everyone who stood on him would be able to reach the heights.

But women didn't stand on him. They grabbed him and hung on for dear life. The outrageous shenanigans didn't stop even after Venya married Katya.

"Believe me," Venya would tell his wife, "they don't want sex. They want light. We're just friends now..."

Maybe Katya believed it and maybe she didn't. But she didn't argue with it, since she loved Venya and was fully intent on living with him to the day she died. Katya had no intention of arguing with death. But she thought up punishments for all of Venya's other women: they wouldn't be able to get shoes in their size, or their plastic surgery would be botched, or they'd get married far away and never come home again. Also, a hiccup that wouldn't stop, or infertility (but only if they stayed in touch with Venya), or permanently being on a thousand-calorie-a-day diet.

Katya didn't have the time or the bloodthirstiness for any more than that. She even started to like the ones who got married.

Marina was one of the ones who married happily, maybe even permanently. Because she had two kids, a mother-in-law who was good as gold, and her own car, a Škoda.

Marina called Katya. Although she usually called Venya.

Marina called Katya and asked, "Can I come over now? I need to talk to you..."

It was eight at night.

Cold pickle soup. Kvas. Sour cream. Cherries, black as coal. And two cottage cheese pancakes, one of which Venya had managed to take a bite out of.

Katya loved feeding people. Venya's dad used to say, "Feed your guest and treat him well, so he'll be there when you need help." But Katya disagreed: "No, it's just that when one person's busy serving food, and the other person's busy chewing food, it's harder to say something stupid."

As she set the table, Katya hoped she'd be able to bury Marina's weighty truth under savory, and sweet, and soup, and dessert, and that a sated Marina wouldn't cause Katya pain.

Right.

Except that Marina didn't even sit down at the table. She went to the sink and turned on the water and let the water run over her palm. Without turning her head to Katya, she said, "I took the children to Ukraine. To Mar'inka..."

"You did the right thing," said Katya.

Ukraine started twenty-four miles and two checkpoints from Donetsk. Our army was next to Mar'inka.

Next to Donetsk were the Chechen volunteers. And non-Chechen volunteers, too.

"I was raped. DPR soldiers. Five of them. Don't tell Venya. I'm not telling my husband, either. Our men can't protect us." Marina crouched on her heels and pressed her forehead into the door of the cabinet under the sink where the trash can was. "And, if they want, they'll kill them anyway."

"Venya, don't come in, we're naked!" yelled Katya.

"As though I've never seen you naked before," Venya retorted playfully.

Marina threw up.

"Let's go get washed up," said Katya. Marina didn't move.

"Carrying the wounded is easy. What's hard is believing you might need to know how to do it," Katya's civil defense instructor used to say.

He was right. But they'd all managed to live very good lives between "easy" and "hard."

Katya carried Marina to the bathroom. She brought antiseptic, a needle filled with antibiotics, and some Postinor emergency contraceptive pills. She didn't have any other sure-fire morning-after meds on hand.

"Can you give me something to wear?" asked Marina as she took off her clothes.

"Want to burn this?" offered Katya. "Douse it with gas and fire it up, huh?"

Katya scrubbed Marina in the shower, then gave her the shot, then scrubbed her again. Marina threw up after taking the Postinor. Katya suggested washing the second Postinor pill down with a bite of cottage cheese pancake and a glass of compote. And then to hold her hands tightly over her mouth until she gagged.

"Then we'll know it's staying down. And then we can have our little campfire..." Katya wanted to stroke Marina's hair, but didn't dare.

They folded the clothes and put them in an aluminum basin. Katya did the folding. And Katya did the dousing. Then a couple of matches. The flame was weak, but smelly. The bra gave out black, acrid smoke and the panties turned into a glob of plastic, but the skirt didn't burn, just smoldered in a few places.

"Girls, I don't get it, are we burning because a shell hit us? Or are you driving out demons in there?" shouted Venya, rattling the door handle.

"Put it out," asked Marina. "We'll throw away whatever's left. But do it now. I need to live twenty more years. At first, I gave myself fifteen, but then I realized that my Vanya is so coddled he won't make it on his own at seventeen... So, twenty. And I've already made it through two hours of that. No sweat..."

Venya took the trash out.

Marina asked for vodka. Katya didn't give her any. "No, the pills... You said yourself, you'll still be needing your liver... Let's have a little sedative now and Seryozha will come get you..."

"Seryozha's in Dnipro until the day after tomorrow."

"And a good thing, too," said Katya.

Katya stayed by Marina and sang, without parting her lips, until Marina fell asleep: "Go to sleep, nighty-night, wrap yourself up good and tight, stay in the middle of the bed, my dear, or a little brown bear will bite your ear..."

Venya was sitting at the computer. He sighed. He was smart, and beloved, that darn Venya. And his women were all good, all capable. The cream of the crop. They were all worth avenging. And Katya knew he very well might do it—go to a Duh-P-R checkpoint with a mop, since he had no other weapons. And threaten them with it. And die holding it.

But Katya wanted him to die not with a mop, but with her. And not anytime soon. With her and no one else.

Venya tore himself away from the Internet, smiled, and said, "Hey, listen to this interesting question they're asking: what do you feel when you see a Saint George's ribbon? What about you, what do you feel?"

"Disgust," answered Katya.

* * *

Remember, you were telling me about your Grandpa Pavel? The port electrician in Saint Petersburg? And I was laughing at your inherited dream of running your own bakery?

I wondered, where do these things come from? Because for me, too, out of all the other kinds of businesses I could run, I only want bread and rolls...

It's the genes.

Your mom, Grandma Katya, was baptized in Vladimir Cathedral. Straight out of Dostoyevsky, right? So they must have lived somewhere around there... Not nobility, but not the lumpenproletariat, either... I asked, I remember, but you don't know exactly where.

It's clear that it was somewhere close by, anyway. Why drag a little baby girl, born in winter, across the entire city? Who'd do such a thing? They did their baptizing where they did their confessing. Where they lived and where they expected to die.

But in '17 he took his family and left for Donbas.

You can imagine what that must've been like, and compare it: from the capital to a world without electricity or plumbing.

So, it turns out that your grandpa, my great-grandpa, a worker saving up to open his own bakery, ran away. From whom? From other people of his class? From—and please excuse the Marxism—the proletariat who'd slipped their chains?

Today our "republicans" issued an order forbidding anyone to take ice cream, beer, or the little, ring-shaped crackers we call *sushki* out of the city. They should've kept people from taking out sunflower seeds, too. Kyiv will definitely die without our sunflower seeds.

These people are morons. They didn't know how to study and had no intention of ever doing it. They had no plans to work, either. So, they robbed others. In '17, they robbed people. And now, again.

In the name of the revolution, of course—how else...

And now I'm thinking how well he saw the future, our Pavel. How bitterly and how clearly.

The beautiful city on the Neva lost. The dismal, undeveloped steppe won.

But, in the steppe, you have your free will. If you know what free will even is.

It took our steppe almost a hundred years to fatten up and give birth to abject poverty. For the luxury of some to mock the penury of others. For us to go blind from the desecration of everyone and everything. For the zealous victory of "beer, sushki, and sunflower seeds."

What else did you tell me about great-grandpa?

He didn't go out to repair the mine when the Nazis came. They caned him, an old man even then, twenty-five times. To punish his obstinacy. Both painful and degrading.

Then the reds came, but again he didn't go out to repair the mine.

A suspicious character. But a strong personality, and a strong will.

Blood isn't water. That's why I can't accept idiots in power. I can't stand violence either.

A bakery's no good in the world that our and your fascists are building on my land. We can't use bread or rolls. Too soft...

Hard, dried bread is needed here... Sure, and sushki, too...

* * *

And now the orcs have banned fireworks. The revolutionary messieurs are so kind as to tremble in fear. They think the fighting has come for them.

Although the word "thinking" doesn't apply in their case.

They sense it. They sense the threat.

So now, Lord, it's time for us to place our bets. What will they ban with their next decree? Thunder (Yours)? Or taking my (our) carpets outside and beating the dust out of them?

* * *

YET ANOTHER CEASE-FIRE

Today the cease-fire—during which "our unarmed guys in tanks" seized checkpoints, killed civilians and soldiers, raped women, sold hostages, and gave instructions on how to rob ATMs—will be extended. We found out about this from someone other than the president. The president won't decide for another ten hours.

But Rahshah-TV already announced it.

Over this past week, it has become clear that Rahshah-TV controls us.

I called my sister and said, "We need a Plan B. When and where we're going."

"What happened?" she asked. Seriously, 'What happened'? Don't we live in the same city, read the same news, and wait for one and the same thing…

"He's going to announce a cease-fire again…"

"You know," she said, "peace can only come after war. If we don't fight a war, there will be no more Ukraine to fight for …"

"Hence Plan B."

"Right. Not to Kyiv."

"Not to Kyiv," I agreed.

Someone who surrenders Donbas that easily will surrender Kyiv, too. We want to live in Ukraine. In a place where nobody surrenders.

"Lviv, right?"

"Right."

"We can open a cleaning service. We'll do the work ourselves. And the girls."

"And I can still write... I'll try getting something at the university, but that won't stop us from mopping floors..."

"Nothing will stop us. But what about the parents?"

That hurts. That will always hurt. They've gotten little, our parents: helpless, dependent. They've gotten weak. And we'd like to rock them sweetly to sleep, spoil them, coddle them, and comfort them... We'd like to give them an old age where every breath they take is a reflection of our own tranquil, protected, and very spoiled childhood. They definitely won't be working in any cleaning service. Going hungry, living out of their suitcases, looking for apartments, begging and scrounging... No to all of it.

We don't say this in so many words, but we both know that, in the panic of moving, in a situation where we're leaving everyone and everything, they'll be a liability. Our little store of energy, already depleted by waiting for freedom, could run out. True, it would run out in a good place for a good cause: in our parents' hands, in their knees, in their cheeks and eyes... But it could actually run out. And we still have to raise our kids, see them out into the world.

We can't abandon our parents. But dragging them into an unknown, one I see for some reason as a draft, a gust of wind blowing badly-hung doors that flail back and forth... No, we can't do that either.

"Two months in Rahshah?" my sister says.

"Two or three. Then we'll go get them," I agree.

"My share of the parents will go to Taganrog."

"Mine and ours will probably go to Petersburg."

We sigh. We love them to the moon and back. But we can't make them take this leap into another life. We can't do that to them. Change must bring them nothing but joy. They've lived through so much dirt, tears, and disappointment already...

"When?" I ask.

"When we lose our jobs. The money will come in handy, so we've got to keep plugging away as long as we can."

"Misha should go to school... On the other hand, he can go later... He'll catch up. Maybe there'll still be school by the time we lose our jobs..."

"We have to try to sell our apartments... Even for half of what they're worth..."

"Yes."

Apartments. Books. The green teakettle. The trunk I figured out how to paint and then distress. The table with delicately curved legs, slender as a ballerina's. The throw, the thick knitted colorful throw on the bed... It's huge, six feet by six feet... We bought it at a flea market in Milan... The giant monstera I raised from two leaves... The embroidered pillows... I won't have any of it anymore. The things we're taking with us are divided into just two categories: heavy and light. For winter and for summer. Clothes and ID. And the indigo teacup. Nothing more.

"We will win," says my sister. "You and me. We, personally, will win. Some people begin living their best lives at fifty. Italians in America, for example."

I can't answer. I want to cry but I can't. For four months now, the "tears" option has been blocked by the men in camo. They can take my life from me, but they won't get my tears.

Tears are a luxury. Tears are for later. For "after-we-win."

"You know what? It feels better now we have a plan B, right?" my sister says.

My sister. Natasha. She and I have a really hard time explaining the complex interplay of our kinship, which we didn't create, to outsiders. It's even harder to explain what we feel toward each other. The ones who don't understand, who purse their lips, scoff, and try to pin us down on "actual blood relatives" will be outsiders permanently.

I was five when her dad married my mom. You remember...

She was eight. According to all the laws of the genre, she was supposed to have hated me: the man she loved had become mine. She was supposed to take revenge on me for it. And me... I was probably supposed to feel constant guilt and try to get her to forgive me...

Not that long ago, this is what she said to me, my sister Natasha: "You were so funny. So kind and touching... From the moment we met, I knew it'd be impossible not to love you..."

And I... From the moment we met, I knew that this little girl was my sister.

* * *

Update. Up, up, up...

We can go to Kyiv. The country's still there. Plan B is still in force, but we can go to Kyiv.

Yesterday, I thought about this: if she, my little girl, my Ukraine, ceases to be—what will change for me personally?

Nothing.

If she dies under the new Russian boot, if she dies from the old Hetman betrayal, if she's smothered by the manicured hands of her West-European mourners, nothing will change for me. I won't stop loving her. And I'll be grateful to her for all the days and nights I had her with me. For her smiles, her caprices, for the stumbles, the scrapes and scratches, the words. For the smell—that newborn-baby smell of the crown of her head, that wormwoody, just barely bitter smell of the palms of her hands...

She will be with me forever. My baby motherland... My little child who didn't make it to adulthood...

* * *

THE POLICE ARE WITH THE PEOPLE

TUESDAY

JULY 1, 2014

DONETSK

The police were with the separatists from the very beginning. Not all the police, sure; but, on average, they were. The cops directed the seizures of the first buildings in March, and again later in April. They created corridors, opened gates, and obligingly opened weapon vaults and other peoples' safes.

Then, later, the police became fast friends with the terrorists who were already good and well-armed. In June, they all walked the city together, keeping watch.

The highway patrolmen were also doing quite nicely. They would set up their "bush traps" near seized buildings or checkpoints and wait for their "prey" with the radar guns at the ready. If there was any trouble, "peaceful protesters" would come help fleece the chumps.

The mutual love of these groups was explained in various ways at various times. In March, for example, the higher ranks were expecting Russo-pensions; the lower ranks, Russo-paychecks. They dreamed big and worked in service to their dream. They told themselves, "In Russia, cops run everything. Everything!"

In April, they also dreamed: they organized referendums, stood duty in police stations, and printed ballots on their home printers. Joy! Pure joy...

But once May rolled around, when the bearded volunteers—Chechens—started outnumbering the local idiots, our cops were just plain scared.

The police had no weapons. The weapons were gone early. Some were taken away "so the enemy doesn't get them." But a large portion of them had already been gone before that: business deals. The cops were sad. "The first month, we sold our firearms to the *opolchentsy*. The second month, we sold our bulletproof vests to patriots and peaceful citizens. The third month, when peaceful citizens no longer wanted to be peaceful and were paying super-unbelievable prices for 'hardware,' there was nothing to sell them anymore. All that was left were riot batons." The mournful cops sighed, "Darn it, we sold too low."

So, anyway, there were no guns. But there was fear. And with each new tank, BRDM scout vehicle, or APC, with each new "Donetskite" from Ossetia, "Horlivkian" from Samara, or Chechen from Kadyrov, with each ripped-out heart or eviscerated corpse, the fear increased.

The police were "with the people" so firmly that, at first, they turned into that very "people," but then later, in June, they turned into pure, grade-A punching bags.

The locals kept their eyes peeled for this sign in spring and summer 2014: if you can see cops and highway patrolmen in the city, it means the "peaceful protesters" aren't planning on shooting today. No shooting, no explosions, no kidnappings. Robbery, sure, but when have the police ever been a problem for robbers?

The opposite was true as well: if there are no people with insignia out, expect trouble... Explosions, exchanges of fire, more mines, new checkpoints... All that and more...

Afterwards, of course, they'd come tiptoeing back out again. Doves of peace. No big deal.

By summer, there were a lot of "Saviors of Donbas." Ten out of ten of them aspired to legal status and an imposing name. We were being "saved from the junta" by entire armies. There was the Russian Orthodox Army, for example, or the Army of the South-East. There were also the militants of Oplot and the Vostok Battalion. The Donbas People's Militia. The "DPR" Army...

At the end of June, twenty or thirty locals and out-of-towners gave birth to the Kalmius Battalion, which famously seized a military base. Some other volunteers proclaimed themselves to be the Eighth Company, named according to the same principle as Chanel No 5, to wit: it was the eighth even though there had been none before it...

Once the border had been more or less closed and the flow of weapons from the Russian Federation slowed, there was a shortage of AK automatic rifles and similar pleasant attributes of the lovely, easy life of the liberator.

The armies and battalions started filching things from each other. Just on the level of personal contacts made and ideological differences discovered after the first shared bottle of vodka. After these folks parted ways, some had acquired more AK automatic guns, while others, sadly, had lost theirs. It was insulting. The insulted parties complained, as was their habit, to the police. Criminal cases were even opened.

No, not on the basis of illegal possession of firearms. On the basis of theft...

The police tried as hard as they could to be with the people.

And what did they get? Pitch-black ingratitude. It happened on the first day of July. The first day of the continuation of the anti-terrorist operation.

The oblast police HQ was attacked.

And the attackers didn't shoot the way they used to, in a friendly way, by prearrangement. They shot for real. At cars, people, windows... One police officer was killed, a couple dozen others wounded.

That wasn't the main thing, though. The main thing was the blatant bad sportsmanship of the "peaceful protesters," who in four months of close cooperation had been given everything: the weapons, the offices, and all the rest of it. Except for their honor. Not the honor of their uniforms. No sir.

The distressing news spread all over Facebook and social media. By then, those were the only news media in the city. The newspapers had been closed a long time ago by decree of the Kingdom of the Apes, and the average age of the mail carriers—predominantly grandmas—prevented them from playing at underground messenger. There was our paper, but, of course, nobody bought it...

The vivacious LieNews anchors informed the old ladies that the Right Sector had taken over the police HQ.

Some people were so sick of the "Rescuers of Donbas" that they wanted to welcome the Right Sector with bread and salt. But this turned out to be impossible. The terrorists had blocked off Fire Station Square and were shooting at passing cars, and even, for some reason, at the number one tram.

This all happened in broad daylight. During the day. It started around two and lasted for about three hours. Maybe a little longer. The press service of the Ministry of Interior Affairs proudly announced that the police HQ was under attack. According to them, the police had barricaded themselves in and were resisting the attack. There was no assistance coming, but their fighting spirit was high.

And just as a reminder, the Ministry is in Kyiv. All of us have seen that resistance, that fighting spirit. We're not blind. We've gotten used to it, even...

To make a long story short: four hours later, we got the real story. The one who'd attacked the police HQ was Bes.

Bes (the Demon) was a comrade from Horlivka. Bes is his pseudonym. His real name's Igor Bezler. He's got a long, difficult medical history. He used to be a GRU officer. Then he was a coffin maker. In the course of those duties, he managed to get into various kerfuffles with all the local authorities. He held such a grudge that he started a countdown not only for those authorities, but for all the businesses in Horlivka, which had previously been uninterested either in dying or in buying a plot in his cemetery.

In just a couple of months, the countdown reached zero and Bes buried everyone in power. People said he even buried his boss, another "defender of Donbas" against the junta, a man with a nickname very dear to the Russian ear: Abwehr.

Then he let himself truly express all the breadth and depth of his *l'esprit militaire*: his brigade stole explosives from mines and laid them along railroad tracks. No, he wasn't a maniac. It was his new way of extracting tribute from freight forwarders.

It might seem strange, but the cities were at work. They unloaded the cargo. But the railroad tracks were still blown up at least twice a day. Some stubborn individual definitely did not want to pay.

Once Horlivka's supply of goods ran out, Bes realized Donetsk was better. So he went to seize it.

Since all the good buildings—like the public prosecutor's, the Ukrainian Security Service, the law school, and the military bases—had already been taken by other "peaceful rescuers," Bes decided to move into the oblast police HQ.

All the mortars, machine guns, and automatic rifles were right there. And it was dark. Although everything happened in broad daylight.

It was dark because Vostok, Oplot, the Eighth Company, and some others all came to help the police who, according to the minister, were putting up a strong defense, but, according to eyewitnesses, were obediently abandoning their posts.

The ensuing battle was no joke. It was a matter of principle. All these different "units" hadn't been created just to sit back and give fat Donetsk up to be milked by a deeply provincial interloper like Bes.

The Duh-P-R's press office announced that Vostok was bravely fighting against the terrorists. This gave Lie-News fits of cognitive dissonance.

Closer on toward evening, the minister in Kyiv announced that the attack on the police HQ had been repelled.

And now we were the ones having fits of cognitive dissonance. We couldn't wrap our heads around it. We couldn't get it through our thick skulls...

If the attack was repelled by Vostok, and if the minister is the one telling us this, then... This means that... Vostok is now a unit taking part in the Ukrainian anti-terrorist operation?

But, on the other hand, what difference does it make... It makes no difference...

"Granny Halya! Where are you going?! There's a lot of shooting. Go home!"

"But I need to get my shoes fixed. They're worn out..."

"I'm telling you to stay home. There's shooting!"

"That's on the next street over. By the time it gets here to us, little ol' Rustam's gonna get me some new shoe plates on. They'll be shooting every day, but I'm supposed to walk around in worn-down shoes?"

* * *

New billboards appeared that morning in Donetsk. "Armored cars. For you and your family."

I called them on the phone and asked, "What's your guarantee?"

"Free passage through checkpoints. Because they act like they're going to shoot, those Duh-P-R sons-of-bitches..."

* * *

Also that morning. A few things became clear.

The Duh-P-R issued a press release. It stated that "Igor Bezler, aka Bes, and his unit took over the police oblast HQ building. At the present time, an anti-terrorist operation is underway and in the event of resistance from the terrorists, they will be destroyed."

To be clear: this is a matryoshka doll.

Ukraine is carrying out an anti-terrorist operation against the Duh-P-R, the Duh-P-R carrying out its own operation against Bes, while Bes is carrying out his own operation against the police, and the police are carrying out their own operation against us.

So which one of them is that swell guy Robin Hood?

* * *

When the minister of interior affairs is an active Facebook user, the Security Service had better keep up. If not on the actual Internet, then at least in terms of the style.

They've got the style. And they're not afraid to use it.

This is considered good news: "On July 1, the Ukrainian Security Service detained Vladimir Kolosniuk, one of the fighters' leaders and the self-proclaimed 'mayor' of Horlivka, and remanded him to Kyiv as part of the active phase of the anti-terrorist operation. Kolosniuk, who reported directly to the terrorist Bezler ('Bes'), was responsible for supplying weapons. He also organized and took part in kidnappings and torture as well as armed attacks on the checkpoints of anti-terrorist operation forces."

Kolosniuk was apprehended by Ukrainian Security Service agents in a café in Berdyansk, Zaporizhzhia Oblast, in the act of purchasing two million hryvnias' worth of large-caliber machine guns, grenade launchers, automatic rifles, and explosives. The terrorist attempted to resist law enforcement during the arrest.

In a café. Buying grenade launchers.

After this, we'll say Putin's lying. But he's not lying. He's mistaken.

You can't buy guns in every store here. There's nothing like that in any of our stores. But in our cafes, now—in our cafes you can buy whatever you want.

* * *

Olya's mother-in-law used to tell this story: "In '73, we bought a set of living room furniture that goes from one wall to the other. Yugoslavian, with a high-gloss finish. The glass doors were so pretty, like windows in a medieval castle. It had these metal lattices like twining boughs... We bought it, installed it ourselves... Of course we were happy, what did you expect! We were so happy we couldn't keep our hands off each other. We got to sleep late... The next morning, I hear his tender whisper, 'My beauty, my beauty...' I don't open my eyes, but I smile, and snuggle up to him, and put my arms around him... But he's got his back to me, the jerk. He's gazing at that Yugoslavian wall unit, all cuddled up to it... So, of course we started calling it 'the beauty.' And now little Kolya's the same way... Learned it from his father..."

Kolya is Olya's husband.

He's a fashion designer now. It's a funny profession, especially if you live in a mining town, not in Paris. But Kolya's got a very narrow specialty: dress shirts. He made his first one out of curiosity and hate.

All collars were criminal. Every shirt went bad in its own way. One collar choked him, another chafed his neck, a third wouldn't even button, a fourth would button but it somehow ended up looking "hostile to the working class." Kolya did not accept that it's impossible to make a regular old collar. So he sewed one.

And crapped his pants from joy. In his new perfected design, the collar didn't pinch, pull, chafe, or make him look like a professional hangman.

In short, he took off. Shirts, trousers, suits...

He even got a little bit rich. He got a slightly used Lexus. He wanted to name it Olya, but she popped him in the face with a rag. He settled on Lyalya.

Olya would've preferred a different sort of name. A man's name. But Kolya demurred, citing the classic Soviet-era comedy *Letuchaya mysh* (*The Bat*): "When Schultz named his dog Hector, it died. It died as Hector, but, deep inside, it was Alma..."

"You're weird," acquiesced Olya. "Can you really want to name your car Hector, though? That could kill it..."

"Wait, what film are you talking about now?"

"Well, let's just say I'm talking about *Troy*."

"Whereas I, let's just say, was talking about *Letuchaya mysh*..."

So, basically... Lyalya, Lyalechka.

Once the "rescuers" arrived, Kolya's trousers and shirts, along with his stores and a couple of workshops, all closed for vacation until better days. He refused to make "camo," let alone tailor it. Although there were willing clients... Especially among his old friends...

Kolya got good and truly fed up. First, with the evil clowns calling themselves "ministers," then with the

Ukrainian government's generals. Maybe even more with the generals. Because it was obvious just looking at the soldiers that the generals' habitual thievery was the same as a chronic disease: death's the only permanent cure. Kolya and some of his cutters and distributors formed a group to procure food, medicine, and soap, and then army boots, body armor, and combat helmets that went right to the front... The army wasn't far from the city. Kolya drove all over Ukraine, passing through local and foreign checkpoints. But everything he got he put directly into people's hands. He traveled with a measuring tape. In a special notebook he wrote down the measurements of the fighters standing guard on the highway to Zaporizhzhia. The figures looked like a code. Or like phone numbers.

Kolya, who was no dummy, drove a rented Daewoo Lanos on business during the day. But, in the evening, although he was still no dummy, he did for some reason drive his Lyalechka around town.

His Lyalechka was nabbed near the Covered Market, on a Saturday at the beginning of June. A hefty boy holding a heavy portable grenade launcher told Kolya, "Your property is being requisitioned for the good of the revolution!" The rest of the boys had AK automatic rifles. They just nodded. Kolya said, "Any way the revolution would be okay with a Lanos?"

Then the frailest member of that chorus of proletarian rage popped Kolya in the face with his rifle stock. It hurt.

After that, Olya and Kolya lived how they lived. Kolya continued supplying the army, driving around between the fields and the warehouses. He wouldn't get back until after midnight. And in the mornings, he'd tenderly whisper "Dearest Lyalechka..." then abruptly wake up.

He developed yet another quirk. Like a mother whose child has gone missing, Kolya peered frantically, yet piercingly, into the "faces" of other people's cars. Not only black Lexuses, but also grey ones, and midnight-blue ones... Once Olya even caught him stopping short in a car park when he glimpsed some completely different make of car. Kolya sighed and suffered from grief and longing. He wasn't losing hope, but he had completely lost any sense of self-preservation. He posted receipts and photos of items procured for the army on Facebook. First and last names... Photographs... There were no addresses, granted. But Kolya was betrayed. And then he was picked up.

They didn't get him by his address. They got him by his car. While he was driving on business. They found vodka and cigarettes in the trunk. Nothing military. Thank goodness.

Four days later, Olya found the people who were holding him. They wanted twenty thousand dollars for him. They settled for five. The "Orthodox Army" liked dollars. And haggling.

Kolya had broken ribs and burns on his arms. A whole lot of little circles. Cigarette burns. And his eyes were completely dead.

"We can't deal with them... We can't... They're just murderers... That's all they are... And we can't deal with them..."

He lay in bed at home, staring at the ceiling. Didn't eat, didn't drink, didn't talk. He had a movie playing constantly in his head. A horror movie. Olya understood this. She kept saying, "Let's leave while we still can. Here, eat. Drink this." And always, "Let's leave."

But Kolya wouldn't speak.

One day she suggested, "What if you just go for a walk? Half a mile. And then one mile. And then one and a half. Just go for a walk. Hm?"

Then, after a week of the ceiling, she exploded. "Go for a walk! I said go for a walk!"

So Kolya started going for walks. Olya watched from the window to make sure that he didn't sit down on a bench, that he didn't stumble over his own feet, that he didn't forget to breathe...

Half a mile. One mile. Just around the building at first. But within a week he was already walking around the city. Kolya walked all the way to Donetsk City, then to Dytia-chyi svit toy store, and then to Bilyi lebid mall. He took sel-fies and sent them to Olya for her approval. She approved.

But, one day, her cell phone rang and it was him, shouting, "Olya! The second set of keys. The suitcase. The documents. The keys are in the second desk drawer. It's my Lyalechka! Bring them as quick as you can!"

He'd found his car by the seized oblast state ad-ministration building. It was unhurt. Dirty, and sad, but unhurt.

So they stole it back. Olya and Kolya. They snatched it right out from under the Duh-P-R's nose. Their own lit-tle beauty, their little girl. Their Lyalechka.

And they skedaddled to Dnipro. Olya was a tiny bit offended. He wouldn't take her away to Dnipro, no way, no how... But he'd take his "Lyalechka" in a minute.

"Just like his dad!" her mother-in-law laughed.

* * *

SATURDAY
JULY 5, 2014
DONETSK

I have to be happy. I have to be happy. I have to be happy. Slovyansk was freed today... And Kramatorsk, too, and Druzhkivka, and Kostyantynivka, and Artemivsk.

But I have to be especially happy for Slovyansk. They've gone through so much... So much...

But I can't get my happiness to turn on.

I just can't.

The column was over a mile long. But orderly. With all their equipment, ammunition, and people, Girkin and his maniacs entered Donetsk.

The clown show is over. That's it. No more pretend-ing. No more playing at playing.

Nazism. Sadism. Ruscism.

Nobody welcomed those scum. When they came into the city to "defend us from the junta," nobody threw flowers, nobody shouted "glory to the liberating warriors," none of that. They came into Donetsk the way the Nazis came into Donetsk: accompanied by the stares of gawpers and professional Ukraine-haters. But not even they would risk running up to the soldiers to hand out flowers. Nazis... Those people came into our city like Nazis.

There's a photograph where a column of soldiers is walking along empty streets, a long, drawn-out column, and they're dragging their rifles behind them on the pavement. It's a long, long column, stretching out beyond the horizon. The caption is "Donetsk. July 1942."

Why wasn't that column destroyed while it was still on the move? I don't have an answer for that. Who gave a city with a million residents to be held hostage by a maniac who has killed in Bosnia, in Chechnya, and in Slovyansk? I don't have an answer for that, either.

There is no answer.

JULY 7, 2014

Separatists take over four dormitories at Donetsk National University.

* * *

MONDAY

JULY 7, 2014

D O N E T S K

The question "How was your day today?" is now considered indecent.

We measure things here by the hour now. Sometimes by the minute.

One day... A day's so long, goes by so slow... You might not live long enough to see the end of it.

JULY 11, 2014

Positions of the Ukrainian armed forces and the State Border Service near Zelenopillia in Luhansk Oblast are shelled by Russian regular army units, killing forty-four Ukrainian servicemen.

* * *

FRIDAY

JULY 11, 2014

DONETSK

Hell in Ukrainian is *peklo*. Peklo is heat. The root of the word, which comes from "pek-/pik-" or "pech-/pich-", is basically good: *pich*—oven; *zapikaty*—to bake; *pechyvo*—cookies...

Peklo is a nice word, not a scary one. Peklo is the likelihood of eternally answering for our venal sins, and we regard it with a slightly narrowed, calculating gaze.

But what's happening now is hell. And hell in the Ukrainian dictionary has to be a Russian word. Hell isn't heat.

Hell is evil that freely does whatever it wants. And what it wants is a lot of pain. A lot of pain that does not end.

You probably have to see hell to see God.

And we have seen hell.

There's no tomorrow, no today, no yesterday. There is pain. It seems there's no way for it to hurt worse than this. It seems this is already the absolute limit. But it can hurt worse.

It can hurt much, much worse.

We've been living through the history of evil for five months. The only thing missing is the fires of the Inquisition. We have everything else. The NKVD's execution walls. Kidnappings. Eviscerated corpses. Special elimination lists.

And fear. Fear. Fear.

Evil laughs, flashing its gold teeth. Evil lies. Evil controls space. Evil sets up Grad multiple rocket launchers in residential neighborhoods to shoot at other residential neighborhoods. Evil calls itself good: Satan trying on the Savior's clothes. But the crown of thorns... The pain, wounds, and death... None of that will be his. All of it will go to other people.

Heroes don't die. But evil doesn't care.

It's cold in hell. No heat there. There's emptiness in hell's eyes. And in its mouth, too. It can't talk, but it does all it can to make people hear nothing else, listen to it alone.

Hell. And, at first, we wish for all of them, for every single one of them who came to spill our blood, to spend some time in that hell. To get their fill of it.

But then, later, we don't. We stop wishing it.

Nobody deserves that.

It's probably only in hell that you can truly see that you believe. That you believe and trust in God.

Evil seems strong. So strong that there's not a single logical argument for faith.

But you don't need one for faith.

Only grace. Only a miracle. Only God can save us.

Trust is what begins after hope.

JULY 12, 2014

A fake report about a boy being crucified and his mother executed on the central square in Slovyansk by Ukrainian fighters is aired on the main Russian state channel, Pervyi Kanal (Channel One). The report causes a public outcry. It is shown to be entirely staged as a means of informational warfare against Ukraine, particularly on the territory of the Donbas where Russian TV is watched by local residents.

JULY 14, 2014

A Ukrainian military transport aircraft AN-26 is shot down by Russian regular units in the Luhansk Oblast, about 3 miles from the border with Russia, using the Buk missile system. Two crew members are killed.

* * *

TUESDAY

JULY 15, 2014

D O N E T S K

Do you know what burnout is?

Dad says there's no way you don't know. He's always defending you.

"He has a really hard job, honey. Psychiatry is a terrible profession. You have to love your patients, take pity on them. And all his patients, or almost all of them, are murderers. What's he supposed to do with that? He doesn't have enough heart for all that. Remember the patient who brought him the head of another patient from his ward? As a present, a friendly token? Nobody could have enough heart for that. It's impossible not to burn out... Who can love murderers? How is that possible? But the place where love is, there's just that one place for all of it, honey. Your kids, and life, and food, and women... Just one compartment, you understand?"

"No!"

I don't understand. Every day "peaceful protesters" bring somebody's head, take somebody's life. Every day. My profession is not psychiatry. It wasn't me who arranged these Russian maniacs' summer tour of Ukrainian cities. I can't love them. I can't understand them, either.

But yes. Yes, Dad: just one compartment.

You're right about that.

I'm burning out.

Twenty people died in Moscow due to an accident in the metro.

There was a similar event in Moscow a few years ago. I don't remember whether it was a terrorist attack or just a disaster. But right away I called all my Russian, or rather my Muscovite, friends and colleagues.

And I sighed happily: it didn't happen to them. Thank God, it didn't happen to them.

Do you know what I ask about now, after this recent accident?

"Does Rahshah-TV have enough food now? Even just three days of food? Enough for it to talk about itself, and not about us? Will those twenty deaths be enough for it to grieve, instead of barking and lying? Is that enough?"

My husband shakes his head. "Don't hold your breath."

* * *

TO BE A MAN

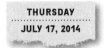
THURSDAY
JULY 17, 2014

Donetsk is at work. Bread, milk, sausage, jam, metals, fertilizer, chemicals for domestic and industrial use, ice cream, candy. And lots of other stuff, too. The factories and plants have been robbed and looted five times each, but they haven't stopped working. People have to live, have to make money to eat.

That's what Dad says. Misha listens. He doesn't know yet what he'd do if he had a family, on the one hand, and a despicable war like this, on the other. He's both distressed and happy that he doesn't have to know yet. Ten years old is not an age for making decisions. That's also from Dad. It's easy to quote Dad because Dad knows the answers to all the questions.

This knowledge is why Dad shouts and gets upset a lot. The surface of Dad's mind bubbles, like boiling water, and spits out painful epithets. Misha doesn't take it personally.

You don't argue with Dad, and you don't whimper, or else he'll land you one upside the head for not acting like a man.

Dad's worse in the morning than in the evening. But right before bed, when all his strength has left him, he gets worried and fearful himself. He gets like Misha. And, at night, you can call him to chase away the monsters that cast shadows, that whisper and gnash their teeth, that come for you when you're asleep. All boogeymen disappear as soon as Dad comes into the room...

"Factory's gotta work," Uncle Valera is saying. "Why should we stop because of a bunch of scum? How'll we fill client warehouses then? I signed up for a month, so far. On contract. Yes, with the army, 'cause if we sit it out, in two months 'Rahshah' will be in Kyiv. If we have to smash it with sheer volume, well, I'll be the volume."

"I signed up, too," says Dad.

"Nope. Just one of us can. One for the factory, the other for the war. Three hundred people. You understand. They'll all be left without money."

"I agree. But I don't agree," fumes Dad. "Why you? Your Anya's pregnant. She's due any day now. Don't you have a conscience?"

"Sure do!" beams Uncle Valera. "A whole bucketful. Yesterday, I come home and the apartment's been sealed with this shitty little piece of paper, and somebody's scribbled—get this—somebody's scribbled "Enemy of the DPR" on it. Those sons-of-bitches carted off everything but the kitchen sink. My rifle, my vest, our money—everything. Except the pistol. Get this: it was right there on the desk. With pictures from last year's vacation on top of it, like it was a picture stand. They didn't find it! So, yeah, I've got a bucketful of conscience now. For them."

"Where's the pistol?"

"In your desk drawer. And two grenades. They have a twenty-six-foot kill zone."

"Don't teach your father," bristles Dad. "I was trained to throw grenades back in 1989. But I still don't see the logic. Why you?"

"Ah, screw it; screw the logic," agrees Uncle Valera. "Let's flip for it. I call heads. Misha! Mishuk! You got a coin? Your dad's gonna take tails."

"I never said I would, but fine. Go ahead, Misha. We'll flip to see who goes first. And screw you."

They're in the car on the way to the train station. Misha flips a coin. And drops it, of course. It lands somewhere on the seat. He tries to find it, scooting this way and that. The coin rolls off the seat and now he has to look for it in the footwell.

"Let's take a break," suggests Uncle Valera. "Pull over. Might as well have a smoke, too."

Dad burns Misha to ash with a look. That gaze is composed of two unrelated sentences. One sentence has no verb, the other has no subject. "Butterfingers!" Dad's look yells at him. Then it adds, "No blubbering."

What Dad says aloud, he says mean, with long pauses between words: "No. Breaks. He. Will. Pick. It. Up. Now. And. Flip. It."

Uncle Valera turns to Misha. He smiles. His gaze also contains a sentence. This one has neither a subject nor a verb. "Deal?" asks Uncle Valera without speaking.

Misha and Uncle Valera waited in the car while Dad got the train tickets. Uncle Valera told Misha that he and Misha's dad were going to flip a coin. And that whatever happened, whatever fell face up, Misha had to call heads.

"I won't lie. I don't even know how. And my parents don't let me," said Misha, shaking his head firmly.

"You will, Mishuk. You have no choice. Look, here's my logic. First of all, I'm younger than your dad. Second of all, the factory'll be worse off without him than without me. Third of all, one of my sons is already grown, and the other one hasn't even been born yet. You see where I'm headed here?"

Misha nodded.

"My oldest had me for eighteen years. And the one that hasn't been born yet—he doesn't even know me. But you're already here. And you know your dad. If anything happens, your loss will be greater. Understand?"

Misha nodded again. The tears came pouring out. He felt sorry for the new little guy who'd never see Uncle Valera. Uncle Valera looked like the hero Ilya Muromets. Misha had gotten a bad grade for his description of Viktor Vasnetsov's painting "Three Bogatyrs." Not so much for the description as for his stubbornness. He'd said that Ilya Muromets had red hair and freckles. The teacher had said, "That's the first time I've heard something that stupid." But Misha had said, "He's got red hair. You just didn't notice."

Uncle Valera coughed. "Hey," he said. "None of that. Let's not have none of that. If a person hasn't had something, then it doesn't hurt to lose it. Like the song from *Ironiya sud'by* (Irony of Fate), right? 'If you don't have a dog, your neighbor won't poison it...'"

"You're not a dog," said Misha.

"Exactly right. I'm not a dog. So there's a chance I'll go up to heaven and take care of my son from up there. Although I actually wasn't planning on dying. I was going to win. And so, either way, it's heads. Deal? It's hard to be a man. But on the other hand, we don't give birth. So we're lucky. Aren't we?"

"Yes," agreed Misha.

"There you go," sighed Uncle Valera.

"Wait, did you just trick me into saying yes?" asked Misha.

"Stranger things have happened. But you gave your word. All you can do now is keep it."

Misha gets down off the car seat and feels around under it. He whispers to himself, "Dear God... I mean, Respected Lord... No, wait, I mean, Our Father. Our Father, I really ask you to help me do the right thing. Follow my logic, please, okay? First of all, I really love Dad. And I don't know how to live without him. Second of all, Uncle Valera tricked me. Third of all, it'll be just as hard for his new little boy as it will be for me, and maybe even worse. How can I get out of it if my word was given by accident? How do I get out of this, dear Lord? No, wait, I mean Our Father? How?"

Tears roll down Misha's cheeks. He sobs and catches hold of the coin.

"I found it. I'm flipping it..."

The coin flies gently upward, hits the upholstered underside of the car roof, and falls quickly. Misha gets his palm under it and immediately closes his hand into a fist. He screws his eyes shut and asks, "Help me, Lord. Now. And later, too, when one of them goes off to war..."

"So, what it is?" Dad asks, irritated.

"Heads," wheezes Misha, swallowing his tears.

JULY 17, 2014

Malaysian Airlines Flight 17, a Boeing 777, is shot down near Torez in the Donetsk Oblast by a Russian Buk missile system, registered with a rocket brigade of the Russian army in Kursk, Russia. All 298 people on board the airplane are killed, most of them citizens of the European Union.

* * *

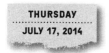
THURSDAY
JULY 17, 2014

The airplane.

* * *

FRIDAY
JULY 18, 2014
D O N E T S K

In all likelihood, they were alive.
     Struck by a missile launched from a Buk—"beech tree"—missile system. At thirty-two thousand feet. No chance of escape. They didn't even have time to embrace each other.

Their birds were in cages.

And their children were in seats. Buckled-up children. Crucified children, you could even say...

Thirty-two thousand feet. They hurtled toward earth alive.... Aware...

No skin, no flesh, bone shattered to smithereens. That is my body falling from the airplane. Those are my children, my parents. Two hundred and eighty-three times.

That is my land hurtling into Russian hell, my land destroyed by a rocket launched from a beech tree.

* * *

The "peaceful protesters" are glad.

Igor Girkin gave an update: "We shot down an *ukrop* bird.[25] It's by a mine in Torez."

LieNews arrived fifteen minutes later. To rejoice.

What a terrific story! A downed Ukrainian plane!

When the plane turned out to be Malaysian...

I thought you'd be horrified. I thought Girkin would shoot himself. I thought the LieNews journalists would take the tonsure.

But no.

We haven't been on speaking terms for a long time now, you and I. And what is there for you to be horrified about? After all, this has nothing to do with you...

Girkin's removing his Facebook post. LieNews is furtively pulling the news from their site.

That's it.

You aren't people.

None of you are people anymore.

By evening, the stories start. The performances.

And boy, is our Donetsk People's Asylum killing it!

Girkin, the "defense minister," reports that the people in the plane were already dead, and that the corpses had vials of blood in their hands.

The "people's governor," Gubarev, doesn't agree. He's sure that they were all alive, all real, but that it was Kolomoyskyi who shot them down. With a rocket from Dnipro. But, as the Yid Banderites had planned all along, it fell to the ground in the "DPR."

You know what? Not a one of you is grieving.

Your TV is spewing out paroxysms of stories. One more fake than the next. But you have no space for grief.

* * *

FRIDAY

JULY 18, 2014

DONETSK

...and another thing about languages. Ever since I was little, hearing German has induced in me the sensation of threat. No matter what a German person was saying, what I heard was "Hände hoch!" and "Schneller, schneller, du Schwein!"[26] That's all. I saw point-blank executions, concentration camps, murdered children, the dangling corpses of hanged partisans. War movies were my only experience with spoken German.

That lasted for a long time. My fear of German grew up along with me. It had no intention of being left behind in my childhood. It's true that, a little later on, pornos with their "Jaaaaa, das ist fantastisch!" did help ease the stress. My fear began to fade. And it disappeared for good once the people turned up. German people. Good ones and bad ones. But still guilty all the way up to this very day.

And here it is again. The same disease.

When I hear that flat "ah" accent, that rapid rat-tat-tat pronunciation so foreign to my ear, that pretentious intonation, that swallowed vowel in the first syllable of a word... When I hear spoken Russian, I imagine point-blank executions, mass murder, torture, lies, and Grad multiple rocket launchers in residential neighborhoods. And that Malaysian airplane.

I see maniacs and murderers in everyone who asks Mom to pour some milk, pronouncing its genitive form as [m-lah-káh], instead of [muh-lah-káh]...[27]

I shudder. And I hate.

★ ★ ★

SATURDAY

JULY 19, 2014

DONETSK

The provocative Russian poet Orlusha writes, "I'm one of the ones who despicably shot down the plane headed for Kuala Lumpur." And again, at the end: "I'm guilty, because I'm Russian."[28]

What about you?

Are you guilty?

What'd they use to cauterize your conscience? Greatness? Or profits from natural gas?

Let's dispense with the euphemisms. Thanks to you, my world now looks like the Planet of the Apes. And there's worse to come. Maybe we haven't descended to the level of, say, Columbian neckties yet. But we're close. We're already pretty close. They call the wives of dead soldiers, did you know that? And make the wives listen while they shoot a whole clip into their husbands' corpses...

My tongue's turned flat, my soul won't forgive, my eyes can't distinguish different tones. But I can still see...

I see Russian contract soldiers on the city streets. I see Russian heavy weapons. I already know the difference between an IFV and a BRDM scout vehicle, and I can tell a Grad and a Nona apart...

What will you do with me if you win? With all of us who have no scales covering our eyes? Who aren't affected by the mind-control radiation from the Strugatsky brothers' Noon Universe?

Will you force us to forget?

How?

Arrest? Exile? Execution?

How will you force me to forget that Russia launched this despicable invasion and started ripping the body of my country to bits, gorging on corpses and washing them down with the fuel of no fewer than six downed airplanes?

Will you gouge out my eyes afterwards, like you did with the architect of Saint Basil's Cathedral? Or rip out my tongue, the way you did to any "thieving brigand" who encroached on the "sovereign empire"?

Maybe you'll pray for my eyes to be opened?

I know what you'll say. "Don't generalize!"

Okay, deal. I won't generalize.

You're good, of course. You're worried about me. And sure, your heart is crying blood.

Do you remember the film *Father of a Soldier*?[29] You should.

An old man, Georgii, becomes a soldier and goes through the whole war just to see his son.

Did you become a soldier?

Did you pick up a cobblestone and head to the Kremlin?

Did you come here to understand, to see everything with your own eyes?

No?

Then say "hey" to your new and improved "passion-inducing chip." The implantation was a success.

Oh yes—and "hey" to North Korea, too.

It won the 2014 World Cup.

What do you mean, "no, it didn't"? The North Koreans are pretty sure it did. They saw it on TV...

* * *

ASSHOLES

THE LAST TEN DAYS OF JULY, 2014

D O N E T S K – S L O V Y A N S K

The photographer's wife was killed on July 21 in Pisky, just west of Donetsk. She'd set up a field hospital there. She was treating people, saving people's lives. Because of their "yes is yes, and no is no"—well, you remember.

The photographer couldn't retrieve the body. He didn't even know if there was a body left to retrieve. He was informed of his wife's death in passing, by accident. At a "DPR" press conference. "Many of ours were lost. A female doctor was killed..." "Was her name Katya?" the photographer asked. "Who?" asked one of the few local ministers, jerking his head. In his past life, the minister had been a Pekinese breeder. "I'm asking if the woman doctor's name was Katya?" the photographer asked again. "Who the heck knows what all those people's names were... Hold on, I'll find out..."

He found out. Katya had come under a burst of heavy fire from the airport. She'd died against Ukraine.

She wanted to be buried in Slovyansk. That's where she was from.

The photographer went to Slovyansk without the body. To find a place. And to arrange the burial service and funeral banquet.

At the cemetery, he quickly found Katya's parents' graves. Their faces gazed sternly from the engraved marble. He sat down by the little fence around their plot, his back to their faces. "I didn't keep her safe." He sighed. "Forgive me."

He didn't know what he should say or how to behave. He sat. He looked up at the sky. He breathed.

Then a voice from up above: "Who're you here for?"

Okay, so it wasn't really from above, it's just that the fellow was standing, while the photographer was sitting. That was the extent of the "height."

"My wife."

"Me too. Drink?"

The photographer nodded. The fellow looked like a bird—a seagull: fair-haired, tow-headed, disheveled, long-limbed, light. He pulled a half-pint bottle and two small, faceted glasses out of his pocket.

"Mine's name was Tanya."

"Mine's was Katya."

"And so we've introduced ourselves. Here's to the heavenly kingdom for them."

They drank in silence. The photographer either hadn't started or had already stopped feeling the pain, he couldn't say which. It was as though he'd been pumped full of a good narcotic, but the medics had slightly injured his throat lining during intubation. It was difficult to speak. The words were like dry toast scraping his throat and sticking somewhere around his Adam's apple.

"Mine was blown to bits. Separatists had a Nona and were shooting at buildings. I jumped out of the way. She ended up in pieces."

The photographer nodded. He croaked, "Mine, too. They say she was blown to pieces..."

"Her left foot was blown clean off. Hold on a sec, I'll show you. I got it on my phone."

The fellow shoved the picture at the photographer. Right in his face. A foot all by itself lying in green grass. The photographer would never, ever have taken a picture of something like that.

"What do you need this for? Delete it..."

"Nope. Can't do that. What if later my life starts to feel not enough, not quite right somehow? Well, the antidote to that's right here. Tanya's foot. You know what's funny? A year ago, she fractured her hip. Her right one. They treated it for a long time. They were barely able to get it to knit. And then her left foot was torn off. Can you imagine?"

The fellow poured again, and they drank again. The photographer croaked, "You're lucky. At least you buried her..."

"True enough," the fellow agreed. "You know how many people here have disappeared without a trace? Those drunks just grabbed them right off the street. Afterwards, they couldn't even keep track of who they'd killed. Dumped them in trenches, in lakes... So, yeah, you're right. I was lucky. I come here to see her, same as coming home... Might get some dinner... Might have a drink... Because she's not going to yell at me anymore. What's she got to yell about?"

The photographer sighed. He wanted to smile. But, under this damned anesthesia, his muscles wouldn't listen to him. They'd petrified.

"Another one?" the fellow asked. The photographer nodded.

The vodka had no taste. The air had no scent, the sun—no temperature, nor did the moon, or what was left of it in the sky. And time no longer had a calendar. June. The last ten days of June.

"Mine was a patriot, you know? Such a patriot that she slept with the flag. I, she, and the flag," said the fellow. "Yours?"

"Mine was for Russia," answered the photographer.

"Huh," said the man, shaking his head. He poured himself another and drank it down. He exhaled hard in satisfaction. He went red all of a sudden. He punched the photographer hard in the chest, then hugged him. And said quietly, "Well, we're assholes, the both of us…"

* * *

THE RAT KING

TUESDAY

JULY 22, 2014

DONETSK

In the middle of the night, the forward brigade of the Vostok battalion drove up to the dormitory where the Russian Orthodox Army had set up base.

Three tanks, two APCs, and a howitzer. The howitzer didn't work, but the Orthodox Army didn't know that.

This visit was regarded as unfriendly. And rightly so! The Orthodox were considered heavy looters. But that wasn't the worst of it. The main problem with them wasn't that they stole, it was that they didn't share.

The fighters were aware of this little flaw. Every evening, they'd promise that no, really, they'd be better tomorrow. But each new day, as if to spite them, began with temptation. Maybe a car was driving around town, or maybe they came across a store that was open…

Seeing that Vostok hadn't come for tea and cookies, the Orthodox alpha commanded, "Fire."

The volley was pathetic and missed the target.

The target responded with one shot from the tank. It was a warning shot. Didn't kill anybody. Just took out the corner of an apartment building.

"What gives, guys? We're on the same side. We're brothers. Slavs. *Russkiye*," sniveled the drunk alpha.

"You've gone too fucking far!" shouted the prince of the East—leader of Vostok—into a megaphone left over from the March rallies.

"But we're gonna give you some! Take it, right now! Take it all! We don't mind sharing with our own..."

"No bargaining! We'll teach you a little lesson, and then any survivors will know better."

The prince of Vostok brought his hand down sharply. The tank released another shot.

"Fuck, man—it's, like, enchanted," said the Orthodox alpha, with fawning deference. His group hadn't ended up with any heavy guns. Every time it was their turn to step up and get their share of the armored Russian inheritance that was coming in from the direction of the border (Sukhodilsk or Amvrosiivka), the Orthodox were never home. They were busy...

"Either you come out one by one to be shot, or we blow your entire dorm to bits!"

"What are we, idiots?"

"Have it your way. I'll give you ten minutes. Get everyone. Drunk, or whacked out, or with a woman—get 'em all out here."

A foreboding silence ensued. The tanks started moving back a little and getting into good fighting positions. Good in this case meaning their shells would actually hit the Orthodox home base. As opposed to going every which way, as happened quite often.

Five minutes later, bursts of automatic gunfire and brief shouts could be heard in the main hall of the dormitory.

Then again. And again.

Seven minutes after that, a fighter appeared in the doorway. He was uncharacteristically sober.

"Here's the deal. We took care of it ourselves. Had a purge. Shot the battalion commander and the squad commanders. Vasya, bring out the corpses. The guys won't believe us. Get them in the light! Over here, under the light... You see this, guys?"

The residents of the apartment building across the street—not the one that had the corner shot off, but another one that was also nine stories with a once-fashionable Czech floor plan—could see it.

The corpse of the commander—drunk, proud, and jolly—was the first to be hauled out to the threshold. Then two more, dressed half-and-half: one in just his pants, the other in just his shirt...

The corpses were thrown on the asphalt. It sounded soft. Pleasant. Because it wasn't the sound of a Grad multiple rocket launcher. And that's already good.

The blood flowing out of their bodies looked black and inexhaustible. Inexhaustible and black.

"Okay. You took care of it yourselves," the prince of Vostok said gruffly into the megaphone. He clearly looked shaken. Short, swarthy, dark-green camouflage, a tense back.

To Igor, who lived on the third floor, the man looked like the Rat King. But that was only because half an hour ago he'd finished reading "The Nutcracker" to his son. Who was also named Igor.

* * *

ASTRO

FRIDAY
JULY 25, 2014
HORLIVKA

The poodle's name was Astro. The dachshund was Jeri. The rottweiler was Linda. The Airedale terrier was Bull.

Every morning, they emerged onto the grassy field near a block of apartment buildings. They each had their own route and their own bushes.

Bull would run to the pond, then back to the lone bench, which was still good and sturdy, though a bit off-kilter. He would bring back a stick. He'd rest, then run to the pond again.

The dachshund would trot delicately along the paths people had worn through the grass. She'd sniff the stock flowers, tactfully and thoughtfully pee. Then continue on her way.

Linda would roll around in the grass, scratching her back. She was the one who barked the most.

The poodle was shell-shocked. And he knew it. Poodles are the smartest dogs of all.

He didn't run, didn't bark, didn't carry sticks around. He lay under the bench and smiled, remembering the way his owner had called him loudly: "Astro! Astro!" but then bad strangers had fallen flat into the grass, shouting, "Get down, buddy. American paratroopers coming down... Astronauts sending the ukrops backup from space... Those sons of bitches..."

Funny.

By the time Bull retrieved his fifth stick, Dusya the pug had appeared with her owner Vera, along with Robert the mastiff and his little girl Natasha.

Vera and Natasha were the ones who brought food. Vera brought kasha and bones. Natasha brought dog food.

They called all the dogs. Jeri was the last to come. She wasn't used to accepting food from strangers yet. But hunger's a powerful thing.

Astro would have preferred something vegetarian. Or perhaps ice cream. But kasha was okay, too.

They ate in a civilized manner, from bowls. Then Vera poured water into those same bowls. After breakfast, she took the bowls back with her. In the evening she'd bring them back again, clean.

Purebred dogs pick up stomach infections quick as a wink. Jeri, Linda, Bull, and Astro were all purebreds. Linda even had two champion titles. A year ago, she'd come to the field with her medal. But she scratched her back on the grass as good as any stray mutt.

After breakfast, they all went about their business. Bull was now running around with ponderous Robert, not by himself. Dusya was racing through the flowers Jeri had already sniffed to her heart's content. Linda invited Astro to go for a stroll. Linda was also smart. And Astro didn't say no. Together, they left the field and returned, as Astro's owner used to say, "to the block."

Linda would walk up to her building entrance, sniff the whole threshold up and down, and then run to the dumpster, trying to catch a familiar scent in her wide wet nose. Then she'd come back to the entrance. Then she'd sit down and wait for the door to open.

Astro didn't participate in this process. He was just keeping her company.

Then they would all go their separate ways for the day. Astro had business in town. These urban forays wore him out completely. Fortunately, there weren't a lot of cars or people. Unfortunately, the particular car he himself needed was not to be found.

In the evenings, they'd have dinner.

Vera and Natasha would start singing the same old song. The women's faces were dark, their eyes mournful.

"How could they do that? How could they leave and abandon their dogs?"

"I know. Seemed like they were normal people. And they weren't poor. It's not like their dogs would've eaten them out of house and home..."

"Maybe I could take little Jeri home with me?"

"What about the rest of them?"

"Well, but the rest of them... They're big. There's still time before the frosts come..."

"But what if the owners don't come back? What if there's nowhere to come back to? Because there's no buildings here? Neither theirs, nor ours? What if the Duh-P-R is here until kingdom come? No way! But, anyway, I still don't get how you could abandon your dogs. How could you—how do I get by without bad words here, Natasha... How could you be such a brute?"

Astro sighed loudly and gave a warning growl. He was categorically against this. Because Jeri, Linda, and Bull had all been abandoned, yes. But not him.

He was a shell-shocked dog. A casualty of war. And his owner had been killed. Had probably been killed...

Right here, on this field. Seven—no, eight days ago now.

It had been late at night. Astro had sniffed out a field mouse and was trying to dig up its den. His owner had called him by name: "Astro! Astro! Here! Over here!" And a bad stranger had shouted, "It's one of their spotters! He's giving their password! Take him out..."

Astro had run fast. But not fast enough. His owner was lying on the ground. And there was a strong smell of blood. Astro closed his jaws on the arm of the bad stranger who'd just lowered his automatic rifle. The other bad stranger cracked Astro in the head with his rifle butt.

He lost his hearing. And then his sense of smell.

Through a grey, soupy film, Astro saw them wrap his owner in a blanket and heave him into the trunk of a car...

Astro doesn't go back home. Because his home is where his owner is. And his owner is in a car. So that's what Astro is looking for.

Poodles are the smartest dogs. When it comes to imagination, they're firing on all cylinders. Same with their sense of humor. And, as we now know, same with hope.

As he fell asleep that night, Astro thought that maybe his owner wasn't dead. Maybe he was just wounded.

Not Cargo 200, like everyone was saying by then. Just Cargo 300.

His number one man was maybe cargo number three hundred...

Or something like that...

* * *

A CIVIL "CONFLICT"

SATURDAY
....
JULY 26, 2014
....
D O N E T S K

Irina Igorevna was a lecturer in the medical school. She's retired now. Seventy-five years old, thanks be to God. But she still sees patients. Because she's a venereologist, and she uses the old methods. Crabs? Her one and only treatment: yellow oxide of mercury ointment. Quick and cheap.

Her husband Eduard is a railway engineer. A smart-aleck and sybarite who loves eating and philosophy. His strong point's Plato. The new technologies he's comfortable with are Odnoklassniki and Angry Birds.[30]

He's always been satisfied with the outcome of his duels with the pigs.

He voted for the "DPR" because he's no hick and to show Kyiv what's what. He even gave an interview to an Italian paper while he was getting ready to cast his vote. "We, the people's intelligentsia, support it. We want all manner of independence from the junta and its stooges. We dream of dying in Russia."

Their housekeeper, Granny Shura, did not approve of this attitude. But what do you expect? Old-time village mentality. Same now as fifty years ago.

But she cleaned really well. No two ways about it.

Granny Shura asked, "But you didn't refuse your pension, I dare say. Is the junta paying you? Are you taking it?"

Irina Igorevna heard something nasty and insulting in the question "Are you taking it?" She gave as good as she got: "If you don't like it here, then go with God, but just go."

"Oh, ho," said Granny Shura happily, "So that's what your referendum did... Because you were atheists when you left this morning..."

For two weeks afterward, Eduard kept insisting on firing Shura. But he refused to scrub the toilets himself.

When Girkin entered Donetsk, Irina Igorevna wept with joy.

"Our defenders... Our warriors..."

She told Granny Shura, "We're going to feed them. Savory pies, soups, braised cabbage..."

"Wrong season for braising," Granny Shura replied, through gritted teeth, and then took ten days off. To go visit her sister in Ukraine.

She left merely deranged but returned a full-on Banderite.

"Are you feeding your *opolchentsy*, Irina Igorevna?"

"What's it to you?"

"Nothing. Brought them a laxative. So they'll shit themselves…"

"Disgusting!" said Irina Igorevna. "There are a great many acceptable words for describing the process of evacuation. But you, Shura, are irredeemable."

"The junta still paying your pension? Or did those defenders of yours already steal everything?"

At the end of July, they decided to go ahead and let Granny Shura go. The issue was no longer just a political one. It was a personal, you might even say a civic matter.

On July 26, the "peaceful protesters" shot down yet another plane.

The Russian channels announced this with their usual joy.

Irina Igorevna's spirits lifted. Shura, on the other hand, grew morose.

"How many have to be buried this time?"

"I have no pity for enemies," ground out Irina Igorevna.

"How were those Chinese kids your enemies?"

"First of all, they weren't Chinese, but Malaysian, among other things. And secondly, it's still unclear who shot it down."

"The only people it's unclear to are the ones Putin didn't tell. But it took that Duh-rkin five minutes to announce it to everyone else: 'We shot down a bird. The pieces are out past the mine,'" said Shura, and burst into tears.

All dressed up, Eduard came out ready for scandal like for lunch.

"Where are you going, dear?" said Irina Igorevna, concerned.

"The airplane turned out to be a drone—"

"Phew!" Granny Shura exhaled.

"—and, on Odnoklassniki, they asked all conscientious citizens to come out and help look for it. They wrote that it fell somewhere around the Embankment. Are you coming?"

Irina Igorevna gave a dignified nod.

"Don't forget your net," grumbled Granny Shura. "And your string bag, to tote the pieces... The bomb shelter's on the Embankment, by school number five. Go look for your drone there—out of harm's way..."

It was late at night when they got back from their search operation. Eduard with a massive heart attack and Irina Igorevna with broken glasses. They'd gotten caught in the crossfire between the fighters of the Russian Orthodox Army and the militiamen of the Army of the South-East. Who could've known that a downed drone was not only a war trophy but also valuable metal that could be scrapped for good money?

They weren't able to get Eduard into the hospital. Not even with Irina Igorevna's influence from back in the day. Now they only treated injured "DPR" fighters there.

Eduard's IV drip and regime of strict bed rest were administered at home.

Shura briskly washed him, fed him, and changed his bedpans.

And the whole time she muttered, "Just you try dying on me, you old fool. I'll wrap your coffin in the Ukrainian flag. Even after you're dead you'll stand right back up, rather than lie down under that..."

Irina Igorevna did not interfere in her husband's treatment. His heart was not in her area of specialization.

* * *

This war will definitely be conceptualized. It will be called the Fatherland War, the Patriotic War. Like WWII. Because Russia attacked Ukraine. It's simple.

It's the end of July. The Federation can still bring in troops. Everything can be worse than it is now. Although it sems like it can't get any worse. But we already know the rule of "worse."

As long as it—the Federation—exists, anything can happen. These days, the Federation is supervising the Apocalypse. And Satan is in, or with, this Federation.

But we'll win anyway.

Because there is such a thing as light. And darkness. Because there is Truth. Whereas the only home of falsehood is the TV towers, the first things taken by the occupiers in every single town.

There are already heroes in the history of our terrible Fatherland war. We know: they don't die. There is betrayal, there is theft, there is the shadow of the "forgotten" divisions that were surrounded, lost. There are partisans, intelligence agents, prisoners of war, and tortured patriots.

It will be painful to write this history. But it's precisely there that we'll become a country with a shared past.

We'll also call it the war for independence. And, in that light, we might regard this war as inevitable.

We could also say anticolonial. But I like "for independence" better.

* * *

Who's the boss of Donetsk?

Which of them's the *Gauleiter*? Who made the decisions? Who will answer for them?

Oh, dear...

Why ask such difficult questions?

When yet another Saint Petersburg company or Orthodox Army group—doesn't matter which—looted the Donetsk city shopping center, everyone suffered:

First off, nineteen people, primarily security guards, were taken hostage. The ransom was a thousand dollars each. That's Obama's doing, by the way. All transactions are in dollars, not rubles. The White House won't be able to wiggle out of this one.

Their relatives didn't have that kind of money. So they went wholesale. Five thousand for the lot. They were ransomed from the prison that had been set up in Ukrsibbank. From a comrade with the code name Kerch.

The thing is there were 10 or 12 prisons. Every *voyevoda*—"DPR" warlord—had his own. You go figure out which was whose.

Secondly, they confiscated groceries. All of them. They'd confiscated groceries before that, too. Six hundred kilograms of sausage here, two tons of meat there. It took them days to steal 480 sheep. Those did end up getting herded directly to the Russian border, though. From there, it's just a few more days to Chechnya.

And coming in third we have the clothes. Tights, for example. Women's tights. Those were for presents. Obviously.

But the biggest trauma was reserved for car owners. Also—just as an aside—not for the first time. This time it was just on a massive scale and all the cars were good ones. For various purposes and various people. Comrade Borodai, the "prime minister," for example, put out his cigarettes right on the upholstery. Sometimes it was a Porsche, other times it was a Bentley. Every day he had a new four-wheeled ashtray. The former owners felt so bad they could just cry. One city council member took it all the way to Moscow. He made phone calls, he sent letters, he had Skype conversations—but no. Moscow refused him. Cars weren't under their jurisdiction. They just did tanks. But what does a council member need a tank for if he's in Kyiv? He's there, hiding from the junta...

All of them, the champions of Donbas and similar peaceniks, were stuck in Banderite Kyiv. From there, they complained about the despicable new Ukrainian authorities. They complained quite freely. Fearlessly...

But a junta—that's not your "peaceful protesters." It has to convene, and prepare a criminal case, and go through the whole process. "Innocent until proven guilty" and all that nonsense. Can't complain, really.

But I digress.

I was talking about who the boss is.

The boss is the one who can release hostages.

The guy from Transnistria who came out to take responsibility for the security of the Duh-P-R was very impressed with himself. At press conferences, he insisted that all the journalists quote him directly, without omissions. The phrase was unchanging: "The head of the Ukrainian Security Service puts on lipstick before bed."

A few people, the ones who still believed in Rahshn-Federahshn, were taken aback. Then they excused the guy by saying he was giving a password, not his own diagnosis.

But he was a total zero when it came to the issue of hostages.

The governor whose name had been randomly called out by the whole square in March was also a zero. His wife, who returned from Moscow with five bodyguards and still retained the position of "minister of foreign affairs," couldn't help with this business of saving people either. She'd say, "My voice is advisory. All I can do is recommend that hostages be freed. That's all..."

Comrade Purgin, the founding father of the "Donetsk Republic," spread his hands. "Not my purview."

The great Duh-rkin (aka Strelok, or Sniper; aka Strelkov; aka Girkin) obfuscated, muddied the waters, and promised to get to the bottom of it, while sighing and covering his face with his soft, delicate hands.

Not the leaders, not the ministers, not the commanders—none of them could help.

In point of fact, the boss of the city was whoever could release hostages.

But the fact is there was no such person.

People ransomed their near and dear from a diverse array of people. Perverse, but diverse.

The voyevodas still collected Russian journalists at press conferences to drone lazily at them about the bright future of the "DPR."

Meanwhile, their gunmen strode confidently back, stepping across centuries and plunging into darkness.

Spitting on the sidewalks of the empty streets, they went off to their mammoths and loincloths, to a time when people didn't yet believe in the soul, or totem animals, or life after death. Their world hadn't yet given any signs of self-awareness. For them, there was no such thing as the next day. There were only enemies. Only the here and now.

The ones who became the bosses were the ones who still knew nothing—or who no longer knew anything—about what it means to be human.

They had call signs, but they didn't yet have names.

Abwehr, Demon, Motorola, Devil, Botsman, Taiga, Maksud, Crazy...

* * *

THE GAME

MONDAY

JULY 28, 2014

S L O V Y A N S K

The commander's the one in the green underpants. He's a little taller than the others. Maybe a little older. But maybe not.

He shouts, "Did everybody bring some?"

"Yes," answers the smallest, looking nervously at his comrades. They nod wordlessly, mumbling something to themselves.

Some of them brought it in buckets; some of them used plastic bottles with the tops cut off; and some of them just carried it in their cupped hands: dirt.

"Fall in!" shouts the commander. "Show me!"

The boys stand in a row and hold their dirt in front of them.

The one in green underpants walks up to each one slowly and examines the dirt closely. He tests it with his finger, he bends close to it, it seems like he even smells it.

"They're not ours! They are not ours! To the ditch! Bury them! On the count of three!"

He counts to three and everyone runs to the ditch. They throw their dirt and run back. They're in a hurry, pushing and shoving. Getting back first means you won. Whoever wins three times in a row becomes the next commander. "The one in the green underpants is probably the one who thought up the rules," thinks Sanya.

He looks at the smallest boy, the one with the red bucket who always comes in last. He doesn't run fast but he sprinkles his dirt thoroughly, pounding on the bottom of his overturned bucket. And then for a few seconds he tamps the dirt down with his feet. He sniffles, offended: "The commandew owdewd us to buwy them, but evwyone just thwew theiw diwt!"

He doesn't have his *R*'s yet. But his *S*'s are good.

Sanya finishes his cigarette, stands up, and approaches them.

"What game are we playing here, men?"

"Burial," they answer out of sync.

Sanya has a coughing fit. The air went down the wrong throat, or something like that. He can't stop. He's in spasms. The one in green underpants asks, "Want me to thump you in the back?"

Sanya nods.

The commander has a good fist. Only takes three blows. The coughing stops.

"Who are you burying?"

"Unidentified. Not ours. In the ditch. Whoever gets there fastest."

"Any of ours?" asks Sanya.

"We buried ours in April," replies the commander, with a heavy, grown-up sigh. "Back at the beginning. Then we covered up all the ones who aren't ours with dirt. But when the girls come out, then we bury ours. The girls cry really good. They pretend to hand out pies, and we have a pretend memorial... But their mommies don't let them play that game."

Sanya begins coughing again. The wrong throat. Something heavy and lacerating went down the wrong throat. It's tearing his chest apart. He can't breathe.

Sanya is a sapper in Slovyansk. He didn't set out to become one, didn't train for it. He was never interested in mines, or shells, or tanks. He wasn't interested in war, either. Cars were his passion. He has a god-given talent for car repair. In Mykolaiv, he's got a month-long waiting list. But here—everywhere—there are mines. Even in the school. Whose idea was it that everyone in Slovyansk should die? They left, but they mined everything. Death. Death. Death. Three thousand times already—death...

Sanya can't stop. He keeps coughing and coughing.

"Would water help?" asks the commander.

"It's because he wants to cwy," says the youngest. He looks Sanya right in the eye. He sighs.

"Cwy if you want. We won't teww."

He doesn't have his *L*'s yet, either.

The commander in his green underpants scoffs. He shouts, "Fall in! Show me!"

* * *

THE CHECKPOINT

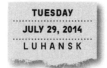

TUESDAY
JULY 29, 2014
LUHANSK

Public transportation's not running. Bread is brought in, but rarely. In stores it's cheap, but it might run out by the time it's your turn in line. And if you buy it from the speculators who drive in, then it's expensive. Nobody's been paid their pension in ages. But for bread, they managed. They pooled their money. They sent Mariya Georgiyevna to get it. She was an athletic woman. A "walrus"—that is, an ice-hole swimmer. Her dad had introduced her to cold water back when she was little. He doused himself with it, and her, too.

At first, it's happy little shivers, but then it's actually hot. Heat and strength in the body. Every Epiphany without fail she dunks herself in the water through the special hole cut into the ice. Her whole body, including her head, three times. She does it faster than it takes to say, "Save me and preserve me, Lord."

Her neighbors, the ladies who lived in the same section of the apartment building, were jealous and didn't support her foible. They foretold that her heart would stop one day. And? As if anybody's heart was going to keep beating forever!

"'Let death, once come, be quick,' girls," Mariya Georgiyevna sang, teasing them with Mikhail Isakovsky's famous war poem. "Let wounds, once got, be small."

And now her foible was coming in handy. She went out for bread. Earlier, she would've gotten on the bus and gone five stops. But that was then. Now, she had to go on foot. On her own two little feet.

There was another thing, too, besides the bread. The thing was called a "humanitarian corridor." Somebody had put up a flier about it in her apartment building section. It was important information. Her building section neighbors included two old people who couldn't walk and three babies. Granny Vera and Granny Manya, who couldn't walk, couldn't be brought up from the basement anymore. So that's where they were fed and bathed.

But they needed to be gotten out of there.

Mariya Georgiyevna knows that all medical care depends on the tenner slipped to the medical aide. The delivery of your pension depends on the monthly five-spot you give the mail carrier. The army, too, as far as equipment goes, depends on people. Everyone gives what they can.

The UN isn't going to accomplish anything with any corridor. Because look where the UN is, and look where Luhansk is. A personal connection's the only thing that works. Family networks. Money.

Mariya Georgiyevna was relying on a personal connection—that, or the authority of age.

She rehearsed her speech as she walked: "We, the old people and children of our section of the building, are asking in good faith: don't shoot! Just for a few hours! Let us leave already!"

She made it to both bread and checkpoint...

They had set up an access control center. A table and chairs from the nearest café. Behind them, trenches with a sheltered area covered in concrete. And an anti-aircraft gun. Not a Grad multiple rocket launcher.

Mariya Georgiyevna and Grads weren't close, so to speak, but she knew them by sight. There was one a couple of buildings away from the shop with cheap bread. Whenever *they* started shelling, it always hit the city center. The hospital was hit especially often. Back when there was still cell service, lots of people were able to reach their friends and family downtown in time for them to make it to the basement. You had about five minutes to make your call while *they* were walking over, preparing it for firing, and checking in with their superiors. That five minutes was enough to save lives.

Mariya Georgiyevna got a white scarf from her bag and, waving it, approached *them*. *They* were gazing up at the clouds drowsily. Mariya Georgiyevna and her neighbors also looked up at the sky a lot. And went straight to the basement if they saw an airplane.

"Good afternoon," she said.

"Whaddaya want, old lady?"

"We, the old people and children of our building section, are asking in the name of Christ the Lord for you to let us leave through the humanitarian corridor. It will pass through here..." Mariya Georgiyevna clearly read the detailed route described in the flyer.

They remained drowsily silent. Then *they* suddenly burst out laughing. Guffawing. *They* bent double, pointing at her with their fingers and rifles. Like in the films about fascists, only in Russian instead of German.

Mariya Georgiyevna straightened to her full height and shouted, "What did I say that was so funny? Are you human beings or not? What's so funny? That we want to evacuate our sick and injured? What's funny about that?"

One of *them* finally got hold of himself and said pleasantly, "What're you getting all riled up for, you old bag? Cracked a good joke and then you get all riled up... Use your brains! Think! If you all leave, who are we gonna defend down to the last drop of our blood? Huh?"

* * *

TUESDAY

JULY 29, 2014

D O N E T S K

Today, they shelled my block, where I live. Didn't hit my building.

* * *

I catch myself thinking that I'm still treating her like a child, a late, long-awaited, only child. I don't sleep if she's not sleeping. I don't eat if she's got "a yucky tummy." I take pictures and videos of her first steps. Her first real teeth. Her first victories. Her songs, her friends. Her camo Kevlar boonie hats. Her baby booties, which we call army boots. Her little armored onesies, her strollers with gun turrets... I show pictures to people I know and even to people I don't. I watch their reactions intently. I suspect those around me of loving her the wrong way; insufficiently, somehow. Not as much as I do.

At night, I ask my husband in my stern teacher voice:

"Tell me: how do you feel about her?"

"Do I have to do this for you to wish me good night?"

"Tell me for real! Or else! How do you feel about her?"

"The same way I do about you." He embraces me with all his body parts. I don't know how, but he does. He whispers in my ear. "The same way I do about you. She's right here, and I don't need anything else..."

I heave a broken sigh. He smiles.

"Was that the right answer? Should I stand at attention to recite it for you?"

He emphasizes the words "stand at attention" meaningfully.

What am I going to do with this guy?

* * *

Severe hangover syndrome used to help with everything. But not from vodka or other alcohol. A dark, hopeless future's what does the trick. If you get good and drunk on that, then both your morning, and afternoon, and, if you're lucky, your whole day will definitely not be good.

The body is honest. It's smarter than the head. If you stuff all kinds of garbage through your mouth into your body, it'll get sick and purge itself in all manner of unpretty but effective ways. Barfing is guaranteed. And, for some amount of time, it won't take any of what poisoned it. In some cases, this isn't for some amount of time, it's forever.

But, judging by some of our fellow citizens, you can stuff absolutely anything into the head, any kind of garbage about a bright, hopeful future. The head takes it and doesn't burst. It's amazing, actually.

As for actual alcohol, it doesn't help. Nothing helps. It's just that after the third glass of hard liquor you get indifferent. Where they're bombing, where they're not bombing—makes no difference... Can't be bothered to go down to the basement. Can't be bothered. They'll kill us and to hell with us.

* * *

WEDNESDAY
JULY 30, 2014
DONETSK

The citizen of the Russian Federation (sometimes I don't know what I'm capitalizing those words for)... Anyway, citizen Girkin announced that Donetsk is now entering a state of siege.

Therefore, the requisitioning of personal belongings, means of transportation, and foodstuffs from citizens and enterprises is now officially allowed.

The decision comes after the fact. The zombies from his (and other) units have already polished off, demolished, stolen, or sold everything.

But my dad started crying. He was born in '41. He remembers bits and pieces of the war. His father, who'd been captured by the other side but escaped, was hiding under the bed. The neighbors turned him in. The Polizei came. My little toddler father kept peeking under the bed and crowing happily. He thought his father was playing. It was a thin line. A thin thread. If it had broken, then my dear dad would have lived his whole life believing he was a patricide. But the Polizei "didn't see" my dad's father. They "didn't notice" him. Seems they were better people than the neighbors.

Now there's a new war. In the role of the Nazis we have the citizens of Russia, led by Girkin.

Dad's crying. "How can they do this? What are these requisitions for? What are these bandits here for? Who asked them to come? My home... My home..."

Home means apartment. In a quiet area of the city center, with flower stalls, the clatter of the tram, the archive, and the road to the Embankment where all the dog owners walk their dogs.

"How? How can they do this?"

My dad's gaze is direct and clear, like a child's. He's still a practicing doctor and he knows better than me how things can and can't be done. It's a psych ward in here, a whole bouquet of diagnoses. The Donetsk People's Asylum isn't joking around. The whole thing is one big mental crisis. But camo isn't a straitjacket. And a Nona isn't haloperidol... They're all long dead. Their brains have been eaten, destroyed. And they joyfully burst through the wide-open gates of death, dragging innocent people with them. Living innocent people.

But Dad doesn't want to leave, regardless. So, like many others, he's not leaving.

His tears sear away the remains of my humanity. The place where forgiveness and understanding should be turns into a nighttime desert. Cold and wind.

I want Girkin, the citizen of the federation, to shoot himself. Preferably publicly. I don't want a trial, I want the death penalty for everyone who came into my city and my country.

I want them all to die.

The veneer of Christianity turned out to be very thin indeed.

I'm entering into an anthropological devolution, along with the orcs and zombies. I don't hear the words of the Gospels. I don't respond to them. There's nothing left in me that can.

My book: the Old Testament.

My prayers: the Psalms of David. "O my God, make them like a wheel; as the stubble before the wind. As the fire burneth a wood, and as the flame setteth the mountains on fire; So persecute them with thy tempest, and make them afraid with thy storm. Fill their faces with shame; that they may seek thy name, O LORD. Let them be confounded and troubled for ever; yea, let them be put to shame, and perish..."[31]

* * *

THURSDAY
JULY 31, 2014
DONETSK

There's nothing they won't do.

Girkin gave a late-afternoon briefing. He announced that special rocket systems had been set up in Kramatorsk that the Ukrainian Army was using to carry out strikes on the Horlivka chemical plant, as well as on the Donetsk and Luhansk wastewater treatment plants. Chlorine, he warned, will explode everywhere.

We are familiar with Girkin's language.

This isn't a warning for peaceful residents. This is his plan. His plan of action. He and his people are going to blow up all the things they named.

It'll be a great image for the Russo-TV channels.

A real-live catastrophe.

Girkin thinks a catastrophe like this will lend the Dickhead confidence, so he'll finally bring in troops.

Girkin's a little fool.

If the Dickhead wants, the Dickhead will make up a reason himself. Or create one.

Grads continue to shell my Ukraine from Russian Federation territory.

Troops from many and varied Russian oblasts are collecting at the border. From Murmansk oblast, for example.

The soldiers of the Russian Federation brag on social media about killing ukrops. The latest Kadyrov assault force has been deployed. The RF air force is with us every day.

Is anything more really necessary here?

Girkin's a murderer. The ones who support him with artillery are, too.

They're murderers. And they know it very well.

* * *

ELCHE. TARRAGONA.
BARCELONA. FIGUERES

SPRING AND SUMMER 2014

GIRONDE

Everything's the same for us here as it is for lots of people. A small mining town. As long as there was coal, the curbs and tree trunks were painted white. They always managed it in time for Easter. But it was officially regarded as being for Lenin's birthday, or else May 1.

A nice little, flat little place that's the same for everyone. The "higher-ups" get a little more; the lower-downs, a little less. Sveta—Svetlana Afanasyevna Golovina—was from the "higher-ups." Her dad was an engineer at a mine. Her mother was an assistant principal.

It was a dyed-in-the-wool Soviet family. They all had principles and were proud of them. Sveta was taught to be honest: you have to always understand the implications of everything, remember where you come from, and know how to carry yourself.

Her mother quizzed her on the implications every evening, automatically correcting her word stress and pronunciation. Her mother was seldom satisfied. Sveta's head was full of wind and mush. Instead of "serve the motherland," Sveta wanted "love and marriage."

Her mom was forced to beat the stupid out of her. Her dad sometimes got in on it, too. They did not employ physical means. Just words. Words and words. They employed them all night if they had to.

Everything didn't fall apart all at once. It was a slow process, thus an imperceptible one. Sveta managed to get her college degree, begin her career of teaching biology, and graduate her first class with two gold medal winners. Best results in the whole town.

But her parents were disappointed. They didn't use the phrase "you've brought shame on the family" on principle, because it's not tsarist times anymore, and because of progress, and all that. So, if a woman decides to have a baby without a husband, then let the tongue wither of anyone who dares say she carried the baby home in her skirt.

All the more so because the baby did have a father. It's just that it took him a very long time to get divorced, which made him start drinking. And then the drink did him in.

Because of the personal failure, the general one went almost unnoticed. Although Svetlana's dad did recognize the dwindling production, and the reduction in government contracts, and the delayed wages.

The mine was dying like a bedridden patient: slowly, steadily, and with complete indifference from the authorities.

Then it died, and that's when things got really bad.

Everything vanished all at once. The only things left were vodka and moonshine. The curbs and tree trunks were no longer painted, neither for Easter nor for May 1.

That year, Svetlana Afanasyevna and her class developed a passion for educational exchange programs. She took the children everywhere: Germany, Austria, Poland, Spain.

They went by bus. And the trips weren't easy. But they were cheap. Each new trip produced new connections, as well as the potential for all kinds of European philanthropy for children from a worn-down industrial region of Ukraine.

On one of their trips, between Miskolc and Nyíregyháza in Hungary, or between Elche and Alicante in Spain... Doesn't matter... On one of their trips, Sveta realized that she was not a tourist. She had no interest in castles and kings, in galleries and fountains; she went to the markets and compared prices for potatoes, flour, and grains. How much here and how much there.

And then for apartments, too.

Meanwhile, a situation was developing with a man back home. A situation involving love and marriage. Her heart was tearing itself apart, from his indecisiveness and from her utter certainty that it was impossible to live there. It was impossible now and would never become possible later.

She took her son and left, because she understood the implications of everything and remembered where she came from. Her little boy would be eaten alive. Both by her own people and by others. Even though it was no longer the bad old tsarist days.

Her love also remained in the town. But that was better, actually. It meant she could dream. Dreams are more valuable than actual presence. They last longer, they've got more healing power. You don't know what might have been.

She settled in Elche, which is in Valencia. She struggled to make ends meet. She struggled so hard she hadn't time to sigh nor cry.

First, she was an aerobics instructor. Winters in the gym, summers on the beach. Plus, bedridden Grandpa Diego, whose eyes were blue-black as plums. Plus, language lessons.

There was a lot more after that: a checkout clerk in a supermarket, a house painter, a hotel maid, a pizza delivery lady... Plus, Grandpa Diego, who'd forgotten his native language.

Things stabilized a little after ten years or so. She started giving Russian lessons, along with English lessons (for which there was always a big demand among wait staff, entertainment concierges, and anybody in any beach-related job). Not traditional lessons, she didn't have that level of knowledge. More just sharing her experience of using international signals. Plus, Grandpa Diego, whom a drop of red wine made completely content.

Everything was turning out okay for her son Alyosha—here, Alejo. Knock on wood. Language lessons, school, skeet shooting.

But after Grandpa Diego's death, things started looking up for Svetlana herself, too. Diego Senior's son was also Diego. And it had also been Diego Senior's idea, actually, for her to live with them, so she and Junior would marry once Senior was gone.

Sveta had little interest in "later." But it was an excellent choice for "now."

She maintained a connection to the motherland through Odnoklassniki. An easy-to-use platform where she could share photos and exchange a few words.

Her friends and family back home were also struggling to make ends meet. They'd already lost hope in anything good coming along. Although they did hope for some sort of success from Sveta.

Diego Junior was a success. He was a joy. And the fact that he was her father's age—well, you couldn't tell that from the photos. A well-preserved Spanish macho. He snored, he smacked his lips, he tippled. He was grumpy first thing in the morning. Same here as anywhere else. But the difference here was the apartment he paid for himself. She was able to work a little less.

Something new emerged: time. And with that time came an idea: that for her, for Sveta, everything had turned out right. Things were good. Not like back there. She was sure that back there it definitely had to be bad. Otherwise, why'd she leave?

That spring, a young woman—her former student—wrote her in Odnoklassniki. The message was bursting at the seams in ecstasies of patriotism: "We're battling against the junta to save the Russian language! Our grandfathers fought, and we are fighting—against fascism and the Banderite horde, against gay parades and same-sex marriage! Down with the junta!"

Junta is a Spanish word. But it's also a Soviet one. Sveta remembered: military power, a military takeover.

Horrible.

Her horror expressed itself as a fit of emotional engagement. She responded, "Europe is with you."

Then came the photographs, songs, and poems. Suddenly Sveta herself started writing poetry. She remembered her expertise with school shows, her nights spent working on the scripts and performances that always got her class first prize.

She got so involved in the process of opening a second, European front in the battle against the junta that she stopped eating and sleeping. She lost weight. Diego said it suited her. He was affectionate.

But how could she bother with affections when refugees from Slovyansk were walking on foot to the Russian border?!

"Look!" Sveta shouted. "Those are my people. They're fleeing the junta... Here's a photo of the place where it's all happening!"

Diego looked. Then he looked again. Then he said, "Do you have mountains and snow there now? Is your motherland in Australia?"

"What mountains? Why are you talking about Australia?"

"Well, you see here, in the background? Mountains. And people are dressed in warm winter clothes... It's winter in Australia. But in Europe, it's summer."

Sveta's feelings were hurt. She burst into tears. She wrote a song all of a sudden. The lyrics included the following: "Arise, inflamed by curses vile, our dear, beloved, great Donbas! Since days of yore, we've kept at bay all critics of our working class!"

Just one line was borrowed. But at school performances, those kinds of borrowings were actually encouraged. They had the whiff of big history about them.

She joined battle. Photos of dead members of the Slovyansk people's militia, of children and women, also dead—just torn to bits. Vivid. Horrific. She posted them in her timeline, adding a curt "We won't forget, we won't forgive" underneath. Her former student thanked her profusely. Sveta wept. The junta attacked.

It was clear that emigration wasn't just the correct move, it was the only possible move. And now it was also a means of saving her own native Russian tongue. Her student wrote that the junta was hanging people for it. Not directly for the language, but symbolically, "for every Russian word." A nightmare. It was a nightmare. She was drowning in it.

She oversalted the polenta. She bought not-quite-fresh squid. She forgot which was leeks and which was green onions. She stopped bargaining at the market. Diego said he was ready to get married and promised to take her on a trip around Spain. But she had no time to be happy about it. The news from home was terrible. There was no water, groceries, or natural gas; many buildings had disappeared; schools no longer had roofs; and the mayor of the town was taken captive. Sveta didn't ask who had captured him. She knew: the junta.

And then that junta shut off her former student's electricity. The messages stopped.

Sveta and Diego got married. They even had a wedding. A beautiful Catholic ceremony. A beautiful ring passed down in Diego's family. Sveta gazed at it and cried.

"There's a civil war at home, but here I am in gold..."

Whether it was ulterior or just base, her motive was clear and thriving. Underneath those tears, a triumphant sensation throbbed. It was shameful, yes, but that's the truth of it. Sveta understood the implications. A habit of hers since childhood.

"Everything'll turn out all right," Diego would say.

"Civil war. Brother against brother... How can this be? The poor working people only want justice."

"The poor people don't want justice, they want to take from the rich," fumed Diego.

This was the only subject about which he was always angry and intractable. He called Hemingway a prejudiced scribbler of made-up trash. He called himself a Francoist.

They went from Elche to Alicante. Then to Gironde. It was very French. Whereas Figueres was, for some reason, Italian. Barcelona wasn't like anywhere else, only like itself. The kind of place where life's funny and easygoing.

Sveta posted photographs. The captions she added were meaningful, though short: "City of genius," "The sun says hello."

From time to time, Sveta plastered her online "wall" with tragic news of the special punitive squads' outrages. But, by now, she was doing it sort of half-heartedly. Without pathos.

At the end of July, her former student wrote. The latest news was good: the electricity and water were back on, there was food in shops, the trolleybus was running. And her roof was going to be repaired any day now.

Sveta didn't bother asking who was going to fix it. She knew who: the junta.

* * *

Girkin has forbidden cursing. He threatened to apply military law to people who use bad words. And that's why, with the clean conscience of a Ukrainian underground fighter, I would like to convey to you the brief contents of our shared national idea, so brilliantly formulated by the provocative Les Podervyanskyi: "Leave us the fuck alone!"[32]

Would you leave us the fuck alone already?!

* * *

SUNDAY
AUGUST 3, 2014
BERDYANSK

Lyusya and Grandpa have been in Berdyansk for over two weeks now. That's not very long. There are people here whose children or parents brought them right after what happened at the airport. Back in May. Those people are considered the old-timers of the Donetsk colony. They argue over terms: refugee, resettler, emigrant.

Grandpa chimes in. "Probably emigrants, though..."

"No, we're on our own land, in Ukraine..."

"Here, yes. But there—it's some kind of 'DPR.' In relation to it, we're definitely emigrants..."

"In relation to whom?" Lyusya manifestly disagrees. "To those occupiers? To those looters and murderers? Not a bit of it..."

Grandpa is seventy-three. Lyusya is five years younger. His hair's grey and he's often out of breath. She is a beauty. Not a former beauty. A timeless beauty. Lyusya is what her grandchildren call her. It's what everyone calls her. A mark of respect for her beauty, for the family line. Even the littlest tongue can't bring itself to call her "Grandma." So that's the names they've been stuck with, for years, for family and strangers alike: Grandpa and Lyusya.

The ocean out on the spit of Berdyansk is troubled. It's deep, and the water's choppy, too. It's good to look at. The seagulls are good to look at, too; the birds hang in the air, they catch the right gust of wind and float, frozen, on one spot.

Grandpa and Lyusya don't like the word "refugees." In this, they're just like the Ukrainian state: no word means no problem.

"Resettlers" is even worse. It's even worse. You can't say "resettle" when Lyusya was born and raised in the house on Chelyuskintsiv Street. Her grandpa lived there, her father, brother, and mother. They all died a long time ago. Lyusya has been an orphan since she was twenty-four. But she has that house. She has the piano her dad bought. She has the wall between rooms, the one that used to have a door in it. Her grandpa bricked it up. If you put your hand on the red bricks there, it'll be warm.

If she has the house, it means she's no orphan.

"Maybe we're evacuated?" Lyusya ponders.

"That's it," nods Grandpa. "By our kids, pulled out by the scruff of our necks…"

Grandpa's like a child. He resists somatically. Traumatically, too. Diabetes, arthritis, thrombosis… He doesn't follow his diet… He gets severe pancreatitis… And then again… In the Berdyansk hospital's emergency room, he's welcomed like family. "Oh, you've come to see us again…"

Lyusya watches over him. She doesn't let him overeat or eat what's bad for him. So, Grandpa, like Don Quixote, enters into battle with a door that's letting a draft blow on him. He emerges victorious. His battle trophies include a wound and four stitches on his finger. And again, they're happy to see him in the Berdyansk hospital. They forbid him from getting the stitches wet until they heal.

The next morning, while the Donetsk colony is sleeping, Grandpa puts on a surgical glove and heads for the ocean...

He wants to go home, too. At home, he has his books, his stove, and his steam cooker. The market's not far. Grandpa loves cooking. He understands it, he's good at it, he knows food and its secrets. And he has his work. His workday starts at two. He misses his work as well as his kitchen.

He is a man. So his unease is greater than Lyusya's. He's used to being the breadwinner and to never getting tired. But here, in Berdyansk, he's slowly becoming dependent on his children. And on free time. On a great big raft of time that's choppy, like the ocean out by the spit of Berdyansk. He feels like a useless freeloader. Like a seagull, frozen in the sky. He used to dream of flying when he was younger. But now he just hurts.

His children say, "Dad, this makes us happy. Really. It makes us happy to be able to do something nice for you."

Grandpa and Lyusya exchange a look. They're not entirely convinced that Berdyansk is nice. They have an escape plan. And money for a taxi.

"Even if the occupiers are there for good, we're going to go on back. We're going to be citizens of Ukraine. We'll never surrender to them. But let us go on back home. The neighbors are saying there's no shooting on our street yet. Just craters in the sidewalks. Can we go already?"

The kids talk them into staying another week.

It'll be the fourth.

Fresh air. Lots of iodine in it. There's fruit. Vitamins in it. The kids laugh. That makes them happy. Music comes from everywhere. Music's better than the whistling whisper of a Grad multiple rocket launcher.

Grandpa and Lyusya are sitting on a bench, looking out at the nighttime ocean.

"Do you remember that film, *Air Crew*?" asks Lyusya.[33]

"What's that, my pet?"

"*Air Crew*, with Georgii Zhzhonov?"

"He spent seventeen years in camps under Stalin. He was still young... Yes, of course, I remember. It's a good film."

"I want to do just like her," sobs Lyusya all of a sudden. "Like the woman from the plane. Tell our son-in-law that, when he takes us to Donetsk, he has to stop right at the entrance to the city. I want to lie down there on the asphalt and kiss it. Do you hear me? Do you have your "ears" in? It's not too windy here for you? You're not dizzy?"

Grandpa slowly shakes his not-dizzy head. He says, "Okay, my pet. I'll tell him. But, in the meantime, you can kiss *me*..."

Lyusya kisses the top of Grandpa's head, his grey hair, his small, almost invisible bald spot. He takes her hand, turns it palm up, and brings her palm to his lips. He presses a kiss onto it. He doesn't let go for a long time.

* * *

SUNDAY
AUGUST 3, 2014
A KITCHEN IN DONETSK

We're talking. In five voices. I don't know which of them is mine...

"Ten tanks from Rahshah again. They're headed to Donetsk."

"Come on, how were they allowed in? How?!"

"How were the other ones let in? There's a hole there, in the border. Who would've thought they were shoving their way in here to fight us? Brothers, right? Fucking hell..."

"They robbed the last delivery service. They got ten million. That's the end of the mail."

"But they got their TV up and running again. That bomb landed so perfectly on the TV tower yesterday. But today—hello! All fixed again. How could they survive without Rahshah's brain stem. They sweated all night over it."

"I heard an ambulance came and got them because they were coming down so hard off their high."

"Damn them. Let them all die of withdrawal."

We go silent. A prolonged pause into which my daughter seamlessly inserts herself. Ever since she was a baby, she has been able to insert herself into all situations as though they were created specifically for her. The war's an exception. She inserts herself noisily, tenderly, almost even languorously. She sighs: "Here you all are, just like everybody else. All you can talk about's the war. And here I am, sitting with you like a dummy. Every night, I dream of a girl. A little baby girl. Button eyes, white eyebrows, really white, and her hair's also white. And her little mouth, with a little lower lip that's almost as though it were painted on... What a pretty little girl..."

"It's a portent. A sign of a miracle. You've got a pleasant surprise coming," says Grandma.

"No. For you it means a miracle. But for me it means a little girl. I know for sure."

Before the war, we would've demanded, in four stern voices with various intonations from panic to curiosity: "Are you pregnant?"

But not now. Now, we just sit. In silence. Smiling. I imagine this little baby girl. It occurs to me that she might get my ears. So we won't get them pierced. Such little bitty ears. So sweet.

* * *

SUNDAY

AUGUST 3, 2014

DONETSK

It feels like they've already stolen everything. All the cars, anyway. But no.

There were still the parking garages under apartment buildings. Cars were stolen from them selectively. First, the orcs took pictures of the cars, then they posted them on a website. People from Russian border towns picked out cars based on looks. Just point your finger and say, "I want that one!" "That one" is then stolen...

The moment Girkin legalized looting, all the parking garages were emptied.

Every single car that had been left was stolen. Down to the last one. Bad or good, all were requisitioned to serve the orc army's needs. Their needs were varied. Joyrides through the city. Crashing into telephone poles, fences, and ditches. Or into each other. Cars that had served the needs of the *opolchenie* were just abandoned on the road.

Orcs of a lower rank took the ruined cars to scrap metal recycling centers. Once these centers ceased to exist, the wounded and murdered cars just sat there waiting to be towed away.

Every night during curfew, stolen cars raced all over the city, brakes squealing. They were calling out to their owners, howling out their grievances... But their merciless killers slowly murdered them anyway.

The locals called this little show "Pricks on Parade."

* * *

MONDAY

AUGUST 4, 2014

DONETSK

Granny Shura's ninety-five years old. She sleeps most of the time. Doesn't talk much. Her clear spells are rare.

But in her clear spells she recognizes everyone and smiles.

The fifth floor of a *khrushchevka* apartment building.[34] It's hot. She catches cold when the air conditioner is running. But, when it's not running, she stifles. Last night was hard. First, her blood pressure leaped to one-sixty, then it fell to ninety. It was impossible to bear. Just like we couldn't bear fifteen hours of her urinating.

The ambulances weren't running. Couldn't go to the pharmacy. Curfew. You'd get shot. Her daughter, Irochka—the last, late-born, long-awaited girl child, as good as she was beautiful—suffered terribly that night. Everyone they knew helped take care of Granny Shura, by phone or, in the neighbors' case, in person.

By morning, things got better.

Granny Shura sat down by the window to look out at the street, at Ilyich Avenue. The locals called it the McHighway.

"What's that, Irochka? Is it war? Did the Germans attack again? Tanks, Irochka. Ten of them? Did the Germans attack?"

"No," the tired Irochka responded curtly.

"Those our tanks? Training?"

"No," her daughter said again. "Not ours. None of our tanks are in the city."

"What are you getting me all mixed up for then?!" scolded Granny Shura. "If there are tanks driving down McHighway, but they're not ours, then it's the fascists. The fascists again. What's happening, Irochka?"

* * *

MONDAY
....
AUGUST 4, 2014
....
M A R I U P O L ,
K Y I V ,
D O N E T S K
Yesterday, the Ukrainian Security Service detained the editor-in-chief of the Donetsk city council newspaper. She, this woman we're talking about, was a die-hard. A believer, even. No standards of ethics or journalism apply in matters of faith. But it lets people feel bold, entrusted with a mission. This person eagerly posted pictures of Balkan refugees, saying they were Slavic. Children's corpses, too—children of all times and peoples—featured in her paper under titles like "The Junta's Victims."

This fortress of faith was tested a couple of times a month by her Ukrainian salary. She didn't observe religious fasts on paydays. She took the money.

I'd ask Maks: "How can she do that? Hryvnias must burn her hand to the bone. There are all kinds of symbols on them: the national emblem, a picture of Lesia Ukraïnka…"

Maks would shrug. "Simple: it's the Donetsk custom of taking advantage of chumps…"

"The chump being Ukraine?"

"That's what it looks like."

I'd go to the paper's website every so often. There were whole days, even weeks, when the moaning about "peaceful protesters on tanks" was replaced by completely psychedelic pieces about the damage wreaked on roses by the tansy beetle. Or about how to use tree rings to tell the age of trees.

She went into raptures about fountains, paving stones, how to fix your teeth, and cubic feet of trash. But then a lament would again burst forth, for the murder of innocent "peaceful protesters" who had just happened to accidentally get into two tanks, so they could look at the stars through the cannon sights. She sobbed—and called on society to sob—over passages written by that Horlivka bastard, Bezler, passages he'd written using primarily interjections; she painstakingly turned them into complete sentences for him.

And then relief, again. Remission. Harvest scenes. Weather reports. Anti-aging tips.

A minder would probably pull on her chain. Bring her back to her senses. But this little kick in the pants wouldn't last long. All it took was the tiniest taste of Lie-News and she'd be off on another bender.

During one fit of faith she even took on a new job. She became the director of the "DPR's" Information Department. She did not get the position of information policy minister. That post was firm in the grip of our old mutual acquaintance, a chronically combative neighborhood weirdo. He does have a name, of course. But, in this case, it's only meaningful for his psychiatrist.

She didn't keep the job long. She left because she disagreed with their methodology. She didn't end up liking theft and hostage-taking.

You can see where she's coming from.

But she didn't change her views after she quit. People advised her to go to Ukraine. Get some medical treatment. But it didn't work. She came back from her native town devastated by traditional Ukrainian embroidery and suffering from aggravated hatred for the flag. "Everywhere! It's everywhere! On every balcony! How can anyone live out there in the middle of that Banderite horde!"

I don't know what on earth prompted her to go to Mariupol, not to Belgorod. She had so much strength, so much faith, that it seemed like she could die the death of the brave along with her "peaceful protesters" who'd just happened to accidentally pick up a few Grads at the Silpo along with the milk and bread.[35]

She could've. She just didn't want to.

From Mariupol she went to Crimea. And from there, as happens often enough, she ended up in Kyiv. On Volodymyrska Street. In the Ukrainian Security Service building.

She, this woman we're talking about, isn't a stranger. On the contrary: she's one of us. Somebody I know. Somebody we all know.

People have had coffee with her, laughed together, shared the search for sensations large and small. People talked a lot about the acute form of her Ruscism.

About her arrest, too.

She had a lot of defenders. She was even praised for her honesty, for her openness about her position, for not being wishy-washy, like some. For being brave, too, and steadfast.

Her critics were nonplussed. "What, should we praise Dr. Mengele too? For being honest and steadfast?"

The Facebook discussion distracted the city from the war for a whole evening. Everything in that discussion was like it used to be... Just like it used to be...

I didn't participate in the argument. By that time, I was already a barbarian. An unapologetic barbarian with a bad case of tunnel vision. I couldn't be allowed to be with people. Neither virtually, nor in real life. Not at all.

But you know... My friend Maks...

He said, "Two children. She went to Crimea with two children. Somebody has to figure out what happened to them. Somebody has to find them..."

When I look at Maks, when I listen to him, I understand that everything in the *Lives of the Saints* is true.

But being a human being is really hard. I can't do it anymore. I can't do what it takes anymore.

* * *

GOOD NEWS

DONETSK

"Hey, the orcs aren't taking prisoners anymore. They don't have anything to feed them with..."

"Good thing. And it seems they can't execute them, either... They don't have anything to shoot them with..."

"Uhm... hooray?"

* * *

THEY'RE NOT REFUGEES

TUESDAY

AUGUST 5, 2014

THE SKY, KYIV

They're not refugees. Not freeloaders. They have money, IDs. They have summer clothes. The husband might even be able to get a job. He's a smart guy. A banker. He held it all together. His department used to laugh: "Soon, we'll be moving money in our pockets." "Or in our underwear," he'd say.

Last week, he arranged for the entire staff to be relocated to Mariupol. They found a space, switched over all the operations.

Some vigilant orc—one of his own people, of course—betrayed him.

Their departure was disorganized. The clothes on their backs plus the "emergency bags."

Katya had four bags, one for each family member.

Her mom called before they left: "Have your banker get us our pensions. Otherwise... Well, you know..."

"Your 'DPR' will get it to you," Katya growled, exhausted.

"You meant to say, Russia?" prompted her mom sweetly. "Be sure of this: we have no doubts. Not a one. Putin is coming! He's coming, and here he'll…"

"Hang!" said Katya, and ended the call.

They rented an apartment in Kyiv. Bought groceries. Made borscht. Strolled around the building courtyard.

Katya caught herself sizing up the basements: where they were, were they easy to get to, were they fairly dry.

She made herself stop. She was ashamed of herself. But, whenever fireworks went off, she'd immediately cover her head with her arms and hunker down onto the pavement. Sometimes, she even had time to lie down. But more often than not she caught herself when she was crouching and pulled herself up by her own hair, like Baron Münchhausen. She was afraid of the garbage trucks, too. She'd been afraid of them even back in Donetsk. They sounded like a Grad launching its rockets.

The trash was picked up on a rotating schedule in the neighborhood where they were renting an apartment. For this reason, Katya often found herself and the kids in the partition between apartments. Sometimes, she was still holding a ladle in her hands, other times the potty. Both walls of the partition were load-bearing, and there were no windows. It was safe.

It was safe. It was good. People were relaxed. They argued over nothing. They didn't stock up on food. They didn't hide their cars. They didn't deliver water, food, and clothes to checkpoints. They collected money. But they didn't deliver things. Money was easier than deliveries. But, on the other hand, Kyiv had traffic jams. Nobody was a fan of that. In the traffic jams, everyone yelled at each other and honked at each other. Then they'd laugh. A lot, and often.

They'd laugh. But for Katya, it was painful.

The laughter was painful, and the music, and the comedies on TV. But being in pain wasn't being afraid. It was something different.

When people are in pain, they are still themselves. But when people are afraid, they're not.

And it was good for the kids. Her younger boy built Lego checkpoints. He'd ask, "Mom, what do I make their balaclavas out of?" Her older boy would scoff. He was quiet, a thinker. The thinker part was her husband Igor. The quiet part was Katya. And that's how she knew that her older boy wanted to go home. He won't tell her. He never tells anybody anything. He goes through everything without speaking about it. Wanting something without speaking about it: nobody needs this kind of skill. But this situation isn't teaching him any others...

Every day since their arrival, Igor has insisted in the strongest possible terms that Katya enroll their older boy in school and the younger one in daycare.

She hasn't done it. Igor yells at her. In a whisper, after the kids are asleep, Igor yells at her and calls her irresponsible.

What can he possibly know about her responsibility? What can he know that won't make him laugh, or get scared, or call a doctor, or put her on meds?

Nothing!

Katya doesn't enroll them. Because she's holding up the sky over their home. School in Kyiv is the last line of defense. If she gives in, there will be no more home. They won't go back. They'll never go back.

Everyone's here, everyone's safe and well. They could start over here.

But home is there. Home's there. Not here.

Katya holds up the sky and doesn't budge. If she has to, she can teach the kids for a month or two herself.

* * *

THURSDAY
AUGUST 7, 2014

The citizen of the RF, also known as the "prime minister" of the Duh-P-R, comrade Borodai, announced to his loyal subjects on Twitter that he's stepping down from the post of King of the Apes.

The citizen of the RF, also known as the "prime minister" of Luhanda, comrade Marat Bashirov, announced on Facebook that the junta had completely destroyed Kramatorsk. "Now, there's no glass factory in the city anymore, there are no two parallel streets left..."

He's right about the glass factory. There is no glass factory there anymore because there never was one.

The part about no two parallel streets being left is a lie. Only Muscovites think provincial cities don't deserve to exist due to their non-capital-city inferiority. But Stephen King lives in the state of Maine. He doesn't agree with this. And neither does Kramatorsk. There are a lot of streets. Both parallel and perpendicular ones. And not a lot of destroyed buildings. A hundred thousand residents. Kramatorsk has been lucky.

It's good there.

It's so good there that Girkin, that maniac, is jealous. He said this in his briefing: "The junta has come up with a new way to pay its IMF loans. The Kramatorsk underground reports about the creation of gay brothels in the city where our captured militia members are forced to service European moneybags."

He's really sick, Girkin is.

But the president of the RF, citizen Putin, is healthy. He has banned food imports and promised to address the nation.

He was expected to say, "I declare war on Ukraine" or "I'm tired. I'm stepping down..."

We didn't get our wish. Neither we nor his people.

But Borodai's "I'm stepping down" is better than nothing. One less rat.

We'll trust in the law that good things come in twos.

If such a law exists, of course.

* * *

THURSDAY
AUGUST 7, 2014
D O N E T S K

A mortar has a three-mile kill zone. Once you hear the sound "trr-trr-trrr," it's five seconds till detonation. A Grad multiple rocket launcher whistles: "fshuuu-fshuuu-fshuuu." You count ten or eleven seconds, and only then—boom. Its kill zone is also bigger.

We have no army or National Guard in the city.

But what we do have is the sound "tpr-tpr-tpr" and missile strikes. Today, they've hit the hospital and residential buildings.

A mortar or an anti-aircraft missile.

The orcs set up their artillery in one area of the city and shoot at another area. Anyone in camo vanishes off the street before the event. The locals know: this is a sign.

If there's no guys in camo, it means residential areas are going to be bombed.

What for?

Do you even have to ask?

Five or ten minutes after the shelling, right there, next to the residential buildings and civilian corpses, out pop the TV crews of LieNews and the other Russian garbage.

Our suffering is broadcast to Moscow and the Far East.

It's called, "the junta's shelling the city." And you don't even need to ask how they know it's safe for their TV crew, that there won't be any more shelling in that area.

They don't just know it. They're the ones directing the whole show.

Putin must have fervor and justification, without a moment's pause.

"Putin, put it in!" This game has already lasted five months now. The deaths aren't ending. He hasn't made the decision yet: when. And whether.

But just as a reminder: if there aren't any orcs out on the streets, they're getting ready to kill civilians. They themselves are sitting tight in basements. Cowardly devils. Petty demons. Taking care of themselves.

* * *

THE ANTI-AIRCRAFT GUN

FRIDAY
AUGUST 8, 2014
DONETSK

Anna Petrovna's the head of the local housing and utility management department. She's a real force of nature. If a plumber goes off on a bender, she can sober him up better than any medicine. She can bawl and box the booze out of anyone.

She's not afraid of dying anymore. The only thing she frets about is her hair and her nightgown.

She puts her curlers in every day, so her hair's done in time for bed. She washes and irons her nightgowns every day. She's got some to spare, thank God. Three total. One's just plain gorgeous: cotton batiste and lace.

"If I turn up dead, they'll show me on TV. For sure. So, what then?! I'm supposed to just lie there all frowzy?! No sir! I'm used to being pretty! I'm getting ready for my film shoot!"

Some might have begged to differ regarding the being pretty. But, in general, her initiative was greeted with solidarity. Young people—especially those with something to show off—even decided to sleep naked. Katya from the fifth floor colored her hair. Nelya got her hair cut. Short, but stylish. You'd never give her sixty.

When the other side set up artillery on the roof of an unfinished apartment building nearby, Anna Petrovna got good and mad. The buildings under her care had maybe earned a stray bullet, but not targeted fire from our own army. Anna Petrovna had no intention of becoming her own side's collateral damage. She didn't want to burden their conscience. Her building agreed with her.

Nelya with the new haircut said, "Let's go up there. Have a little talk with them..."

Nelya was a big lady and it wasn't easy for her to go up the stairs in an unfinished building: the steps are there, the handrails aren't. They stopped twice for cigarette breaks, although Anna Petrovna couldn't stand the smoke. Just hated it.

They made it to the top.

The roof. The cannon. Two guys sitting there. Working on their tans. Automatic rifles lying there next to them.

That fact lent the women courage. "We'll have time to say something before they can get ahold of them and start shooting..."

Anna Petrovna hit the ground running: "What the hell are you doing barging up here with that bandura of yours?![36] What are you calling death down on our heads for?! Don't you have a conscience?!"

Nelya joined in. "They don't have any conscience! They probably drank it away!"

"Hello, women," said one of them politely. He was neither young nor old. He looked tired to death. His eyes were flat, no spark. This one you'd have to feed and coddle for a while yet to bring him back to his right mind and his real self. And his accent wasn't Russian.

"What you shouting for? What you bothering us for?"

"What are you bothering *us* for!? Nothing else to do?! Is that it?! Come work for me! I could use a plumber. And an electrician! I'll give you work!"

"War is our work. You understand, woman?"

"They pay us. We work. Why electrician? We don't know how to do electrician," smiled the second. He had a nice smile. Nelya's son used to smile that way. But not anymore. He was a doctor. There was nothing to smile about at all anymore. And when would there be again? Nelya scowled and said, "This is bad work. Shameful..."

"What you say is true," said the older one. "It is bad here. War here is wrong. First shoot over here. Then shoot over there. Where is the front? Where is the enemy? Who are we fighting? Who are we killing? Why different directions all the time? This is not how it's done."

He sighed. The second one glanced at him and then sighed, too.

Anna Petrovna was coming to a full boil. She knew this audience well. First, they get you to feel sorry for them, next they wangle a tenner out of you for some hair of the dog, and then they disappear and don't do the job. Meanwhile, the faucets are leaking and the residents are complaining. Makes you want to murder the whole lot of them. And rip the faucets right out of the wall.

"Ah, you stump of a human being!" she shouted terrifyingly. "What did your mother birth you for? So you could come kill me right here in my nightgown? What did your wife love you for? So you could trade in my children for your rubles? Ah, you soulless trash, you rotten sacks of..."

Nelya tugged at Anna Petrovna's sleeve. But she was now unstoppable. In her family, this was referred to as "Here comes the hurricane."

The younger one lowered his gaze. The older one hung his head.

"What!? You afraid I'm going to hit you? You scared? Well how scared do you think *we* are?! Ah, just look at you... And you're *men*..."

"Woman. You know what?" said the older one. "Come take it away! Can you come take it away at night? Then, in the morning, we'll come and it's not here. We'll say it's ukrop sabotage. You understand, woman?"

And he smiled. It was a despicable smile. Because it was a nice smile, too. Anna Petrovna had fallen in love with that kind of smile as a schoolgirl: teeth and dimples. On his left cheek, he even had two dimples. Her schoolgirl crush had also had two...

"We will take it away," she said sternly, fending off a surge of tenderness.

That night they brought Palych along. They'd never have managed the hulking thing with just the two of them, on stairs with no railings.

Palych, an electrician and a watchman at a pricey parking lot (but what kind of parking lots do we have now?), said they couldn't manage it with just three of them either.

"We have to take it apart!"

"I'll take you apart!" roared Anna Petrovna. "Last time you took my gas meter apart, there were fifteen parts left over! And it counted down, not up! I'll end up in jail thanks to your taking things apart!"

"Well, but then it won't kill anybody," he noted philosophically.

"Let him take it apart," agreed Nelya.

There didn't end up being a lot of parts. Anna Petrovna tried to memorize everything, even to write it all down: what it was, what it was for, where every little nut and bolt went... But she couldn't keep up. It was dark, the notebook was small, the pen wouldn't write...

They started carrying it away. Nelya took the screws. Palych picked up a wheel. He exclaimed and sat down.

The same exact thing. First the feeling sorry, then the ten rubles on account of severe alcohol-induced lumbar pain.

"Don't even think about it!" Anna Petrovna shouted at him. "Get up and carry it!"

"Oh, for the love of..." whined Palych. "What an idiot... Oh, this idiot woman... And when me and this giant doohickey fall off the stairs, what are we going to screw onto the cannon instead of a wheel?! Your tits!?"

"I'll give you some tits! You watch your mouth!"

"We need a winch. I'm telling you. Do you have a hundred on you? I saw one on a construction site here..."

"What do you need a hundred for? You're not going to steal it for free?" asked Nelya.

She was resting between flights. Smoking. She shouted up at them, "I've got a hundred. Go get the winch..."

Palych nodded and darted down past Nelya. Like a bird on the wing. Didn't care there were no handrails.

"He's not coming back," sighed Anna Petrovna. "I know what men are like when they get together..."

They waited an hour or two. The night thickened. It was quiet in their area. They usually shot at the airport, so the "booms" came from a fair distance and weren't scary anymore...

"Look," said Nelya. "What do we need a great big cannon for? You want to install it in your office? You going to shoot at something?"

"Well, I..." Anna Petrovna furrowed her brow.

"'Well, I...' Let's take the barrel, and that—the thing that's inside it, and just push it off the roof. If we have to, we'll drag it away afterward. But if it breaks, then to hell with it. And let the rest of it just stay here..."

They pushed it off the roof. One-two-three lift, one-two-three heave...

The cannon parts and the barrel hit the pavement below with quite a crash and the sound of screeching metal.

"Now the patrols will come running," said Nelya apprehensively.

"They'll be too busy shitting their pants to run over here! Sons of bitches!"

Gradually, they made their way downstairs. They dragged the barrel out past the garages and left it in a ditch. They had enough strength left to throw some dirt over it. Then they pulled "the thing it shoots" over to the substation. They put it next to a big hole that was there not because there'd been an attack, but just because the road there wasn't paved.

It was getting light. They could hear the explosions more and more clearly. The sounds weren't coming from their area yet, but they were very close.

"We aren't fit for television," said Anna Petrovna. "My hair's dirty, my nails are all torn up…"

"Yeah. Two sweaty carcasses on prime-time channel ORT.[37] This isn't what I've been dreaming of," said Nelya seriously.

"Still, it's better somehow, without that cannon. Right?"

Nelya sighed.

It really was a lot better without that cannon.

* * *

CLASSIFIED AD

Apartment to let in Donetsk. Amenities in the courtyard. Artesian well + hand pump. Great water pressure. Diesel generator. Fully-equipped basement. Not cheap.

* * *

"Shakhtar," he says. The Miners, the Donetsk soccer team.

My dad took me to the Shakhtar stadium. Forty years ago. I don't remember the match, just the ice cream and the delirious joy. What it was like to be a grown-up. You can shout, stand up from your seat. You can talk. It's not like it is in the theater. Soccer is freedom. I formulated it right there. But, back then, I just felt it. My father's gone now. And so Shakhtar is my father, too. He taught me everything. To run, to jump, to not be afraid. Volleyball. Checkers. Chin-ups. He took me all over the city by tram. I knew all the tram routes by the time I was six.

My dad was worried I'd get lost. The trams were supposed to save me. That, or comfort me. I've never gotten lost in my life. This is my city. My city...

Now they play in Lviv. They're one man down. They're intense. They're winning. I don't care. The Shakhtar inside me is dying.

Shakhtar's owner is responsible for the war. He could have done something. But he wasn't able to. He'd used up all his steam on the whistle. On the factory whistle, to be precise. And then he cut and ran. Remember how he was talking back in May: "The bullet hasn't been born that could chase me out of Donetsk." But it worked out without the bullet. He ran...

He's responsible. It'd be better if he'd sell the club. Or give it away.

His Shakhtar is his joy. What do I need it for, if death's in the city?

It's not soccer anymore. It's not freedom. This is the coward's team, the team of war...

I think my father would've understood me...

* * *

I don't like carnations. They're formal flowers. They're the property of Soviet power. They're for monuments, ceremonial openings, and bad poems: "The bright red carnation comes out for our sorrow. The bright red carnation's our hope for tomorrow."

After being put to such wooden, official use, they can no longer be given to women. It's in poor taste.

But they can be used at funerals. They're good for cemeteries. Long stems, no thorns. They don't hurt your hands. Just your heart. They even look nice with the black mourning band. They smell like woe.

Today, in Donetsk, there's a whole bouquet. Five of them. Five Carnation self-propelled howitzers. 122 millimeters.[38]

Moscow has ordered a "humanitarian catastrophe."

So the Duh-P-R saluted: "Yes, sir!" A maternity ward, hospital number eighteen, residential areas...

But good Duh-P-Rites happened to be walking by the Topaz military radioelectronics plant, the one that makes Kolchuha radar systems, and gave them a little heads-up: "In sixty to ninety minutes, there will be shelling here. Hide." People no longer asked, "How do you know?"

Clarity is when every person knows that the Duh-P-R has been shooting civilians for the third straight day.

It identifies its victims in advance over and over. Then, along with Rahshah-TV, it mourns them loudly.

The "good" Duh-P-Ritesare probably locals.

They still have the capacity to take pity on someone...

* * *

SUNDAY
·····································
AUGUST 10, 2014
·····································
DONETSK
The terrorists hit a penal colony with a shell. One dead. Ten wounded. The prisoners fled in all directions. Recidivists were panicked. Those are terrifying people, but they ran like regular people, peaceful people who haven't been sentenced twice.

They lived for a day in something like freedom. In the "DPR." Then they shrugged and went back to the penal colony. "There's food in prison. And—it's safe, somehow..."

* * *

Women are giving birth in basements. In basements. While they're being shelled. The apes are shooting over and over again at the Vyshnevskyi hospital.

* * *

NOT ENOUGH

MONDAY
·····································
AUGUST 11, 2014
·····································
LUHANSK
OBLAST
A volunteer Ukrainian battalion. The general's headache. Short on discipline, long on self-esteem. "Why aren't these tents in a row?" "You an idiot, pops, or what? 'In a row!' So it's easier for the enemy to mow us down?! We're actually doing some fighting over here. Want to join us?"

Generals come out to the anti-terrorism operation zone so they can get their pictures taken. And get their status. Everyone in the zone gets the status of participant in military action.

There's no such thing as a general who's full. They can never get enough.

But they aren't the only ones who hate the battalions. The local authorities do, too.

In the cities, there's not a single civil servant who doesn't have some sort of connection to the separatists. Not all civil servants and police are the Polizei. There are some heroes. There truly are. But only a few...

Our fighters found the public prosecutor's body in a ditch. Some of our fighters know him. Knew. They were from the same town. Compatriots.

In March...

That March was so long ago now. A carefree month, when idiots strolled the streets singing old war songs...

The battalion commander smiles but doesn't laugh. He's forgotten how.

The dead body bears signs of torture. The commander has seen more than enough of them. But there's no way the eyes can get used to such things. It smarts, every time. Like somebody's sprinkling sand in them... Rub them or cry, makes no difference...

In March, that public prosecutor had worn a Saint George's ribbon and demanded that the "peaceful protesters" be treated with all due respect. At a word from him, the prosecutor, people from villages near and far were driven in for the demonstrations. But they went back home on their own. Cursing to beat the band. They made sure to cuss out the prosecutor specifically. But they left no one out. They used expletives for Yanukovych. And the junta. They just piled on the swear words. But not at the demonstration itself. There, they were all by the book, knew exactly who was ours and who was theirs. "Come back, dear one! Come back! Down with the junta!"

"What the hell are you doing, you piece of crap?" That was the commander giving a virtuoso solo on the "horn"— his cell phone. He also knew the public prosecutor. From way back. You could say from childhood: they'd gone to the same school. And then the same college. Then they parted ways at the starting line. The commander gave up on his legal career without ever even starting. But the public prosecutor went into civil service. And he served. Oh, how he served. He wasn't the worst of the lot. No, not the worst. But there just hadn't been enough evil yet, back in March. He could have been an idiot and crossed some lines. But he didn't; he wasn't stupid. He wasn't the most despicable. And, as far as crossing boundaries went, he was okay.

"Do you get what this could lead to? And I'm not talking about an article in the Criminal Code, I'm talking about the real issue here! You're not an idiot!"

"Stay out of this. You can see it yourself: we're being coerced. We got a phone call ordering us to. So we did. If we don't, it's curtains. Our own guys will throw us in prison..."

"Don't you dare start talking about a vicious circle!" he yelled. Not at full commander yet—more like just your average office IT hamster. But then: "Don't you dare! Now I'm asking you: what are you doing, you son of a bitch? And do you have any idea..."

The conversation wasn't a success. Not a success at all.

Signs of torture. He had a furrow in his throat. The skin was ripped off his back. He'd been dragged behind a car. Naked. Naked was how we found him. Naked and dead.

We hadn't talked since March. I'd heard bits and pieces. The guy had had it. At some point, he just got horrified and decided to jump ship. He wanted to escape. He called his patrons. They wouldn't talk to him. Every man for himself.

"He should've come to the battalion," thinks the commander. As far as that goes, nothing's changed: still have to pay the price in blood.

Well, here's the blood. Not much of it, and it's congealed, but it's blood...

Looks like he paid the price.

A fighter sighs. "They got him at a checkpoint. The apes. A band of Russian brothers. The sons of bitches. They were probably after money. But why'd they torture him, too? His money was in his money belt. Same place they keep it, same place everybody keeps it... But they went and tortured him."

The second fighter taps the commander on the shoulder. "Can I see you a minute?"

The youngest in the battalion. They celebrated his quarter-century under tree cover. Everyone drank water, but he got Pepsi-Cola. That was their big present. They celebrated for all of forty-odd minutes. Then Rahshah started pouring it on again from the border.

For about four hours. They'll spare no expense when it comes to us. No amount of guns or coffins can be too much.

But at least nobody died. They decided it was a good sign, the kid was lucky. He'd bring luck for everyone.

"Commander, look, here's the situation... You know... Him..." the fighter nodded at his compatriot. "Him and me... Nobody else will... I mean... The thing is that if you look at this a certain way... With some human decency..."

"Will you stop dragging the elephant by the tail!?" burst out the commander.

"Hey, my mom says dragging the cat!"

He smiled. But he quickly wiped the inappropriate smile off his face.

"To be brief: the deceased had two sons. One was a buddy of mine, the other was a little kid. His father and mother are alive. His wife... Widow, I mean... Let him die a hero. And those signs of torture—it wasn't for the money. It was, like, for the country. Like he was a patriot. He died but didn't surrender. Let's write that in the report to headquarters. It's up to us... To you... You hear me, Commander?"

The commander nodded. He mumbled, "Fine. Deal."

He walked a short distance away. He sat on his heels with his back against a tree. He covered his face with his hands. He rubbed his eyes, his head. He slapped himself on the chest. It made a hollow sound. He looked at his fighter and felt something like jealousy, but in a good sense. He thought about how, back in March, there hadn't been enough evil.

But now, turns out, there wasn't enough good. Not enough good. So, then the question arises: where did it go? And can it ever come back? Or is that hollow sound in his soul here to stay?

* * *

SO HAPPY

MONDAY
AUGUST 11, 2014
DONETSK

A humanitarian aid convoy from the RF. But we know. It's the invasion. How many times now has this happened: meat from Kadyrov, bullets from Tula, and peacemaking tanks in a compact vacuum-sealed package.

In March, it was very scary. In April, too. But now? Not really.

They've already invaded. It's just that now they will reinforce their contingent. Or not.

That's the only difference.

Well, but no. Actually, there's another difference. In Donetsk, Luhansk, Ilovaisk, and Shakhtarsk, it's not as scary as it is in Kyiv, Sumy, Kharkiv, and Chernihiv.

Five months with war versus five months without it. They still have no idea what hell it is.

They're numb with horror. But we're not. We're bleached out, faded.

We no longer call each other asking, "How are you?" We call saying, "We're alive."

Roll call.

My friend Ira, Iruntiya, she laughs into the phone: "Listen, I'm so grateful to you, words can't do it justice!"

She lives in the Smolyanka neighborhood. It's "incoming" there for the third night in a row. Everyone's in basements. Whoever has them, that is. Iruntiya has one. She brought all the old people who couldn't walk to her basement. There's more people who aren't hers than are. Her closest people, her parents, are in Horlivka.

But here she is, laughing: "Do you remember leaving a pack of cigarettes here? At New Year's? When we were shooting pool in the basement? And Pyotr Vasilyevich let you smoke?"

"Yeah, so?"

"Yeah, so I found it! Just sitting there, what a beauty, almost a whole pack. You're my girl! Everyone in the whole block got a real nice smoke. So happy..."

* * *

We call explosions "booms." Like children. When something hits, we say, "A package was delivered." Artillery is "arta."

We can tell Grads, mortars, and howitzers apart by the sound. And now we have Uragans, too...[39]

We've learned how to hear the "start" and count down to the "delivery."

Do you really think anyone should have to learn this?

* * *

MONDAY
AUGUST 11, 2014
A N T R A T S Y T

Antratsyt. Yes, the town's named after anthracite. The "Russian world" has been in this town for a long time. No water, no light, no groceries. There isn't much entertainment either. Just track and field. Sprinting. Into and out of the basement.

But what they do have are tanks, Grad multiple rocket launchers, and the hope that Putin's coming.

But he hasn't come yet, and the "liberators" are bored.

If it wasn't for their captured ukrops, they could just die. Although they might actually die anyway. At any moment.

But today they have come up with an amusement.

They are going to fight back against the homos and Eurogays.

They forcibly dressed their ukrop prisoners in thongs and bras they got from local gals. Skirts, too.

They bound the prisoners' arms behind their backs. They drove behind the prisoners in a tank, herding them through town. They had their armored vests and automatic rifles.

They shot off their rifles in victory. And to make sure people saw the prisoners' shame.

Fun times.

The prisoners walked. Their balls hanging out. One of them shouted, "Women, don't look. Don't look. Don't!"

But those dumb broads... They just stood there, crying...

* * *

Let's call that story from Antratsyt fake. Let's forget about it. I want to. But the only way I can forget it is to die.

* * *

War isn't how it's described in books. You somehow never get to the stage of acceptance. It's impossible to believe it's really happening, to completely believe it, all the way down to your core. "It's not happening to us. It's not happening to me. All of this isn't happening to me." Even if you get a "delivery" right under your nose. Or if the next building over gets one. Or the business center. It doesn't matter. As long as you're alive, it's impossible to believe it.

Did you know the communal services are still picking up the trash? In Luhansk, they're not anymore. It's an utter catastrophe over there. But out here: yep, still picking up the trash. My friend says that, as long as they're picking up the trash, it's not a real war.

AUGUST 12, 2014

First reports arrive of a direct incursion by Russian regular army units into Ukraine. Thirty-four Ukrainian servicemen are killed.

AUGUST 14, 2014

The Marynivka border crossing is taken over by separatist and Russian forces, allowing an uncontrolled flow of goods and people into Ukraine from Russia. Ihor Plotnytskyi takes over as the leader of the "DPR."

* * *

FRIDAY

AUGUST 15, 2014

SOMEWHERE NEAR CRIMEA; DONETSK

"Hey, you heard that over in Crimea, on the Kerch bridge, there are thirty-five hundred cars stuck in a traffic jam? They have to wait in line for up to thirty hours. There've been two deaths. And one birth. And one lady who tried to cut in line had her head smashed in!"

"But why don't they drive through Ukraine?"

"They're afraid to! They're afraid we'll recognize our cars and take them back!"

* * *

I don't know what things will be like ten minutes from now. Much less tomorrow. Will my city still be standing? Will my apartment building still exist? The navy-and-grey one, on the left-hand side of Trenyova Street, and then you go on through almost all the way to the end of the courtyard... Will I still be here on earth? My family? My friends? Where will they be, and will they be alive? Where's the next delivery of a peacekeeping Grad or a humanitarian land mine, who's going to get it? Who else will they manage to kill, and which of us will manage to escape...

I don't know.

But I do know two things very clearly.

The first thing is simple and old. Like the apple tree my great-grandfather planted in Kostyantynivka back before that other war.

The government of Ukraine can be beaten. Generals steal, civil servants take their cuts from city budgets and make bank off our soldiers' deaths, politicians tell lies and tremble in fear of losing their positions and MP seats... The wheezing government is hawking up its long, drawn-out nonexistence, but the worms and parasites are stupendously experienced at surviving. They eat and eat. They eat until whatever's alive becomes dead.

The government of Ukraine can be beaten.

But the people can't.

This is a very simple concept. It has some irrationality in it, things like truth, faith, strength, prayer. But there's also something quite pragmatic: people, the friends and strangers who—today, and tomorrow, and always—will stand next to me on a long road, one leading all the way to the horizon, and maybe further... These people will rescue, and build, and cook, and forgive, and give, and heal, and defend. For as long as it takes.

This is what we will do. So we can't be beaten.

The second thing I know is a little more complicated. It's personal.

At the end of February, I escaped from my birthday to Rome. A city that couldn't care less about me. Nor I about it. Which is maybe the reason I could actually live there.

My husband and I were walking around the Campo de' Fiori where Giordano Bruno stands. He stands with his back to the Vatican. There's a great deal of dignity and freedom in that defiant position. Yes. He's a statue. But statues can also be free.

Here, on the Campo, there's a market, restaurants, a café. A young waiter, catching sight of two women speaking in Russian, shouts gaily, "Rahshn! Rahshn! We have Rahshn menu!"

They walk past. They're chatting. Smoking while they walk. And then one of them turns her head abruptly and says in English, annoyed, bitter, and proud all at once: "Exactly I am not Russian. I am Georgian."

I roll these words around in my mouth. I know they are correct. I like them. I repeat the phrase to myself. I smile, completely carefree. I'm having fun...

Rome couldn't care less about me. Scipio Africanus still walks her streets. The Caesars, too... Constantine the Great...

And Emperor Augustus, too, who wanted the title "divine" and went to see the Sybil about it. She lit a burnt offering and, in its smoke... They both saw it, both the Sybil and Augustus... "The divine one has already been born," she said. He, the emperor, didn't want to accept this.

So he took the title.

How was I supposed to see the Sybil in that short woman with the funny crochet handbag? How was I supposed to see the smoke of a burnt offering in the smoke of her cigarette?

Ukraine has already been born. In me, and in others.

"Exactly I am not Russian. I am Ukrainian."

We are Ukrainians.

Or something like that.

Wait. No. It is *exactly* that.

* * *

SUNDAY
AUGUST 17, 2014

The "DPR" has instituted corporal punishment. As the strongest measure of social security.

Now they'll be killing people on the streets not in a drunken rage, but in full compliance with the law.

* * *

SUNDAY
AUGUST 17, 2014
L U H A N S K

The terrorists shelled a refugee convoy with Grad multiple rocket launchers. People burned alive in their cars. Children, too.

That Malaysian airliner turned out to be very big indeed.

AUGUST 18, 2014

The Donbas volunteer battalion enters Ilovaisk with the support of the Ukrainian armed forces. Ukrainian forces encircle Horlivka in Donetsk Oblast and enter the city center of Luhansk. A convoy of civilians from Novosvitlivka and Khriashchuvate fleeing the war zone is shelled by separatist forces, killing eighteen people.

* * *

MONDAY

AUGUST 18, 2014

B E R L I N

Steinmeier, the German minister of foreign affairs, said Russia is fully capable of invading Ukraine. What's happening now is not the worst of it. Europe is again "deeply concerned."

* * *

MONDAY

AUGUST 18, 2014

And you know something? Putin's not a Dickhead. He's the Antichrist. And he's not going to stop. Ever.

* * *

My dad says that you're old and that I can't do this to you. He's probably right. I'm old, too, now. Which means both of us might go at any time.

Parting the right way, saying goodbye the right way, is an art. We could really use that medieval cult of the macabre right now. Some kind of handbook for how to say, in a fitting way, "Until we meet again…"

I do not address you by your name. I actually don't address you at all. But I'm very grateful to you, and I will be for… For as long as I live.

You never laid any claims on me. You could have. You had the legal right.

That legal right meant you could tear me to pieces, rip out my heart, and turn my eyes into eternal waiting zones... Waiting for the next time I'd see you...

Many cruel people do this. But not you.

I don't know if it was your conscious choice, or whether it was the ease of youth. I never really thought about whether you rejected me, or abandoned me, or just forgot.

I never had any pain for you.

You're not in any of my childhood memories. I was five when Mom got remarried. To Misha. To my dad.

And, from that moment, I remember all my days. As though somebody'd turned on the light. Lyudmila Ulitskaya has this great phrase: "Her feet never touched the floor growing up."

My feet did, of course. I walked around on my own two feet. But I was held in an embrace the entire time.

No matter what I did, I was always good. Mom corrected that as much as she could. But nevertheless, Dad's eyes only showed love. There was so much of it, there is so much of it still... It's just that now I can't hide in it, dissolve in it. There's war here. War. We've entered into our sixth month of it now....

As an adult, you know, I've only lately understood what a feat that was on your part. To go off to the side, to not get involved, but somehow to still be there... Once a year. Sometimes more.

You let me go. You let me and Dad go. Into our own happiness that you weren't part of—really that the whole world wasn't part of. There were books in that happiness, and generosity, and something else, something that's hard to put into words.

But I have my patronymic and last name from you. Because...

Because it doesn't matter. They're just letters and sounds. They don't confer belonging to a family line. I'm guessing I've completely lost my voice when it comes to the call of my blood. People love people, not erythrocytes. All these games, the playing at dynasties, at being legally-born, at being adopted...

But I did call my son Misha, so I'd hear and say that name until the day I die. It warms me. I'm at home in that name.

Forgive me. It was probably painful for you. But all's fair in love...

How do I say this to you, so that I'm saying farewell, not trying to hurt you? How do I keep from pounding home the nails I might not live long enough to regret?

There is one thing. One time the relics of Saint Spyridon were brought to Donetsk. It was early spring, it was cold, the line was long... I had business with Spyridon.

You can't do business inside a church. But people do. They stretch their luck.

I wanted to buy a little icon of Spyridon. But they'd just run out. The caretaker offered me my choice of various others. I bought an icon of Saint Viktor to give to you.

But I didn't give it to you. I carry it in my purse. I transfer it from my winter purse to my summer purse and back again.

Whenever my fingers touch it, I think about you and give thanks.

And so, you see, Ukraine, to me, is like my dad. It's my light. My home. When we're together, I can do anything. I can be Russian, I can make mistakes, I can be weak. But I'm always held tight in an embrace, and I'm always forgiven in advance for everything. Ukraine loves me, my precious girl loves me, just for what I am.

And as long as she lives, I do, too.

* * *

All war diaries are histories of suffering. Anne Frank. Tanya Savicheva... "Everyone is dead..."

But you know something? All my people are alive. Kotya, and Surikova, and the photographer, and Granny Shura, and even Astro the poodle.

We're alive. Heroes don't die.

AUGUST 24, 2014

As Ukraine celebrates its Independence Day, a "March of Shame" takes place in Donetsk downtown, also dubbed "the parade of captives." Captive Ukrainian servicemen are led through the streets of Donetsk in a humiliating procession between two rows of militants bearing rifles with bayonets. Four battalion task groups of the Russian regular army with over 100 units of heavy weaponry enter Ukraine, crossing the border from Russia and moving toward Starobesheve to the southeast of Donetsk, thus cutting off Ukrainian troops at Ilovaisk and encircling them.

AUGUST 27, 2014

An attempt to break the Russian encirclement at Ilovaisk fails. Forced to retreat under heavy shelling by Grad multiple rocket launchers, the Ukrainian National Guard units lose sixty-three servicemen who cross the border into Russia and are captured there.

AUGUST 29, 2014

After a "humanitarian corridor" is negotiated by Russian president Vladimir Putin to allow Ukrainian troops to withdraw from the encirclement at Ilovaisk, Ukrainian troops are shelled by separatist and Russian forces and 254 servicemen are massacred during the retreat attempt.

SEPTEMBER 5, 2014

The Minsk Protocol (Minsk I) is signed. The protocol requires a full ceasefire on both sides. On the same day, the Aidar volunteer battalion of Ukrainian forces is ambushed at Vesela Hora and thirty-five servicemen die.

NOVEMBER 4, 2014

Oleksandr Zakharchenko takes over as the leader of the "DPR."

JANUARY 21, 2015

The battle for the Donetsk airport comes to a close with the withdrawal of Ukrainian forces, counting around one hundred casualties on the Ukrainian side.

JANUARY 24, 2015

"DPR" head Zakharchenko announces an attack on Mariupol. The Skhidnyi neighborhood of the city is shelled, killing twenty-nine people.

FEBRUARY 10, 2015

Several neighborhoods and the airfield in Kramatorsk are shelled by separatist and Russian forces using heavy artillery.

FEBRUARY 12, 2015

A new package of measures within the Minsk Accords (Minsk II) is agreed upon at the Normandy Format summit of Ukrainian, Russian, German, and French leaders, and signed by Ukrainian, Russian, "DPR," and "LPR" representatives. On the same day, in the battle for Debaltseve, Lohvynove is taken over by separatist and Russian forces.

APRIL 30, 2016

A new agreement for an immediate ceasefire is reached by the members of the Trilateral Contact Group on Ukraine (comprising representatives of Ukraine, Russia, and the OSCE).

SEPTEMBER 1, 2016

Another agreement for an immediate ceasefire is reached by the members of the Trilateral Contact Group.

(...)

(...)

FEBRUARY 21, 2022

Russia officially recognizes the "Donetsk People's Republic" and "Luhansk People's Republic."

FEBRUARY 24, 2022

A new stage of the war begins with Russia's full-scale invasion of Ukraine.

(...)

(...)

(...)

(...)

The war continues to this day with millions of Ukrainian citizens fleeing their homes or emigrating to escape violence, and thousands of civilians perishing in Russian attacks on Ukrainian cities and villages.

AFTERWORD

ANNE O. FISHER

Olena Stiazhkina's *Ukraine, War, Love: A Donetsk Diary*, written in 2014, is a book about war. Specifically, it is a book about a war that is ongoing to this day. Notably, it is also a book that is being first published in translation. So, as a witness, as a mode of record and engagement, this book will first exist not as itself, but as its interpretation: the translator's interpretation. *My* interpretation. This is a big responsibility. The ethical impact of my ability to render Stiazhkina's aesthetic accomplishment is daunting.

And this book is an aesthetic accomplishment. Stiazhkina's narratorial genius, psychological precision, and love of language make my task a delight. Is it ethical to savor wit, wordplay, and pitch-perfect characterization in a text about war? It is. It's not just ethical, it's imperative. After all, the Russian invasion of Ukraine is predicated largely on the myth that Ukrainian culture and identity don't exist, since they're supposedly just regional variations of Russian culture, Russian identity. What better way to dispatch this lie than for Ukrainian writers to show what their culture and identity really are!

Olena Stiazhkina writes brilliantly in many modes, from academic to genre fiction, from short story to journalism. In my mind's eye, I see her intellect and talent as an elemental force, acting on readers with everything from icy snowstorm to hot sun, gentle breeze to hurricane, soft rain to flooding downpour. She educates, entertains, berates, and comforts us by turn, grounded all the while—absolutely literally—in the earth of Ukraine beneath her feet. She is fearless in sharing her fears; intimate in her treatment of her characters; daring in her narrative path. As the translator, how much should I smooth the way for her readers?

Well, sometimes, it depends on how easily the key elements of the original can move into English. The particular combinations that make jokes and puns tick are often difficult to transfer. How to render the derisive nicknames for separatist organizations and institutions? The "Donetsk People's Republic," or "DNR" in Ukrainian and Russian ("ДНР"), is nicknamed *Dyra* ("hole"), given that "N" in Cyrillic is "Н" and how close that is to the letter "Y" in *Dyra* when spelled in Russified Ukrainian ("ДИРА") and in Russian ("ДЫРА"). But calling the "DPR" (in Latin script abbreviation) a "hole" in English is weak sauce at best, plus, it fails to pun on "DPR." So I came up with Duh-P-R, which implies stupidity, and which also transfers well to Girkin, whom one Granny Shura calls "Dyrkin" ("hole-kin"). In translation, she calls him Duh-rkin.

When the separatists took over the DonODA (the Donetsk oblast state administration building) and proclaimed it—the building—the "Donetsk People's Republic," it didn't take locals long to start calling the DonODA the *Durdom* ("loony bin, lunatic asylum, crazy house"). No snappy English translations of Durdom start with D, though, and maintaining the D for Donetsk is a strong pattern that should be retained. So, I took a different tack and called the *Durdom* the "Donetsk People's Asylum."

In some cases, I use a stealth gloss—a phrase in the translation that gives some information or meaning that would be understood by readers of the original—to allow the reader to get the point without having to stop and look it up. An example is "along with the milk and bread" in the sentence "She had so much strength, so much faith, that it seemed like she could die the death of the brave along with her 'peaceful protesters' who'd just happened to accidentally pick up a few Grads at the Silpo along with the milk and bread" (218). Knowing that a Silpo is a grocery store is key to preserving the sarcasm here. So, how to convey this information? I could've simply used "grocery store" instead of "Silpo," but then the local flavor is lost. Hence the stealth gloss indicating that a Silpo is a place to get groceries without explaining it in so many words. (Look up Susan Bernofsky's interview in *Words Without Borders* from April 30, 2013, for more on the stealth gloss strategy.)

You might also notice the Grads in that last example—the multiple rocket launchers that are picked up at the grocery store along with the milk and bread. Names of heavy weaponry are tricky. NATO identifies Soviet and Russian weaponry by its own system of reporting names that have nothing to do with the taxonomy established in the USSR: for example, NATO calls different types of Buk ("beech tree") missile launching systems Gadfly and Grizzly. So, I could've used the reporting names. Or I could've just transliterated the names as Stiazhkina uses them, since these are also relatively well-known: Grad ("hail" as in "hailstorm": a truck-mounted multiple rocket launcher carrying 40 rockets), Gvozdika ("carnation": a self-propelled howitzer, or medium artillery), Tyulpan ("tulip": a self-propelled mortar, or heavy artillery). But Stiazhkina specifically contrasts these words' lexical meanings with the weapons they identify. To preserve this effect in English translation, the words have to retain their lexical meaning, not just function as conventional identifiers. It is jarring to the English-language reader to see these powerful weapons identified as "Tulip" and "Carnation" and "Beech"—but that's the point. Stiazhkina *wants* to jar us. In the end, a hybrid approach was adopted, with some names retained in transliteration since they are already well-known to US readers that way. In the case of some terms that are particularly load-bearing in the original, like vata, opolchentsy (or opolchenie), and kopanka, I explained the word at first usage and then continued to use the word in transliteration.

Stiazhkina wrote this book in Russian, whose morphological and syntactical features are as different from English as an octopus is from a dolphin. Russian disdains the copula; it loves the kind of impersonal construction that English barely tolerates; its past-tense singular verbs must indicate gender (unless it's an impersonal construction)—and so on. Stiazhkina plays on all these features beautifully. At moments, her language condenses, gets too heavy to be that small, like a shiny piece of hematite you roll around in your palm. At other times, Stiazhkina's ear for dialogue, her virtuoso play with register, and her psychological insight make you gasp (or laugh) and reread a passage. The vividness stems from Stiazhkina's astonishing capacity for empathy, her fiction writer's appreciation of situational absurdity, her historian's long perspective on current events, and her half-humanistic, half-devout conviction that love is a valid mode of engaging the world, even—or especially—when the world offers you cruelty, desperation, and ignorance.

Sometimes it's hard to love, to not succumb psychologically to the enemy. "But being a human being is really hard. I can't do it anymore. I can't do what it takes anymore" (219). Stiazhkina shows us how hard her people fight to remain themselves. A mother comforts herself along with her young son:

> As long as we're here, nothing bad will happen.
> As long as we're here, there's a here...
> As long as we're here, there's a we... (137)

The wordplay borders on word-magic, incantation:

> Fear looks for a safe place to hide.
> Russia seems to be just what it's looking for.
> Russia seems to *be*.
> But it isn't. Russia *is not*. (95)

Humor, like love, is also an effective mode of engaging the world. Irony's a good buffer. There's the occasional wink at academic debates, like the Shakespeare authorship question: "The play *Titus Andronicus* is considered the worst thing Shakespeare ever wrote. It's so bad there's doubt as to whether *they* even wrote it" (73). Chronic sarcasm flares up. In the diary entry "Rumors" from June 1, Stiazhkina mocks the separatists' barely-literate communications, but pauses to take her own side down a peg, and even throws in a little self-deprecation for good measure:

> Why? Why must I read this!? Although there's this, too, a patriotic missive, apparently from our side: "Donetsk! Everyone go back home! Don't go anywhere else! There is fighting in the city's Kyiv district! Everyone sit inside at home and don't go fucking around right in front of the window!" But it doesn't make me feel any better. Because I'm old. What else is left for me besides going and fucking around right in front of the window? (121)

In fact, self-deprecation plays a symbolic role in Stiazhkina's book. Here and there, an entry will end with a shrug: "or something like that." It's possible, in other words, that a better formulation or explanation could be achieved, but—oh well. It is what it is. Do your best and move on. A practical approach. But, at the end of the book, Stiazhkina turns it inside out, from diffidence to confidence, a transformation that's the leitmotif of the entire book:

Ukraine has already been born. In me, and in others.
"Exactly I am not Russian. I am Ukrainian."
We are Ukrainians.
Or something like that.
Wait. No. It is *exactly* that. (243)

* * *

A note on notes: Stiazhkina's individual diary entries occur during the chaotic, day-to-day takeover of Donetsk in
2014. For Ukrainians, no context or explanation is needed. They lived this. But most readers of the translation
will benefit from some basic cultural and political notes.
I compiled these and they were later expanded by the
Harvard Ukrainian Research Institute (HURI) editors—
they are interspersed with individual diary entries in
such a way that they're easy to find and won't interrupt
the reading of the diary entries themselves.

I thank Sergei Sychov and Nina Murray, as well as
HURI editors Oleh Kotsyuba and Michelle Viise, for helping me double-check hunches and work through questions. I'm indebted to the peer reviewer provided by HURI
for their perspicacious and apt comments. It has been
fun and rewarding to consult with my "author sibling,"
Dominique Hoffman, who was working on her translation of Stiazhkina's novel *Cecil the Lion Had to Die* while
I was working on my translation of *Ukraine, War, Love:
A Donetsk Diary*.

Lastly, I'm grateful to the author for her generosity and for the model of her courage. She reminds me of
the diary entry from August 5, about a family that flees
Donetsk to Kyiv, and the strength and determination of
the mother, Katya: "Katya holds up the sky and doesn't
budge." Thank you for holding up the sky for us, Olena.

March 14, 2023

NOTES

1   On January 16, 2014, the Ukrainian parliament, in support of the pro-Russian president Viktor Yanukovych, passed a package of ten laws that were later dubbed the Dictatorship Laws, seeking to suppress civil society activities in Ukraine and introduce harsh punishments for protesters, now considered to be "extremists." The laws mimicked and to some extent surpassed repressive laws previously passed in Russia. President Yanukovych signed the legislation into law the next day, and the heretofore peaceful protests on the Maidan in Kyiv turned violent three days later, on January 19, 2014. For a timeline of events during the Euromaidan Revolution (also referred to as the Revolution of Dignity), see Stanislav Aseyev, *In Isolation: Dispatches from Occupied Donbas* (Cambridge, Mass.: Harvard Ukrainian Research Institute, 2022) (ed.).

2   On February 20, 2014, special forces of the Ukrainian police and Secret Service of Ukraine (SBU) shot and killed 47 protesters, the largest number of victims in one day. The killings took place within the regime's "anti-terrorist operation" in Kyiv, aimed at squashing the protests and removing the protesters from the city's streets. In total, 98 protesters (often referred to as the Heavenly Hundred) have been identified as killed during the Euromaidan Revolution in Ukraine, with several other victims remaining unidentified to this day. The official pretext for the "anti-terrorist operation" was the claim by the pro-Russian government of Yanukovych of a terror attack which was allegedly being prepared by Pravyi Sektor (the Right Sector), a Ukrainian ultra-right group and later political party. The ultra-right movement in Ukraine has often been associated with Stepan Bandera (1909–59), the leader of the militant wing of the Organization of Ukrainian Nationalists (OUN), whose members were accordingly called the Banderites (in Russian, *banderovtsy*). The Soviet Union used the specter of Ukrainian nationalism—and the figure of Bandera in particular—for unjustified,

ruthless repressions against Ukrainian culture, language, and prominent figures (ed.).

3   The conflict around the Tuzla Island has been seen largely as the first Russian act of aggression against Ukraine raising the fears of an armed confrontation. In 2003, Russia disputed the status of the island and began building a dam to the island from the Taman Peninsula on the Russian side of the Kerch Strait. Tuzla Island was a peninsula connected by land to the Taman Peninsula until 1925, when it was disconnected by a strong storm. After 1991, the Ukrainian status of the Island remained not settled with Russia, even though the Island was transferred to Soviet Ukraine in 1954 along with Crimea. Thus, Russia continued to lay claim to it after 1997, even after formally recognizing Ukrainian authority over Crimea. In 2003, Russia attempted to connect it to Russian Federation lands with a 2.4-mile dam from the Taman Peninsula, stopping only about 100 yards short of the Ukrainian border. Because of its location, Tuzla Island was of strategic importance, controlling passage from the Black Sea to the Azov Sea through the Kerch Strait. After clandestinely occupying and then illegally annexing Crimea in 2014, Russia built the 12-mile-long Kerch Bridge, unveiled in 2018, to connect Crimea with the Taman Peninsula. Part of the Kerch Bridge was built on Tuzla Island (ed.).

4   Sunday, March 2, 2014, was Forgiveness Sunday according to the Ukrainian Orthodox Church liturgical calendar (trans.).

5   The region south of the main Caucasus ridge populated predominantly by Ossetians, an Iranian ethnic group. North Ossetia was an autonomous republic within the Russian Soviet Federative Socialist Republic during the Soviet Union and after its collapse, while South Ossetia lay within Georgia, a former Soviet republic and an independent state after the USSR's collapse. Following a war with Georgia in 1991–92, South Ossetia declared independence in 1992, but was recognized only by Russia and a handful of its client states. In 2008, Russia used the pretext of defending South Ossetians from Georgians to justify a full-scale invasion of Georgia in 2008, resulting in the Russian-Georgian War (2008–09). Since the war, Russia has held *de facto* control over

South Ossetia and Abkhazia, another part of Georgia where Russia fanned a separatist movement and recognized the region as independent (ed.).

6   The author refers here to breaking news about the Russian Federation Council's granting Vladimir Putin permission to send troops into Ukraine. That permission was granted in the evening of March 1, 2014 but the author read about it in the news only at 7:22 pm Moscow time the next day (ed.).

7   March 3, 2014, was the first day of Great Lent in the Ukrainian Orthodox liturgical calendar (trans.).

8   Kyiv is named after Kyi, the eldest of three brothers who are mentioned as the founders of the medieval city in the Primary Chronicle (*Povest´ vremennykh let*), a chronicle of Kyivan Rus´ from the mid-9th to the early 12th centuries. The three brothers are usually mentioned along with their sister, Lybid, and are depicted in monuments in Kyiv that have become the city's unofficial emblem (ed.).

9   Andrii Fedoruk (b. 1968), member of the pro-Russian Party of Regions and head of the Donetsk Oblast Council from August 2011 to March 2014. Fedoruk was closely aligned with President Yanukovych's older son, Oleksandr, and worked for several of Oleksandr's companies over a period of time (ed.).

10   In this passage, italics indicate Ukrainian (trans.).

11   March 8, International Women's Day, was traditionally celebrated with pomp and circumstance in Communist bloc countries and the former Soviet republics. While originally devoted to women's rights—reproductive rights, equality, and the struggle against the abuse of women—in the Soviet Union, the holiday turned into a superficial celebration of traditional femininity, women's beauty, and the idea of women primarily as mothers and wives. In Ukraine, leftist feminist organizations such as Feministychna ofenzyva, Svobodna, Hender Lviv and others have organized annual Feminist Marches on this day trying to reclaim the holiday for the struggle for women's rights (ed.).

12   Ihor Kolomoyskyi (b. 1963), a Ukrainian businessman of Jewish descent, oligarch and part of the so-called Dnipropetrovsk (now Dnipro) clan. He made his wealth importing Western goods to

Ukraine, Russia, and other former Soviet states, and exporting natural resources. With the founding of the Privat Group, Kolomoyskyi and his partners expanded into many other branches of business over the decades, including oil and mining, banking and finance, Ukrainian and international air transportation, and mass media. In February 2014, Kolomoyskyi was appointed governor of the Dnipropetrovsk Oblast by the then Acting President Oleksandr Turchynov. He was dismissed from office by President Poroshenko in March 2015 (ed.).

13   The abbreviation "NKVD" stands for the notorious People's Commissariat for Internal Affairs, initially established in Russia in 1917 and expanded to the entire Soviet Union in the 1930s. For decades, the NKVD had a complete monopoly over law enforcement in the Soviet Union, combining regular police functions with those of secret police. The NKVD carried out the Great Purge political repressions under Joseph Stalin; tortured and executed Soviet citizens on a mass scale; formed, populated, and administered the Gulag system of forced labor camps; and brutally suppressed any and all opposition to the Soviet regime, including that among the peasant population (ed.).

14   1937 is a reference to the Great Purge (also known as the Great Terror) under Joseph Stalin from 1936 to 1938, in which the NKVD first targeted Stalin's potential challengers within the Communist Party (so-called Old Bolsheviks) and the regional party leaders, then the leadership of the Red Army and the military high command, and then widened its arrests, violent interrogations, torture, and executions in search of enemies and "saboteurs" of the regime to the general population. 1939 is a reference to the beginning of World War II, when the Soviet Union and Nazi Germany jointly attacked Poland and annexed parts of it. 1941 is a reference to the beginning of the German invasion of the Soviet Union, opening the German-Soviet front of World War II (ed.).

15   Accordingly, the slur "Pindosia" in Russian stands for the United States (ed.).

16   One-seventh of the earth's land mass is a popular notion in Russian propaganda in reference to Russia's size. With 6,612,074

square miles of territory, Russia is the largest country on the planet, though this fact does little to curb its appetite for further territorial seizures (ed.).

17   Bologna sausage for 2 rubles and 20 kopecks per kilogram (2.2 pounds) is a popular reference to the price of groceries in the Soviet Union, implying that it was affordable for general population in comparison to the prices after the USSR's collapse. Nostalgic attitudes for the lost utopia of the Soviet Union usually omitted any mention of food scarcity in Soviet times, long lines and uneven distribution between the capital cities of the Union and the regions, as well as between urban and rural places. Critics of such attitudes often point out that they reduce the complex situation of living in the Soviet Union, including its political and economic regime, to simple terms such as sausage (ed.).

18   In this passage, italics indicate Ukrainian (trans.).

19   As part of the Russian effort to portray the takeover of Ukraine's territory as a homegrown civil conflict, both separatist "republics" in Ukraine's east adopted names with "people's" (*narodnyi* in Ukrainian and Russian) in them: the "Donetsk People's Republic" and the "Luhansk People's Republic." Similar to the clandestine takeover of Ukraine's Crimea before that, both regimes were established by Russian mercenaries, operatives and officers of Russian secret services, and locals under Russian leadership, using Russian money and weapons (ed.).

20   The pro-Russian Vostok (East) Battalion—also known as the 11th Separate Motorized Infantry Regiment "Vostok"—was founded in May 2014 by Oleksandr Khodakovskyi (b. 1972), who gathered under his command former agents of Alfa and Berkut special forces, which were later joined by Chechen mercenaries. Before his treason, Khodakovskyi was a high-ranking officer of the Security Service of Ukraine (SBU) where he served as the commander of the Alfa special operations unit (ed.).

21   Ramzan Kadyrov (b. 1976) is the notorious leader of the Chechnya region of the Russian Federation who is known for his brutality, especially in dealing with members of the LGBTQIA+ community. Kadyrov's fighters—referred to as Kadyrovites

(*kadyrovtsy*)—participated in international conflicts, including Russia's war on Ukraine, and are known for their cruelty and ruthlessness. Kadyrov is closely aligned with Vladimir Putin who has granted him virtually absolute power and impunity in Chechnya in exchange for his undivided loyalty (ed.).

22   Italics in the quoted line here indicate the Ukrainian language (ed.).

23   Volhynia is the historic name of a region in Central Europe that is currently split between Ukraine, Poland, and Belarus. The name is also used for the Volyn Oblast in Ukraine's west, with the city of Lutsk as its capital (ed.).

24   The Ukrainian language has both the voiced [ɦ] (in the Ukrainian version of the Cyrillic alphabet, represented by the grapheme "г") and voiceless glottal fricative [h] (represented accordingly by the grapheme "х"). In addition, although used only in a small number of words, Ukrainian also has the voiced velar plosive [g] (represented by the grapheme "ґ"). In contrast, the Russian language has only the voiceless glottal fricative [h] (represented by the grapheme "х" in the Russian version of the Cyrillic alphabet) and the voiced velar plosive [g] (represented by the grapheme "г"). Given the prevalence of the voiced glottal fricative [ɦ] in the Ukrainian language, residents of Ukraine speak Russian with an accent that is clearly distinguishable by the use of [ɦ] where [g] is used in standard Russian. Similarly, a Russian accent in Ukrainian is evident when the speaker struggles to use the Ukrainian voiced glottal fricative [ɦ] and falls back onto voiceless glottal fricative [h] familiar to them from Russian (ed.).

25   *Ukrop* (meaning "dill" in Russian) is a Russian ethnic slur for Ukrainians and Ukrainian soldiers. Bird refers here to an airplane (ed.).

26   From German, "Hands up!" and "Faster, faster, you pig!" (ed.).

27   In the original, "kto prosit 'mamu nalit' mlaka'." In Russian, "milk" is *moloko*, with the stress on the last syllable and the unstressed syllables with [o] pronounced as an [a]: [malakó]. In the original, the vowel in the first syllable is not pronounced in certain regions of Russia—an accent that strikes other Russian speakers as pretentious (ed.).

28 Andrei Orlov (b. 1957), Russian poet known under the penname Orlusha, a critic of the Putin regime who signed a letter by Russian intellectuals from March 2014 protesting Russia's war on Ukraine and takeover of Crimea. Orlov is known for his pro-Georgian stance during the Russian-Georgian war (2008–09) and his pro-Ukrainian stance since the beginning of Russian aggression against Ukraine (ed.).

29 In the Georgian film *Jariskats'is mama* (1964), directed by Revaz Chkheidze, with a script by Suliko Jgenti, character Georgii Makharashvili goes into war to find his son Goderdzi who was sent back to the front after a serious injury. Georgii finds his son but the latter is injured and dies in his arms (ed.).

30 Odnoklassniki is a popular Russian social network that launched in 2006 with the promise of helping people find their old classmates (from the Russian *odnoklassniki*, "classmates"). The network has become known for fomenting anti-Ukrainian sentiment in its groups and radicalizing users against Ukraine. Per Russian laws from August 2014, Russia's Federal Security Service (FSB, the successor to the KGB in Russia) has full access to the private data of all users. Ukrainian users constituted some 35% of the network's audience and fell to around 10% after it was sanctioned by Ukraine in May 2017 (ed.).

31 Quoted here from the King James Bible, "Psalm 83," https://www.kingjamesbibleonline.org/Psalms-Chapter-83/ (ed.).

32 Oleksandr (Les) Podervyanskyi (b. 1952) is a prominent Ukrainian writer and playwright known for his use of Surzhyk (a mix of Ukrainian and Russian that is spoken in regions of Ukraine heavily russified during the Soviet period) and obscene language in his works. In the original, the phrase mentioned here goes as follows: *Ot"ebites' ot nas!* (ed.).

33 *Ekipazh* (Air Crew, 1979), directed by Aleksandr Mitta, script by Yulii Dunskii, Valerii Frid, and Aleksandr Mitta was the first Soviet disaster film. The first part of the film focuses on the personal lives of the flight crew, while the second follows the escape of the Aeroflot TU-154 plane from a fictional disaster-stricken city in the mountainous region of Asia. The main characters all show an ability to deal more coolheadedly with extreme emergency situations than with challenges in their private lives. The character of the commander of the crew, Andrei Timchenko, was played by Georgii Zhzhonov (ed.).

34   Named after Nikita Khrushchev, *khrushchevkas* were mostly five-story apartment buildings developed in the 1960s to satisfy the high demand for urban housing in the Soviet Union. They were constructed with prefabricated panels made of concrete or bricks. These apartment buildings were known for their tight space, ranging from 320 to 640 square feet for one- to three-room apartments, with small kitchens (around 65 square feet) and tiny bathrooms that combined a toilet with a small bathtub. Up to three generations often lived in each apartment (ed.).

35   Silpo is a popular Ukrainian supermarket chain. The name originates from *selpo*, an abbreviation in Russian for "village consumer society," a kind of cooperative that would collect money from its members in order to purchase consumer goods wholesale directly from manufacturers and then sell them in their own stores (ed.).

36   The bandura is a lute-like Ukrainian folk instrument with strings ranging in number from five (in an early instrument called the *kobza*) to sixty-eight (the modern-day concert bandura). Because of the considerable size and weight of the latter versions, the name of the instrument is often used to refer to bulky and large objects (ed.).

37   ORT is the abbreviation in Russian for Public Russian Television (*Obshchestvennoe Rossiiskoe Televidenie*), the main state-controlled TV broadcaster from 1995 to 2002, after which it became Channel One (*Pervyi kanal*). ORT had been the successor to the Soviet First Channel, inheriting much of its infrastructure, copyrights, and programming. Channel One is currently controlled by the Russian state through an opaque ownership structure and has been actively spreading anti-Ukrainian propaganda and manipulations in its news programming (ed.).

38   The name of the self-propelled howitzer is *hvozdyka* in Ukrainian (*gvozdika* in Russian), meaning "carnation." It was originally developed in Soviet Ukraine in Kharkiv in the late 1950s and entered service in the Soviet Army in the early 1970s. A number of

modifications exist in over two dozen former Soviet states and client states of the USSR (ed.).

39 *Uragan* ("hurricane") is the name of the Soviet self-propelled 220 millimeter (8.65 inch) multiple rocket launcher that delivers cluster munitions. The system is known to be effective in laying extensive minefields behind a retreating army (ed.).

Recent Titles in the Series
Harvard Library of Ukrainian Literature

Forest Song:
A Fairy Play in Three Acts

Lesia Ukrainka (Larysa Kosach)

Translated by Virlana Tkacz and Wanda Phipps
Introduced by George G. Grabowicz

This play represents the crowning achievement of
Lesia Ukrainka's (Larysa Kosach's) mature period
and is a uniquely powerful poetic text. Here, the
author presents a symbolist meditation on the
interaction of mankind and nature set in a world
of primal forces and pure feelings as seen through
childhood memories and the re-creation of local
Volhynian folklore.

2024 | appr. 240 pp.

ISBN 9780674291874 (cloth)	$29.95
9780674291881 (paperback)	$19.95
9780674291898 (epub)	
9780674291904 (PDF)	

Harvard Library of Ukrainian Literature, vol. 13

Read
the book
online

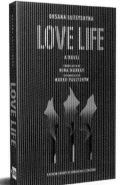

Love Life: A Novel

Oksana Lutsyshyna

Translated by Nina Murray
Introduced by Marko Pavlyshyn

The second novel of the award-winning Ukrainian
writer and poet Oksana Lutsyshyna writes the
story of Yora, an immigrant to the United States
from Ukraine. A delicate soul that's finely attuned
to the nuances of human relations, Yora becomes
enmeshed in a relationship with Sebastian, a
seductive acquaintance who seems to be suggesting
that they share a deep bond. After a period of
despair and complex grief that follows the end of the
relationship, Yora is able to emerge stronger, in part
thanks to the support from a friendly neighbor who
has adapted well to life on the margins of society.

2024 | 276 pp.

ISBN 9780674297159 (cloth)	$39.95
9780674297166 (paperback)	$19.95
9780674297173 (epub)	
9780674297180 (PDF)	

Harvard Library of Ukrainian Literature, vol. 12

Read
the book
online

Cecil the Lion Had to Die: A Novel

Olena Stiazhkina

Translated by Dominique Hoffman

This novel follows the fate of four families as the world around them undergoes radical transformations when the Soviet Union unexpectedly implodes, independent Ukraine emerges, and neoimperial Russia begins its war by occupying Ukraine's Crimea and parts of the Donbas. A tour de force of stylistic registers and intertwining stories, ironic voices and sincere discoveries, this novel is a must-read for those who seek to deeper understand Ukrainians from the Donbas, and how history and local identity have shaped the current war with Russia.

2024 | 248 pp.

ISBN 9780674291645 (cloth)	$39.95
9780674291669 (paperback)	$19.95
9780674291676 (epub)	
9780674291683 (PDF)	

Harvard Library of Ukrainian Literature, vol. 11

Read the book online

The City: A Novel

Valerian Pidmohylnyi

Translated with an introduction by Maxim Tarnawsky

This novel was a landmark event in the history of Ukrainian literature. Written by a master craftsman in full control of the texture, rhythm, and tone of the text, the novel tells the story of Stepan, a young man from the provinces who moves to the capital of Ukraine, Kyiv, and achieves success as a writer through a succession of romantic encounters with women.

2024 | 496 pp.

ISBN 9780674291119 (cloth)	$39.95
9780674291126 (paperback)	$19.95
9780674291133 (epub)	
9780674291140 (PDF)	

Harvard Library of Ukrainian Literature, vol. 10

Read the book online

A Harvest Truce: A Play

Serhiy Zhadan

Translated by Nina Murray

Brothers Anton and Tolik reunite at their family home to bury their recently deceased mother. An otherwise natural ritual unfolds under extraordinary circumstances: their house is on the front line of a war ignited by Russian-backed separatists in eastern Ukraine. Isolated without power or running water, the brothers' best hope for success and survival lies in the declared cease fire— the harvest truce.

Spring 2024 | 196 pp.

ISBN 9780674291997 (hardcover)	$29.95
9780674292017 (paperback)	$19.95
9780674292024 (epub)	
9780674292031 (PDF)	

Harvard Library of Ukrainian Literature, vol. 9

Read
the book
online

Cassandra: A Dramatic Poem,

Lesia Ukrainka (Larysa Kosach)

Translated by Nina Murray, introduction by Marko Pavlyshyn

The classic myth of Cassandra turns into much more in Lesia Ukrainka's rendering: Cassandra's prophecies are uttered in highly poetic language— fitting to the genre of the dramatic poem that Ukrainka crafts for this work—and are not believed for that very reason, rather than because of Apollo's curse. Cassandra's being a poet and a woman are therefore the two focal points of the drama.

2024 | 263 pp, bilingual ed. (Ukrainian, English)

ISBN 9780674291775 (hardcover)	$29.95
9780674291782 (paperback)	$19.95
9780674291799 (epub)	
9780674291805 (PDF)	

Harvard Library of Ukrainian Literature, vol. 8

Read
the book
online

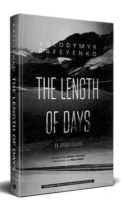

The Length of Days: An Urban Ballad

Volodymyr Rafeyenko

Translated by Sibelan Forrester
Afterword and interview with the author by Marci Shore

This novel is set mostly in the composite Donbas city of Z—an uncanny foretelling of what this letter has come to symbolize since February 24, 2022, when Russia launched a full-scale invasion of Ukraine. Several embedded narratives attributed to an alcoholic chemist-turned-massage therapist give insight into the funny, ironic, or tragic lives of people who remained in the occupied Donbas after Russia's initial aggression in 2014.

2023	349 pp.
ISBN 780674291201 (cloth)	$39.95
9780674291218 (paper)	$19.95
9780674291225 (epub)	
9780674291232 (PDF)	

Harvard Library of Ukrainian Literature, vol. 6

Read
the book
online

The Torture Camp on Paradise Street

Stanislav Aseyev

Translated by Zenia Tompkins and Nina Murray

Ukrainian journalist and writer Stanislav Aseyev details his experience as a prisoner from 2015 to 2017 in a modern-day concentration camp overseen by the Federal Security Bureau of the Russian Federation (FSB) in the Russian-controlled city of Donetsk. This memoir recounts an endless ordeal of psychological and physical abuse, including torture and rape, inflicted upon the author and his fellow inmates over the course of nearly three years of illegal incarceration spent largely in the prison called Izoliatsiia (Isolation).

2023	300 pp., 1 map, 18 ill.
ISBN 9780674291072 (cloth)	$39.95
9780674291089 (paper)	$19.95
9780674291102 (epub)	
9780674291096 (PDF)	

Harvard Library of Ukrainian Literature, vol. 5

Read
the book
online

Babyn Yar:
Ukrainian Poets Respond

Edited with introduction
by Ostap Kin

Translated by John Hennessy and Ostap Kin

In 2021, the world commemorated the 80th
anniversary of the massacres of Jews at Babyn Yar.
The present collection brings together for the first
time the responses to the tragic events of September
1941 by Ukrainian Jewish and non-Jewish poets of
the Soviet and post-Soviet periods, presented here in
the original and in English translation by Ostap Kin
and John Hennessy.

2022	282 pp.	
ISBN 9780674275591 (hardcover)	$39.95
9780674271692 (paperback)	$16.00
9780674271722 (epub)	
9780674271739 (PDF)	

Harvard Library of Ukrainian Literature, vol. 4

Read
the book
online

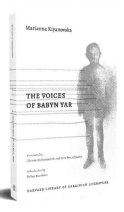

The Voices
of Babyn Yar

Marianna Kiyanovska

Translated by Oksana Maksymchuk and Max Rosochinsky
Introduced by Polina Barskova

With this collection of stirring poems, the award-
winning Ukrainian poet honors the victims of the
Holocaust by writing their stories of horror, death,
and survival in their own imagined voices.

2022	192 pp.	
ISBN 9780674268760 (hardcover)	$39.95
9780674268869 (paperback)	$16.00
9780674268876 (epub)	
9780674268883 (PDF)	

Harvard Library of Ukrainian Literature, vol. 3

Read
the book
online

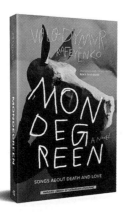

Mondegreen: Songs about Death and Love

Volodymyr Rafeyenko

Translated and introduced by Mark Andryczyk

Volodymyr Rafeyenko's novel Mondegreen: Songs about Death and Love explores the ways that memory and language construct our identity, and how we hold on to it no matter what. The novel tells the story of Haba Habinsky, a refugee from Ukraine's Donbas region, who has escaped to the capital city of Kyiv at the onset of the Ukrainian-Russian war.

2022	204 pp.	
ISBN 9780674275577 (hardcover)	$39.95
9780674271708 (paperback)	$19.95
9780674271746 (epub)	
9780674271760 (PDF)	

Harvard Library of Ukrainian Literature, vol. 2

Read the book online

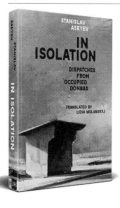

In Isolation: Dispatches from Occupied Donbas

Stanislav Aseyev

Translated by Lidia Wolanskyj

In this exceptional collection of dispatches from occupied Donbas, writer and journalist Stanislav Aseyev details the internal and external changes observed in the cities of Makiïvka and Donetsk in eastern Ukraine.

2022	320 pp., 42 photos, 2 maps	
ISBN 9780674268784 (hardcover)	$39.95
9780674268791 (paperback)	$19.95
9780674268814 (epub)	
9780674268807 (PDF)	

Harvard Library of Ukrainian Literature, vol. 1

Read the book online